The bedroom door opened, and the earl came in bearing a tray. He smiled down at Theo as he set it on the table then went to throw the draperies open to let the morning sun stream through the windows.

Suddenly Theo felt very shy and she pulled the covers high.

"There's no need to hide from me, Theo," the earl said as he sat down on the bed and poured her a cup of chocolate. "I thought we would have breakfast together downstairs. Then I want to show you the Hall from attics to cellars." He looked around and frowned. "Strange, I never noticed how shabby things were in here. We must have the painters in, and the upholsterers—tell me, what are your favorite colors?"

Theo sipped her chocolate and pretended to think. All she really wanted to do was kiss him, he looked so handsome, and yes, so dear. So she had done what she had feared, had she? Fallen in love with him and in only two days' time? She knew that didn't change a thing except to make everything more difficult for her later, but today she didn't care. She was prepared to grab whatever happiness there might be in store for her, even if Lucas never learned to love her as she loved him. Lucas, she thought dreamily. Dear Lucas. My dearest, darling Lucas . . .

SIGNET REGENCY ROMANCE
Coming in June 1998

Emily Hendrickson
A Chance Encounter

Rita Boucher
Lord of Illusions

Sandra Heath
The Faun's Folly

Autumn Vows

Barbara Hazard

A SIGNET BOOK

SIGNET
Published by the Penguin Group
Penguin Putnam Inc., 375 Hudson Street,
New York, New York 10014, U.S.A.
Penguin Books Ltd, 27 Wrights Lane,
London W8 5TZ, England
Penguin Books Australia Ltd,
Ringwood, Victoria, Australia
Penguin Books Canada Ltd, 10 Alcorn Avenue,
Toronto, Ontario, Canada M4V 3B2
Penguin Books (N.Z.) Ltd, 182–190 Wairau Road,
Auckland 10, New Zealand

Penguin Books Ltd, Registered Offices:
Harmondsworth, Middlesex, England

First published by Signet, an imprint of Dutton NAL,
a member of Penguin Putnam Inc.

First Printing, May, 1998
10 9 8 7 6 5 4 3 2 1

For Cynthia Henry Hazard
and for my first grandchild,
Schuyler Grace Lanning Hazard

1

"You wanted to see me, Mama?"

Fanny Meredith looked up from the letter she held. The bright August sunlight that filled the breakfast room did not reach the door where her eldest daughter stood in shadow. Somehow it made her uneasy.

"You are looking uncommonly solemn, ma'am," her daughter remarked as she came forward and took the seat she had vacated only a short time before. She leaned forward to peer at her mother and added, "You have been crying! Did the post bring bad news? Come now, what has overset you?"

Mrs. Meredith waved a hand. "It is nothing, my dear. Well, at least not so very much. And heaven knows I should be used to it by now."

Theodora Meredith began counting back in her head. Yes, her father had stayed occasionally with his sister and her husband when she and her mother had been with them in London for the Season.

"Mama, are you with child again?" she demanded, reaching for the lady's plump white hand and clasping it warmly in sympathy.

"Yes," her mother confessed, dropping her letter to wipe a sudden spill of easy tears away.

"I wish Father would go on a long voyage, to China perhaps, and be so taken with the place he'd elect to stay there."

"Theo! You are too bold! You must not say such things, you must not even *think* them, indeed, you must not! Besides, I . . ."

Just then several pairs of feet thudded across the floor above them and a couple of heavy objects were dropped carelessly as well. Competing with that noise could faintly be heard coming from the direction of the third floor nurseries, the wailing of an obviously unhappy infant.

Mrs. Meredith put her hands to her head.

"Dearest Theo, do go and tell Kendall to please, *please* speak to the boys' tutor and tell him I simply cannot have this noise! Tell him I have the most dreadful headache! And he might have a word with Miss Harpence as well. Your sisters are just as capable of disturbing my peace as ever those rowdy boys were."

Her daughter laughed a little as she went to the door. "In my opinion they are more apt to do so. But I'll restore order, never fear."

As the door closed behind her, her mother picked up the letter she had discarded and read it carefully again. No, there could be no mistake. She didn't understand a word of it even though her husband had written plainly in the brusque way he always used in any correspondence with her. But perhaps Theo would have an explanation?

As Theo Meredith returned and took her seat again she said, "With any luck, quiet will now prevail. We must hope so anyway. And I've told Kendall there is no need to clear just yet, so we may be private."

"Thank you," her mother said, staring down the length of the disordered breakfast table. There were crumbs everywhere. Jam stains decorated what had only recently been a pristine white cloth. A damp trail of milk led from an overturned glass to the edge of the table. The remains of a kipper sat forlornly on one plate while another sported a large serving of fried eggs and ham, now congealing in the butter that surrounded them.

"Remind me to tell Lester he must not take more than he intends to eat. I am afraid he is a greedy little boy."

"But when you do, he will only look at you with those big blue eyes of his and announce in that angelic voice he uses when he is caught out in some mischief, that he truly meant to eat every bit," Theo remarked as she poured them both some tea and added a generous helping of sugar to her mother's cup.

"True. Then he'll smile at me till I won't be able to do a thing but hug him. I fear I am not firm enough with the boys."

Nor the girls either, Theo thought. Her mother was a dear—kind and loving, warm and tender with her ever-increasing brood. She had given her husband thirteen pledges of her affection since their marriage twenty-one years before and of those pledges ten were still living. And now, of course, by next spring there would be another little Meredith tucked away in the family cradle in the over-crowded nurseries of Pobryn Abbey.

Theo looked past her mother to the windows. It was going to be a beautiful summer day. No wonder the children were restless.

"Perhaps it might be wise to declare a holiday, ma'am?" she suggested. "You know how excited the younger boys are now that Teddy is home from Oxford, and Reginald and Huntley from Eton. I do not envy Mr. Farr a bit having to deal with them. As for the girls, poor Miss Harpence! Do let her take them on a sketching expedition, or perhaps for a row on the lake. And let the boys have that fishing contest they were talking about at tea yesterday. It will at least take them, and their noise, outdoors."

"I should not," Mrs. Meredith said with feigned reluctance. "You know your father was most displeased with the boys' progress when he was last home. He ordered me most straightly to see to it. Although I am sure I don't know what I can do about Lester's inability to spell, or William's lisp. As for Teddy's extravagances at Oxford, and Reginald's and Huntley's escapades at Eton, well! I didn't even know of them so I could hardly reprimand them, could I? But there, there is never any sense trying to reason with dear Theodore. He does not seem to understand my difficulties."

"If he would spend more time at home with his children he might realize that their upbringing is as much his responsibility as yours," Theo said shortly.

Her mother looked so stricken she bit back further comments on her father's lengthy absences. She knew she should love both parents but for her father she felt nothing but scorn. What kind of man was he to think that begetting children and providing for their material needs was all that he should be expected to do for them? She had long considered him the most selfish man on earth.

"Was there something else you wished to see me about, Mama?" she asked when she saw her mother was about to lecture her again on her unruly tongue, as well as the proper reverence that should be accorded her father.

Diverted, Mrs. Meredith looked down at the letter she held in her hand. "Yes, there is, my dear. Your father has written to say he is coming home in a few days' time."

"You will be glad to see him, ma'am." And now the damage has been done, it will be safe for you to welcome him back in your bed again, she added silently.

"Indeed I shall," her mother said with a quick smile that recalled the pretty girl she had once been. "He does not say how long he remains this time. Pray it will be for more than a week or two. There are so many things the bailiff wishes to discuss with him; so many decisions about the estate to be made. I simply cannot do everything. You know I can't.

"But enough of that. He tells me he is to be accompanied by the Earl of Canford. Do you remember the earl, my dear?"

Startled, Theo wondered what this was all about. Her heart had begun to beat faster, and she willed it to behave. Oh yes, she remembered the Earl of Canford very well. His name was Lucas Whitney and of all the haughty men of fashion she had observed in London, he was the haughtiest of all. They had never been introduced, for which she was extremely thankful. Just thinking of having to attempt a conversation with the man made her blood run cold. Once, at an evening party, she had seen him observing her through his quizzing glass and it had been all she could do to preserve her countenance. She knew he was in his late twenties and unmarried. And she suspected he was all too aware of his importance as a peer—not only as a leading member of the *ton,* but the object of the most ardent attention of every woman with an unwed daughter to fire off. Theo thought him as spoiled as her father and completely impossible. Still, she admitted, but only to herself, he was fascinating—intriguing, imposing, and quite the most masculine man she had ever seen. It was the first thing about him she had become aware of, and she did not think she was alone in her assessment. Indeed, it had been amazing how exciting a party was when he was among the company, and how terribly dull when he was not.

"Yes, I remember the earl, ma'am," she said calmly.

"But you were never introduced, were you?" her mother remarked, her blue eyes wide.

"No, we weren't. I only know him because it would be hard not to, the way everyone toadies to him and practically swoons whenever he bestows a snippet of attention on them. I can't decide whether the expression 'arrogant peacock' or 'pompous ass' best suits him."

"Oh, dear, your language! Most unsuitable!"

"There now, Mama, don't fret," Theo said, her voice brimming with barely concealed amusement. "I won't call him so to his face, you know. In fact I am sure I can manage to be everything that is polite during his visit. Trust me. But I do wonder why he is coming here. I did not know he and Papa were particular cronies. There is such a difference between their ages."

To her surprise, her mother would not meet her eyes. Instead, she seemed suddenly intent on pleating her napkin. "Out with it, ma'am," she demanded. "What is it you haven't told me?"

The older lady hesitated, then said all in a rush, "Well, I am sure I do not understand it in the least if you have never even exchanged a few commonplaces with him, but there! Men can be strange creatures at times, driven by such odd crotchets it is no wonder women find them impossible to fathom. If I have said so once, I am sure I've said so a dozen times, and . . ."

"Mama, tell me."

Thus confronted, Mrs. Meredith said baldly, "Your father writes that Canford has asked for your hand in marriage and he has given his consent to the match."

There was a stunned silence in the breakfast room as her words died away and she peeked at a daughter who suddenly seemed to have turned to stone.

Theo Meredith felt a roaring in her ears, and she had an irrational urge to slide under the table and hide behind the long cloth that covered it as she had done to escape unpleasantness when she had been a little girl. But surely she had not heard her mother correctly. It was preposterous to even imagine for a moment that that adored peer, that elegant man of fashion who could have any of the most beautiful, accomplished young women of the nobility to wife should have asked for *her* hand.

"What—what did you say?" she asked when she felt she could control her voice.

"He wants to marry you, dear," Mrs. Meredith repeated. Now it was her turn to lean forward and pat her daughter's hand where it lay lifeless on the table.

"Why?" Theo asked.

"I am sure I don't know . . . that is, I mean, well, why should he not? You are a Meredith, one of the oldest and most respected families in England. Remember, we have royalty on our family tree. And your dowry is more than adequate although I am sure Canford paid no-never-mind to that. They say he is as rich as Croesus, whoever *he* might be. And you are a good girl, I've always maintained you were a good girl even when you forget yourself and say those outrageous things you do."

"But this must all be some terrible mistake! For it is not as if the earl could have been stricken by my charms even from afar," Theo said. "I am not beautiful. You know I'm not. In fact, I have nothing to commend me."

"Now there you have gone too far, my dear. You may not be as pretty as your sisters, but you are very ladylike in appearance and—and you have a nice smile!"

Drearily, Theo told herself if those were the only attributes she had to attract a man, it was a miracle the earl had even noticed her, never mind decided she would do for his future wife. But she did not disagree with her mother's evaluation for she knew she did not have the looks of Marietta or Violet or Gwyneth, who even missing some baby teeth was still an enchanting little girl.

"I am sure I am going to miss you horribly when you are wed," Mrs. Meredith mourned, wiping her eyes on her napkin. "How on earth am I to manage without you? Marietta could never take your place. At fourteen she is nothing but a flighty miss with more hair than wit. And if I am not mistaken, and I do not think I am, she is making a dead set at the youngest footman. It will not do. I have been meaning to ask you to have a word with her. And as for Violet, well! She has become so religious I fear for her sanity. I am sure I do not know how she comes by it, do you?"

It was easy for Theo to ignore her sisters' unsuitable behavior, for Marietta's infatuation and Violet's piety were the last things on her mind right now.

"You won't have to miss me, Mama. I am sure I am not going to marry the earl," she said firmly. Her mother uttered a startled cry.

"But you must," she said quickly. "Your father has accepted him."

"I don't believe a word of this," Theo said. "It's my opinion Papa was foxed when he wrote that letter, and he misinterpreted the earl's intentions."

"Yes, well, that might be, of course. He is fond of his port. But somehow I do not believe that to be the case in this instance. I remember him saying he expected you to attract a husband this past Season, and how upset he was when you failed to do so," Mrs. Meredith confided. Theo stiffened as she went on. "I am sure I don't know why he should take that attitude. I can't count the times I've told him what a godsend you are to me, so helpful and knowledgeable. Why, it is as if you are not my daughter at all but

my best friend and confidante. And when you do wed, I do
not know how I shall manage."

"Thank you, Mama. I think. May I see the letter?"

A moment later she was reading the fateful words for
herself. It was true, then. For some reason Lucas Whitney
wanted to marry a female of little distinction and less
beauty. He must have gone mad! But perhaps it was *he* who
had overindulged in the port? Perhaps he was even now regretting his unfortunate choice, even desperately wondering
how he was to escape?

But if that were the case, why would he be coming here
for a visit in a few days' time?

She wondered what on earth she was to say to him when
he came. And was there anything—anything!—she could
do to escape what had to be a marriage of convenience with
a stranger?

2

Not half an hour later, a smart phaeton came up the rutted drive and halted before the front doors of Pobryn Abbey. The driver kept his seat till a groom should arrive, but the older gentleman beside him stepped heavily to the gravel to stretch his aching muscles. Mr. Theodore Meredith thought it all very well to be tooled down from London by a member of the Four-in-Hand Club, but at his age he preferred a commodious, well-padded coach and a sedate pace. Still, he had been loud in his praise of his companion's rig, his team of matched chestnuts, and his skill in handling the ribbons. It would be hard to say which gentleman was the more relieved to have reached his destination, for the Earl of Canford had discovered his prospective father-in-law to be not only a toady but a bore. He comforted himself by remembering Canford was located a good hundred miles to the northeast. Much too far for casual visiting.

He allowed the gentleman to cup his elbow however as he ushered him up the broad steps of his home, cautioning him to watch a loose step and muttering about his wife's negligence in not seeing to its repair. The earl thought the place pleasant, if unkempt. It was made of gray stone and sported several turrets as well as a ruined, roofless wing that surely must have once been the Abbey church. The whole place looked somehow shabby and neglected. Knowing the Meredith fortune, Lucas Whitney was surprised.

No one appeared to answer the clang his host gave the tarnished brass knocker. After a moment or so, he pushed the door open himself, frowning mightily at this inauspicious beginning to the earl's stay.

Later, Canford was to describe the scene that met their eyes to his particular friend, Maitland Grant, as surely a glimpse of the Hell that awaited all sinners. It was, he said wryly, enough to set anyone on the straight and narrow without a moment's delay.

The large, dark hall they entered was filled with people, most of them children of various ages, and all of those making a terrible racket. To one side, a young man of perhaps eighteen was holding a fishing pole over his head while a younger boy jumped up and down and demanded he give it back at once! A little boy clutching the butler's coat was in earnest, shrill conversation, while two others were loudly intent on a game of tag conducted around the other occupants of the hall.

As if that was not enough, three girls stood near an older woman he had no trouble identifying as the governess, demanding cushions, a picnic lunch, their watercolors and, and, and. The earl thought and not for the first time, that governessing was a miserable occupation, and the women engaged in it much to be pitied.

Of his future wife there was no sign, but he saw her mother coming forward to see what the commotion was all about. Catching sight of her husband and his guest, she moaned and swayed. Fortunately a footman standing nearby managed to stop staring at one of the girls long enough to catch the lady up before she collapsed on the floor.

"Teddy, give me back my rod at once! It's mine, it's mine . . ."

"Huntley is a crybaby, Huntley is a crybaby!"

"Boys, a little decorum, if you please!"

"But I must have a parasol, Miss Harpence. My pink one, I think . . ."

"Why does Reginald have to come? He always talks and scares the fish, and . . ."

"Can too carry the water jug! Can!"

"Are you sure there are enough tarts in the basket, Kendall? Are you?"

"Got you! Got you last!"

"Did not!"

"Did too!"

"SILENCE!" Mr. Meredith bellowed.

A sudden, welcome hush fell over the hall. Alas, it was only to be momentary. Frightened, the littlest girl dropped the jug she was holding to the marble floor, where it broke, sending streams of water in every direction. She immediately began to scream, her eyes tightly closed as if to banish the sight of the men who had invaded her home. The earl saw a thin yellow stream run down her stockings to form a small puddle at her feet and was hard put to keep his composure.

"Damn me, stop that infernal shrieking!" the little girl's fond father commanded. "You there, woman, what's yer name? Remove that child!

"And what do you think you're about, Fanny? None of your tricks, now! Here's the earl come to visit. Get up and welcome him at once, I say!"

Since Mrs. Meredith still reclined unconscious in the flustered footman's arms, she could not obey her husband. The efforts of a stout woman wearing the keys of the housekeeper who was flapping her apron in her face trying to revive her did not appear to be doing much good. The earl decided it was more than time for him to take a hand.

"Sir, I believe we have chosen an inopportune time to come," he said smoothly. "With your permission, I shall explore the gardens and grounds for an hour or so. By that time the coach with my man and my baggage should have arrived, and no doubt the household will be in better condition to welcome a guest. Servant, sir."

As he shut the front doors firmly behind him, he heard his host demand, "Well, and what is the meaning of this? Eh? Eh?"

Somehow Canford was not a bit surprised when no one ventured a reply, and he indulged himself in the broad grin he had been so valiantly suppressing.

He had little interest in gardens. Still, even he could see the ones surrounding the Abbey were in terrible condition. The roses were in desperate need of pruning, a small fishpond was full of slime, and the central fountain was rusted and silent.

He did not spend a lot of time contemplating this disorder, for the hot sun soon drove him to seek the shade of the woods. There were some well-worn paths there, and he thought he might find a place where he could sit and ponder how long he might be forced to remain in this madhouse before he could decently take his leave, his wedding plans all in train.

Rounding a bend in the path, he came face-to-face with the young woman he had chosen to participate in those festivities with him. Although he was startled, he did not show it. Theo was not so sophisticated.

"Dear God!" she exclaimed, jumping back, hand to her heart. "*You're* not supposed to be here yet! Why are you?"

When the enormity of what she had blurted out dawned on her, she paled.

Canford saw her look wildly around as if searching for some avenue of escape, and he waited, wondering what she would do. To his satisfaction, she gathered herself together and said, "I do beg your pardon, m'lord. You took me by surprise. I did not expect to see you."

"I am sorry I startled you," he said with a bow and an easy smile. The calm, world-weary air she had assumed did not fool him. He would be willing to wager her heart was in her throat and it was beating double time.

Theo had fled to the woods some time before. She had left her mother conferring with the housekeeper. She knew she was expected to stay for the discussion, but she had ignored the pleading look Fanny Meredith sent her as she excused herself. She could not remain debating whether m'lord would prefer the gold or the green guest chamber, or goose or a brace of ducks for his dinner. No, for she felt she had to be alone to think. She had heard the children above her, racing around as they prepared for their unexpected holiday, and to be sure she escaped them, she had snatched an old sunbonnet from its hook on the back of the gun room door, and hurried to leave the house.

As she tied on her bonnet, she ran toward the woods, and she did not pause nor draw a sigh of relief until she was out of sight of any of the Abbey windows. She slowed her pace then, for even under the leafy shade, it was still a warm morning.

Why? she asked herself again. Why would such a prize on the Marriage Mart as the Earl of Canford decide she was the girl he wanted to marry? Especially since they had never met? Could it be he had chosen her for her lineage alone, not even considering how they might deal together? Had he sat in his prestigious library and coldly perused family trees until he found one worthy of an alliance with his exalted self? That might be it, Theo thought as she stepped over a downed tree trunk that blocked the path. To be sure, the earl was proud enough.

Still, Theo admitted, he did not look like a man who would choose his wife so dispassionately. In her mind's eye she pictured his lean, handsome face and chiseled jaw, those broad shoulders, the powerful yet graceful hands that were the envy of most of the men of the *ton,* his muscular, shapely thighs . . .

Feeling light-headed and aware that somewhere inside she was trembling, she took a deep breath and commanded her body to behave itself.

And then suddenly, as if an evil genie had conjured him up, the earl had appeared before her. And what had she done? Had she smiled and curtsied and welcomed him to the Abbey as of course she should have? Oh no, not she! She had dared to ask him what he thought he was doing here, he, Lucas Whitney, the mighty Earl of Canford. And as if to emphasize her complete unsuitability she was wearing a horrid old gown and her faded, shabby sunbonnet. She wished she were dead.

"Shall we begin again?" he suggested.

Given this second chance, Theo sank into what she hoped was a graceful curtsy. "How delightful of you to come and visit us, m'lord," she said. "Did you have a pleasant drive down from town?"

He drew her up. Her fingers tingled when he released her hand.

"Do you know, although no doubt it is perverse of me, I find I prefer your first words to me," he remarked.

"Even though they were not at all polite?" Theo asked, not understanding him in the least.

"Ah, but they were honest, were they not? Shall we stroll on?"

"Certainly, if you would care for it, m'lord."

Silence grew between them and uneasy, Theo said, "It is pleasant here in the woods, is it not? Such hot weather as we have been having. But no doubt it is good for the crops."

"As long as it rains now and again," he contributed, as if determined to be as socially inept as she felt herself to be. Then he added, "Come, come, Miss Meredith. Surely you can do better than that."

Theo felt a surge of anger in her breast at the cool amusement she was sure she could hear in his voice. What did he expect of her? She was not his equal, and although she had had her nineteenth birthday, she had none of the graces and accomplishments he was accustomed to in young women. If she was tongue-tied, even maladroit, that was too bad, but only what one might have supposed.

"But that was not kind of me, was it?" he added, just before she lashed out at him in retaliation. Theo did not know whether to be grateful to him or disappointed she had lost the opportunity.

"I do apologize, Miss Meredith. I fear my manners are nowhere near as good as they should be. You are placed in an awkward situation, are you not?

"Tell me, has your mother spoken to you about the agreement concerning your future your father and I have reached?"

"She did so this morning when my father's letter arrived," Theo said, carefully not looking at him.

"No wonder you are so uncomfortable," he said, his voice cold now. "You should have had that letter last week. If you had, you would be accustomed to the situation by now."

Theo was not at all sure that any amount of time would have served to prepare her for marriage to the paragon who walked beside her. He was not touching her, but she was very conscious of his virile strength. She wondered at his height. He had not looked so tall across a London drawing room, but now she could see the top of her head only reached his jawline. She was not a short girl either. She had her father's height as well as his looks.

"I am sorry this is awkward for you," the earl went on, and she forced herself to concentrate on his words. "Shall we agree not to discuss the situation until you are more at ease? Yes, I believe that would be best. Take all the time you need, Miss Meredith," he added magnanimously.

For the first time since their encounter, Theo felt a bubble of amusement well up inside her. Obviously the earl could not imagine anyone being less than ecstatic about the match. No, this time he was allowing her was only so she might preserve her modesty. Or perhaps he had been afraid she might betray her eagerness by throwing herself into his arms? Pompous ass, she told herself, feeling much better now that she had his measure.

They had reached a fork in the path and when he would have turned to the left, she said, "Perhaps it would be best if we went the other way, sir. That path goes to the lake. My brothers will be fishing there and it is entirely possible Miss Harpence might have taken my sisters to the gazebo to sketch. Unless, of course, you wish to meet them all?"

"By all means, let us go the other way," he said promptly. "I have, in a manner of speaking, that is, already met your brothers and sisters. They are why I came to the woods."

Theo looked at him, confused. "Yes? But how?"

"They were all in the hall when your father and I arrived. There was a considerable commotion and I excused myself until order could be restored."

"Now that is strange," Theo mused as if to herself. "I would not have thought you a coward, m'lord."

She blushed when she realized what she had said. The earl ignored her complexion as he remarked, "I am not known to be timid. However, it would take a stronger man than I to deal with such pandemonium.

"I see there is a bench ahead. Shall we rest there?"

As Theo nodded a part of her wished she might excuse herself and run back to the Abbey. But another, and equally strong part, longed to stay and hear what else the earl had to say. She smoothed her gown over her knees and realized for the first time she had come out without her gloves. He must think her the worst kind of hoyden.

"How many brothers and sisters do you have?" he asked.

"Nine, sir," Theo said, both relieved and disappointed at the commonplace subject he had chosen. "I am the oldest. After me comes Teddy. He is eighteen and at Oxford."

"Teddy? Is his name Edward? I only ask because I know you are Theodora."

"No, not Edward. You see, my mother named me after my father, thinking to please him. He was not at the Abbey when I was born, nor did he come for the christening, so she did not have the benefit of his counsel in the matter."

Canford heard the disapproval in her voice and refrained from comment. After a moment she went on. "I understand he was incensed when he discovered Mama had bestowed his name on an insignificant female. When his second child was born a year later, he named him Theodore. To avoid confusion since I was already called Theo, my brother became Teddy. My father always chose the names of his sons after that, although he allowed Mama free rein where my sisters were concerned."

"And their names are . . . ?"

"Marietta, Violet, and Gwyneth."

"Gwyneth is the youngest?" he asked. As Theo nodded,

he decided to keep the child's untimely accident to himself. There was no doubt she would hear about it, and her mother's swoon as well, but at least the news would not come from him.

"And the other boys?" he went on smoothly.

"Let me see. Reginald comes after Teddy. He is sixteen and Huntley, nine. Then there is Lester. He is five, and William, three. Oh there is Donald, too. But he's only eight months. I'm sure neither he nor Will were in the hall."

"They might have been," her companion remarked wryly. "There seemed to be at least a baker's dozen."

"You yourself do not have a large family, m'lord?" she asked, feeling a little more comfortable with him now. Faintly she could hear the boys calling as they ran down another path some distance away, and she was glad they would not be interrupted.

"No. I have only one younger sister. She is married to the Duke of Lansmere."

"I believe I saw her in London this past Season," Theo said, her throat dry as she remembered the haughty lady who had never so much as acknowledged her existence even after they had been introduced. She wondered what Her Grace would think of her brother's marriage to a nobody. Perhaps she did not know of it as yet? It almost tempted her to agree to marry him just to find out. She scolded herself for being frivolous. This was a serious business she was embarked on.

"Did you find the Season pleasurable, Miss Meredith?" the earl asked. "I believe it was your first, was it not?"

"Yes. I did not think to, but to my surprise I did enjoy myself."

"London was not as intimidating as you had been led to suppose?"

"It was intimidating all right, but I found it amusing to watch the foibles of society, all the *ton's* pompous stupidity . . . er, that is, I mean . . ."

He held up a tightly gloved hand. "Please. Do not feel you must qualify your statement. If the *ton* amused you, it was performing a service, something for which it is not noted."

She stole a peek at him where he sat close beside her and wondered what he would say if he knew she included him among the conceited overbearing individuals she had met or observed.

"I do not consider myself the least bit stupid," the earl said, almost as if he had read her mind. Theo concentrated on staring straight ahead to where a squirrel sat on a branch, chittering at them in annoyance. "You must not think I am," he continued. "I will admit, however, to a slight degree of pomposity but only on the odd occasion when it is definitely called for. Are you quite clear about that?" he added, turning to look at her squarely.

"I never said *you* were stupid or pompous. I am sure I did not even imply such a thing . . ."

Her voice died away when she remembered that yes, indeed, she did think him conceited. And proud. And unbearable.

Afraid he might continue this unfortunate train of thought, she changed the subject by asking whether he intended to make a long stay. When she saw how his mouth twisted ironically, she realized that asking a guest when he was leaving right after he had just arrived was hardly the height of good manners, and inwardly she cursed her unruly tongue.

"That is, I only wondered if you would be here when we have Harvest Home in mid-October," she hastened to add, hoping to mitigate her mistake. "It is such a gala occasion. We always have a feast for the tenants and their families, with dancing and games and prizes for the children."

"Neither one of us will attend the fete," he said, his voice cold. "I intend our marriage to take place on October first."

"So soon?" Theo breathed, clasping her hands together so he would not notice how they had begun to tremble.

"Forgive me. I am at fault. I said we would not speak of it, and already I have broken my word."

"You also said I might have all the time I needed," Theo reminded him.

"I did not mean you to take months, Miss Meredith. I merely meant a week or so. Surely by then you will become accustomed . . ."

Theo was sure she heard revulsion in his voice, yes, and a tinge of boredom. Did he think she was pretending reluctance to make the game more exciting? She cringed. *It is not like that, it isn't*, she longed to tell him. *I never meant that at all!*

"Besides, since your father has agreed to it, there can be no question of your refusal, can there? Please do not tell me you are in love with the head groom, or one of your father's farmers. I would not believe it if you did. You have too much elegance of mind for such paltry affairs. Quite unlike that sister next to you in age. I saw her flirting with the footman. Someone had better take her in hand before it is too late."

"Marietta means no harm," Theo said, flaring up in defense. "She is only fourteen."

"And that is quite old enough to get into a great deal of mischief, especially if you add a virile young man to the mix. I suggest you have a word with her. No, never mind. I'm sure your father will see which way the wind is blowing and take the chit to task. If he does not, I'll tell him of it."

"My sister is none of your concern, m'lord," Theo said, wondering at her daring.

"You forget she becomes my sister too, when you and I are wed. As such her behavior will reflect on me."

He sounded so grim at the prospect, Theo decided diplomacy was in order. "It is only that she is so gay and pretty," she told him. "Men have always admired her from the time she was a little girl."

"To be sure she is very like her mother. All your sisters are like her. Only you are different."

Theo bent her head over her clasped hands and commanded herself not to cry. She knew she was not pretty.

She knew it very well. But it was hardly kind of him to re-mind her of it. Not kind at all. Still, she told herself, she'd die before she let him know how he had wounded her.

Canford rose then and held out his hand. "Shall we re-turn to the Abbey, Miss Meredith? I am sure peace and quiet have been restored by this time. And I shall be glad of a glass of wine and a change of clothes. The roads from London are thick with dust at this time of year. Sometimes I wonder which is worse, the mud of springtime, the ice of winter, or the dust of summer."

Chatting casually of the journey and the towns where they had stayed overnight, Canford tucked her hand in his arm. Held close to his side, Theo barely heard his polite monologue. She was glad she did not have to contribute to the conversation. Her throat was so tight she was not at all sure she could have managed anything above a croak.

When they reached the weedy, neglected gardens, she saw her father pacing up and down the terrace, and unable to bear greeting him just now and having to watch him preen himself on the match he had made for her, she asked the earl to excuse her. He bowed, his dark eyes searching her face, but he said nothing as she curtsied and hurried away.

Musing over the time just spent, Lucas Whitney strolled through the gardens and up the terrace steps to join his host in a welcome glass of burgundy.

As he did so, he told himself he was well pleased with his choice of bride. She was everything he had hoped she would be, and a great deal more. Indeed, for his purposes she could not have been better.

3

Theo did not see the earl again until evening. As she went down to the drawing room wearing one of the new gowns she had acquired in London for the Season, she wondered what he thought of having his dinner served at six. They kept country hours at the Abbey. She was sure he must be affronted, forced to dine when the sun was still high in the sky, and she was glad. Almost she wished her mother might have had the meal at five, as she often did to accommodate the children when there were no guests and their father was from home. Of course Theo realized there would be no children at the table tonight. Only she and Teddy were to appear. She smiled a little as a footman opened the drawing room doors for her. Her sister Marietta had been highly indignant not to be included. Theo suspected she had intended to try her wiles on the earl. Alas that he had her measure already! Remembering the whispered tantrum that was all Marietta had recourse to since her father's displeasure with his children had been made plain to all of them, Theo was amused again. The assembled guests were treated to a radiant smile as she entered the room.

Beside the guest of honor, resplendent this evening in dove-gray-and-royal-blue broadcloth with linen so white it dazzled the eye, the vicar and his wife, Reverend and Mrs. Covington, and a Lady Barron, the elderly and very deaf relict of the late Lord Arthur Barron had been invited.

"I am sure I wish I could provide a more lively party," Mrs. Meredith had complained to Theo when she captured

her after her return from the woods. "But there! I told
Theodore since he did not let me know the time of his arrival he has no cause to rant at me for the paucity of company, nor for that horrid scene in the hall either. Although I
am sure it was very unfortunate they should have come before the children had left the Abbey."

She had pressed a distracted hand to her forehead, and
interpreting the gesture correctly, Theo had begged her to
lie down. Fanny Meredith was happy to do so. She knew
from past experience that her darling Theo would see to
everything for her, arranging the flowers herself, conferring
with the cook and the housekeeper and selecting the wines
with Kendall.

But in spite of Theo's best efforts, the dinner party could
not be said to be a success. Mr. Meredith tried his best to
keep the conversation flowing, a chore made more difficult
by Lady Barron's repeated pleas for him to "Speak up,
man! Can't hear a word you're sayin'!"

Mrs. Meredith sat, flushed and flustered at the opposite
end of the table, the earl in the place of honor to her right.
Across from him was the Reverend Mr. Covington. Glee-
fully, Theo wondered how Canford liked his lengthy dis-
course on the problems of the local churches, or her
mother's attempts to change the subject by drawing him out
about his estate and London house. To her ears it sounded
as if dear Mama were trying to gauge his suitability as a
husband, and that, of course, was hardly the case. To her
regret, the earl bore it all with equanimity. He even managed to ignore her brother's intent stares. Teddy, aware he
was in the company of a veritable pink of the *ton,* intended
to gather as many pointers on dress and behavior as he
could. Theo ate her dinner demurely. At least Canford
would find no fault with the food he was served.

After dinner, the ladies retired to the drawing room.
When Lady Barron began to question the earl's visit in the
loud voice of the hard of hearing, her hostess was quick to
send Theo to the pianoforte. Fanny Meredith could hear the

murmur of the men's voices clearly. Surely the earl heard this very plain-speaking lady even more clearly.

Theo was quick to begin a rousing scherzo. She had no illusions about her musical talent; she knew she was only an adequate performer. She wondered if Canford intended her to entertain his guests at times. If that was in his plans, he was in for a rude surprise.

The gentlemen rejoined the ladies only a short time later. Theo knew her father kept an excellent port, but she suspected the vicar's prosy conversation, to say nothing of her father's, and the tongue-tied adulation of her brother had driven Canford to the drawing room in short order.

The party drew to a close shortly thereafter, Lady Barron announcing she did not believe in late evenings, and expressing her wish to return to her own home before full dark. The Covingtons were right behind her.

As the door closed on the guests, Mr. Meredith said in a hearty voice that made Theo's hand itch to slap him, "Well, there! I've no doubt you're as glad to see the back of 'em as I am, m'lord! I apologize for the company. Don't know what Fanny was thinkin' of, to ask them. But never fear, we'll have a more lively group in the days ahead. And then we'll be able to enjoy a hand of whist or two. Do you play, daughter?"

Theo was not required to answer for just then the drawing room door opened to admit the rest of the Meredith family. She did not dare look in the earl's direction even as she wondered why her mother thought it necessary to parade the entire family right down to baby Donald, especially after what had happened that morning. Fortunately the baby had just been changed and fed, and he slept through the entire ten minutes, which was all Mr. Meredith allowed his unruly brood to remain.

Theo saw the children were all dressed in their best and on their best behavior. They all stared directly at Canford with the exception of the baby and Gwyneth, who after a quick peek at him lowered her gaze to the floor, blushed, and refused to look up again.

"My dear Mr. Meredith, here are your dear children," his fond wife said, smiling widely. "I was sure you would wish to see them before they went to bed."

Her husband looked at her as if he thought she had gone mad. She ignored him as she beckoned the children closer. "Come and make your bows and curtsies to our guest, children," she prompted. "Mr. Meredith, perhaps you might introduce them, one by one?"

That gentleman looked more than a little disconcerted. Theo knew he was not at all sure of their names. Indeed, during his last visit, he had insisted on calling Lester "Chester," and the baby "Ronald." Now he was quick to ask Theo to do the honors. Before she began, she looked quickly at Canford and saw by the knowing look in his eye, he had recognized his host's dilemma as well as she had, and was amused by it.

She told the earl their names and watched the boys' careful bows, the girls' reverent curtsies. She could tell that although Marietta was indignant at being included in the nursery party, she still gave the earl her most enchanting smile, her dark eyelashes lowered over big blue eyes, and a delicate blush coming and going in her cheeks. As she often did, Theo wondered how she managed that. She had tried to do the same several times in London, for she had seen the effect it had on males of any age, but she had never been able to accomplish so much as a tinge of color.

"Would you and the earl care to hear the girls' new piano pieces, sir?" Mrs. Meredith asked her husband. He was not able to restrain a shudder.

"No, no, not now," he said quickly. "Time they were all in their beds, what? Yes, yes, run along now, all of you. Fine children, fine, don't you think so, m'lord? But hardly suitable for the drawing room, Fanny. Wonder at you, indeed I do.

"A game of billiards, m'lord? Come along with me, sir."

As the door closed behind the two men, Teddy abandoned his careful pose against the mantel. He was disappointed he had not been asked to join them, and he scowled as he sprawled on one of the sofas. "Is what I hear true, Theo?" he asked. "Are you going to marry the earl?"

"Now where did you hear that, young man?" Mrs. Meredith tried to say sternly. "I am sure I never told you anything of the kind."

"That is true, Mama. But you did tell your maid and she told Kendall and before an hour had passed, everyone in the Abbey knew it. You know servants.

"It's a great match," he added before his mother could reply. "Must say I'm surprised, though. You ain't no ravin' beauty, Theo, and Lord, Canford is so high he could have anyone. Plump in the pocket too, from what I've heard at Oxford. It's a coup, my girl, a real coup. And perhaps after you've tied the knot and after I leave university, the earl will sponsor me at Wattiers, and for the Four-in-Hand Club as well. Wouldn't mind staying with you both in London either. It would do me a world of good to be seen in his company.

"Say, did you notice his cravat? I believe that style is called the Waterfall. Ask him, will you? It looks difficult. I wonder how many neckcloths he ruined before he got it right."

"How you do run on, Teddy," his mother interrupted. "Of course Theo will not ask him any such thing. This is all very new to her. You must remember she and the earl were strangers until this morning."

Her son bent his blond head and peered at her. He was nearsighted and he refused to wear spectacles. "Then how does it come about he wants to marry her?" he asked.

"We have no idea," his sister said bluntly when Mrs. Meredith hesitated.

"Surely he must have said something when you were walking together," Teddy persisted.

Theo shook her head. "He seemed to think because *he* was desirous of the match, of course *I* must be as well. Pompous . . ."

Catching her mother's eye, she coughed a little and added, "He was kind enough to say I might have all the time I needed to become accustomed. But then he ruined that magnanimous statement by telling me the wedding would take place on the first of October."

"Never say so!" Mrs. Meredith exclaimed, both hands clasped before her ample bosom as if in prayer. "There is no way we can be ready by then. Why, there are your bride clothes to see to, the guests to invite, the preparations to be made, to say nothing of the many repairs to be made about the Abbey. Mr. Meredith has already given me a list, and I assure you it is a formidable one."

"I am sure there is no reason he cannot see to some of that himself while he is here, ma'am," Theo was quick to say. Turning to her brother, she added, "And perhaps you might be persuaded to lend a hand as well, Teddy. You have little to do until you return to university, after all."

"I say, don't be saddlin' me with any horrid chores," her fond brother said, looking indignant. "I've plenty to do. I'm off to a race meet next week, then I am bidden to visit a friend, and . . ."

"Yes, but surely, dear one, you could do something, couldn't you?" his mother wheedled. "Your dear sister's wedding too! Do you know, Theo, I have been thinking it might be a lovely touch to have all your sisters stand up with you, and perhaps little Will could carry the rings on a satin pillow? What say you?"

Since Theo had heard of Gywneth's accident that morning and wondered how the excitement of a wedding might affect her, she only said, "I do not know what kind of wedding the earl would prefer. Perhaps he will want a small, private occasion."

"But that would be shabby, and . . . and somehow unsavory don't you think? As if we had something to hide?" her mother protested. "When I wed your father we had two hundred guests, even a grand ball. Why, your grandmama worked for months to prepare it all. And that reminds me. I must write to dear Mama at once and tell her the wonderful news. I do hope she will be able to make the journey here from Bath. It is true it is not far, but her rheumatism has been so painful."

Happy the subject had been changed even so slightly, Theo said she would write to the lady as well. She had always admired her Grandmother Hutton. Short and plump and as soft and yielding-looking as egg custard, it always surprised people to discover what a Tartar she could be. She would be sure to speak her mind. She always had. It was no secret to Theo that Mrs. Hutton had not approved her husband's choice for her daughter Fanny, and as the years passed and she had been proved right about him in so many ways, her scorn grew. Mr. Meredith pretended he did not hear her outrageous comments, which only spurred her on to make others, more critical and sarcastic than before. For this reason she was seldom at the Abbey unless Mr. Meredith was from home. Her behavior at the wedding could be as unpredictable as Gwyneth's was apt to be, and with equally dire consequences.

That night, Theo could not seem to find a comfortable place on her pillows for her head, nor could she quiet an overactive mind. It insisted on dwelling on the predicament she was in and worrying at it, like a dog with a bone. It was a long time before she slept.

When she came down to breakfast the next morning, she discovered her mother alone at an immaculate table with the younger children in the nurseries and the older ones banished to a small room near the kitchens. All well out of earshot of anyone in the main part of the Abbey, Theo thought as she selected her breakfast at the sideboard. The nervousness she had felt when she entered the room was gone, for she had seen at a glance that both her father and Canford had eaten sometime earlier. Teddy had disappeared as well.

"Thank you, Kendall. That will be all," Fanny Meredith said to her butler in dismissal. As the door closed behind him, she confided, "I suppose we must be discreet, even if it doesn't do any good. As Teddy said, the servants know *everything*."

"I am happy your appetite has not deserted you, Mama," Theo said as her mother put marmalade on another scone.

"Do you remember the horrid time I had of it with Donald? I thought I would never cease being ill in the mornings."

"Where has the earl gone?" Theo asked before the conversation could turn to a discussion of early pregnancy. She knew it was unusual for her mother to talk of such things with her, but since there were few women in the neighborhood Fanny Meredith cared to call friend, she had always turned to her oldest daughter from the time Theo was fourteen.

"Your father has taken him on a tour around the estate this morning." Fanny Meredith sighed and shook her head. "I am to spend the morning with the gardeners and the other workers, setting all his plans for renovation in motion. Well! I am sure I have enough to do without . . ."

Theo ate her breakfast only half attending to her mother's soft complaints. It was true Fanny Meredith had a great many children and a large establishment to see to, but even though she loved her, Theo had to admit her mother was lazy. She always took the easiest way, sometimes not speaking of a fault if it would make hard feelings among the servants. And there was an army of those servants to see to everything. All her mother had to do was give the necessary orders. It was not as if she had to wield a needle, wash the sheets, scrub the pots or weed the gardens. She did not even have to care for her children. Suddenly Theo had the unpleasant thought that she might have to lead a life not unlike her mother's, and startled, she dropped her fork. As it clattered against her plate, she made herself smile.

"I do beg your pardon, Mama. How clumsy of me," she said absently. Canford cannot want a large family, she told herself sternly. He only has the one sister and I don't think he likes children. Of course he will want an heir, perhaps one or two more, but then I am sure he will go his merry way and leave me back at Canford Hall to see to things. Of course. That is why he is marrying me.

"Why don't we see the gardeners and workmen together?" she suggested, firmly putting the earl and her dismal, loveless future with him from her mind.

"I was hoping you would offer," her mother said, beaming at her. "You are so decisive, my dear, whereas I have the greatest trouble making up my mind. Your father scolded me again last night. He said he was ashamed of the drawing room draperies, and he reminded me he had told me to have them replaced six months ago. Well, so he did, but if you remember I could not decide between the gold brocade or the blue silk and so it all came to nothing."

"Take the gold brocade," Theo said firmly. "I'll send the order and the measurements to the warehouse in London today.

"Tell me, did Papa say anything about when they would return?" she added, her eyes downcast. Sometime just before sunrise, she had decided she must speak to the earl, and the sooner she managed to do so, the better. No one—well, very few people—knew Canford's plans. If the engagement was canceled, it would cause no scandal. Because after a long, sleepless night Theo had come to see that marriage to the earl was something she could not contemplate with any degree of ease. He was altogether too high, too well connected and powerful, too rich and too masculine for a country mouse like herself. She had never been a girl who wasted her time dreaming of the shadowy *someone* she would marry. She had known her husband might be chosen for her, but she had expected to at least be able to get to know the man and feel easy in his company. Earlier she had thought she would have an ally in her mother; that Fanny Meredith would stand up for her if her daughter could not like her father's choice. Now Theo was not so sure. Her mother had not asked her, not once, how she felt about Canford. Instead, she had begun to plan the wedding with anticipation, quite as awed as any other woman with the matrimonial prize that had fallen to their lot.

"He did not say when they would be back. It is a shame too," Fanny Meredith said with a frown.

"What is?" Theo asked idly.

"It's a shame he has gone out," her mother explained. "Haven't you noticed how quiet the Abbey is this morning? The children are all on their best behavior, and now my dear Theodore is not even here to see how good they can be. It is too bad, for depend on it, it will be a miracle if they can sustain such saintliness. I do not expect it. Mark my words, there will be some horrible commotion just about the time your father and the earl return.

"What on earth are you chuckling for, Theo? Have I said something amusing?"

4

Theo was hard at work in the library when the earl found her there later in the day. As he entered, she looked up, distracted for a moment. Quickly, she removed her spectacles, sorry that Canford had discovered yet another unattractive thing about her. No doubt he would begin to think her a bluestocking who had ruined her eyes with constant reading.

He bowed to her a little. "I hope I am not interrupting you, Miss Meredith. I have only come in search of something to read. I shall not be long."

Theo took a deep breath and straightened the papers lying on the desk before her. There was plenty of time to go over her mother's lists but she was not sure when she would have another opportunity to confront the earl alone.

"I—I wish you would sit down, m'lord," she forced herself to say, ignoring her pounding heart. "There is something I particularly wish to discuss with you. If you would be so good," she added hastily as he turned to survey her.

She rose then and went to a chair near the empty fireplace. As the earl took a seat opposite, he crossed one tightly clad leg over the other. Even though Theo knew he had been riding with her father, no one would have suspected it from his immaculate appearance. His high boots shone with polish, his jacket fit him without a wrinkle, and his linen was the usual pristine white. Only the faintest aroma of horseflesh and an even fainter hint of male skin tinged with some soap or lotion he must have used, gave the game away. She wondered, since it was so vague, why it made her feel dizzy.

"You said there was something you wished to discuss?" he asked in his even baritone. He sounded amused and aware she had been staring at him, Theo mentally scolded herself.

"It is very difficult to know how to begin, m'lord," she admitted. She lowered her eyes to her lap and quickly hid her right hand under her left. Her fingers were ink-stained and she wondered why she always had to appear so unkempt when faced with his magnificence.

"Just plunge right in, why don't you?" he suggested. "Unlike a story, a conversation does not have to have a beginning, a middle, and an end, now does it?"

Theo could not smile. Her face felt frozen with the enormity of what she was to attempt. "It is just that this marriage—the agreement you made with my father, I mean—it troubles me," she got out all in a rush. "I do not understand it at all."

He shrugged. "You seem a young lady of reasonable intelligence. What is there about it that is so difficult to understand? I asked for your hand. Your father gave it to me."

"Why?" she asked baldly.

"Because he saw nothing in my suit to disgust him, I suppose," Canford said. His voice was serious, but Theo's startled peek at him revealed a light deep in his eyes. She was sure he was laughing at her.

"I did not mean that and you know it," she said hotly. "Of course he would accept you. I daresay there isn't a father in England who would not and you, sir, in your arrogance, know that only too well."

Once more horrified at what she had blurted out, she hurried on. "I meant why did you ask for *my* hand? You didn't know me when you contracted for me. We had never met, never mind exchanged even the most common pleasantries. Whatever possessed you to decide *I* was the woman you wanted for a wife?"

He was staring at her now, frowning. The silence in the

library grew until Theo found her heart echoing the ticks of the clock.

"I cannot tell you that. Not now," he said at last, his voice stiff. "Perhaps the day will come when I shall be able to do so. But you may be sure, Miss Meredith, our marriage is important to me. And I can assure you, on my honor, you will have no cause to regret it."

"Pretty words," Theo told him as she rose and went to the window, missing the astonished look that came over his face. "How can I know what our marriage will be like? If it comes to that, how can *you* know? We might begin to dislike each other, disagree, argue even—oh, I don't know! And marriage lasts a long time, doesn't it? Forever, in fact."

"Strange, I did not suppose you a romantic," he said. Theo wondered that he should change the subject. "You seemed such a steady girl to me, so sensible. Can it be you are addicted to novels, ma'am? Novels complete with a handsome hero who saves the heroine at the last minute just before he clasps her to him for a searing embrace? I am surprised your parents would permit you to read such things. It is shocking."

"I do not read novels. Well, not so very many, anyway," Theo said, determined to be honest. "And I am not romantic. But I did expect—at least I *hoped*—that I might at least know the man chosen for me. That I might be consulted and my feelings taken into consideration. Instead I am presented with the reality of an almost unknown bridegroom."

"But girls are not supposed to *know* their husbands before marriage," he drawled.

She turned from the window to find him standing close behind her, even smiling, and she was hard put to control her anger.

"I am glad you find this amusing, m'lord," she managed to say. "Well, I do not. I wish this arrangement had never been made. It makes me feel like a bushel basket of grain, a tun of wine—like—like some sort of chattel."

He reached out and captured her hands. "You know, I had not considered how this common custom must seem to the woman involved," he told her, intent on her upturned face. "Know that I do not consider you chattel. Far from it. I chose you deliberately after a great deal of thought. I have no doubt we will get along splendidly. I am not a difficult man. I have a fairly even temper and my manners are not as bad as I have suggested. I am not even as arrogant as you seem to think. I am sure when we have seen more of each other, you will come to feel better about our union. Only consider, Miss Meredith, other men your father might have favored. Someone old perhaps, old and fat and a drunkard. Or someone who had bad breath, one who hardly ever bathed. Surely you must admit I am a better choice than *that*."

She ignored his banter, his teasing smile. "But suppose after I see more of you, I don't feel better?" she demanded. "Suppose you change your mind after seeing more of me? In a few weeks' time the agreement will be common knowledge. But if we cry off now, no one need know of it except my family. There could be no blame assigned to either one of us." She saw his smile had disappeared and she hurried on. "I am not being coy. Believe me, I do not want you to coax me."

"Then marriage does not appeal to you, Miss Meredith? Marriage to anyone?" he demanded.

"I don't know whether it does or not. I hadn't thought . . ."

He laughed harshly. "Obviously. Still, you must know there is no other recourse for you, unless you would prefer to become an old lady's companion, or a strange family's governess. Oh, forgive me. I forgot you are a Meredith and as such would never have to resort to such occupations. Instead you could look forward to becoming your mother's permanent slave, and the elder spinster aunt your siblings would be able to summon whenever there was a crisis in their homes they wanted someone else to handle. Children's illness, huge house parties, in-laws to entertain, that sort of thing."

He dropped her hands and walked away from her. Turning, he said, "But all that is academic. There is no going back now, whatever you feel for me. You said no one knows of the arrangement? You are naive. A notice was sent to the London journals before your father and I left town. He was quick to see to that, no matter how remiss he might have been about informing your mother of the arrangement. By now, all the world and his wife are privy to the secret. I have already begun receiving the congratulations of my friends. I expect your post will soon consist of much of the same."

As Theo stared at him horrified, he added curtly, "Resign yourself, Miss Meredith. On October first you will become the Countess of Canford. There is nothing you can do to change that. You may, however, trust me. It will not be the horrid ordeal you have been imagining."

Theo sank into a chair after he bowed and left her abruptly. She put her hands to her hot face. She was not thinking of her marriage now. She could only think of how she had disgusted him, and she was sure she had done that. His face had shown his revulsion. And it did her no good to tell herself it was about time he had to deal with someone who did not think him a veritable god, and it served him right.

She wondered what he would do. He had told her the engagement could not, *would* not, be broken. He was, for whatever reason he might have, committed to marrying her. The only way she could escape him was to do away with herself.

Theo rose, scoffing at the very idea of it. She had no intention of throwing herself into the lake, off the roof, or under a speeding carriage. She had every intention of living a very long time, God willing. However unpleasant it might be, she reminded herself, married to a leader of the *ton* who was so perfect, so petted, and so proud.

But surely Canford would exact revenge for the defiance she had just shown him. Surely, in spite of his last words, he would make her pay. She shivered. If only she could speak to someone who knew the man, speak honestly and discover what kind of creature he might be.

Her mother would not know, even if she could go to her. Fanny Meredith had moved in a very small circle in London, too shy and uncertain among the sophisticates to try and make new friends. And her father's sister, her Aunt Gloria, had not seemed to care much for her niece and sister-in-law. Or perhaps it was only she had not liked housing them for the three long months of the Season? Of course there was her cousin Charlie. But Charlie was not in England now. He had sailed to Bermuda to see an old friend and spend some time in warmer climes. She loved Charlie. He had been her mainstay in town, always ready to dance with her or introduce her to his friends, to walk or drive with her and share a jest or the latest *on dit*. She missed him more than she could say, especially now. In her mind's eye she saw his homely, good-natured face, the black hair he had such trouble subduing in a fashionable crop, she heard his hearty laugh and aimless, pleasant conversation. She would have married Charlie without a qualm and she knew she wouldn't have regretted it, either, not for a moment. They *fit* somehow in a way she and the Earl of Canford never would.

She recalled her grandmother Hutton then, but she shook her head. She could certainly talk to that lady about anything in the world, but what would her grandmother know? She lived in Bath and rarely left it. And Bath, so fashionable a generation ago, had sunk into a place for the elderly, the infirm, and the parsimonious. Certainly the mighty Earl of Canford would hardly be likely to have spent a moment there if he could possibly avoid it.

Theo wandered back to the window and rested her hot cheek against the cool pane. As she did so, she wondered why she was fighting this at all. The earl had been right. Her father could have chosen a man much worse than Canford for her, in fact just about anyone in the world, for who could compare to him? It was just that the whole thing seemed so bloodless to her, so phlegmatic. She felt like a leaf in a rushing stream, tossed this way and that with no chance to escape the current or find a safe haven away from it.

She wondered how she was ever to look at the earl at dinner or converse in an ordinary way, even laugh at any of his sallies. If he made any sallies, she reminded herself, remembering his grim face when he left her.

But here she wronged the earl. He was his usual urbane self when he entered the drawing room that evening. Mr. Meredith had invited several people to dine, appointed the hour of seven for dinner to be served, and ordered tables set up in the card room for later. Theo was glad to escape those games, for her father asked her to entertain the guests instead, playing softly on the pianoforte. She knew the game of whist, in fact she considered herself an accomplished player, but if she should have been partnered with Canford, heaven knows what mistakes she might not have made! Later, seated before her dressing table while a maid brushed her hair, she thought of the few remarks she and the earl had exchanged. When she felt tears coming to her eyes, she was quick to dismiss the maid. How horrid all this was, she thought. How horrid life was sure to be, married to a man who not only did not love her, but disliked her instead. She wondered if anyone had ever been so miserable.

To her surprise, Theo found herself often in the earl's company during the following days. He took her driving in the afternoons, or for a stroll through the rapidly improving gardens. Sometimes he spoke of his estate near Oxford. Canford Hall sounded magnificent to Theo. She hoped she would be able to manage it, it was so much larger and more impressive than the Abbey.

Sometimes the earl would question her about her life, what she liked to read, what music she enjoyed, who her friends were. One day he asked if she cared for dogs and admitted he himself was fond of spaniels. Did she hunt? He belonged to a local club and looked forward to presenting her to it. Did she by chance paint or sketch? There were several scenic spots at Canford he was sure she would enjoy. If only Theo had not been clever enough to realize what Lucas Whitney was doing being so pleasant, she would have been much happier. Unfortunately she knew very well what he was up to.

One afternoon, they drove into Taunton on an errand for Mrs. Meredith. The parcel collected, they started home again. Theo had been feeling uneasy all afternoon. It was September first, only a short month from her wedding day, and she could not seem to get that date from her mind. When the earl offered to let her take the ribbons, she shook her head.

Lucas Whitney wondered at the little frown she wore, but he did not ask what was bothering her. He had been as angry as Theo had suspected after their talk in the library, but he had been determined not to show it. Instead, he had set out to make her care for him, a campaign as carefully planned and executed as any Wellington and his staff were overseeing on the Continent. Sometimes he was sure he was succeeding, her laughter would be so gay, her smile so warm. But then, in a moment, she would become the solemn, watchful girl he had first met in the woods, her eyes huge on his face, her hands trembling and her posture rigid. Only with her sisters and brothers did she truly relax, and he found himself hoping some of them would join them more and more often. He sensed her favorite was Lester, an angelic-looking little boy who knew exactly how to manipulate the females who surrounded him. He could tell Theo tried hard to like her sister Violet. This twelve-year-old miss had once had the temerity to ask him if he put his faith in the Lord before worldly considerations, assuring him she would pray he had the strength to do so. He had been so taken aback by her impertinence he had not even been able to give her the set-down she deserved. He saw how patient Theo was with three-year-old William, how expertly she took the baby Donald from his nurse and cuddled him until he smiled at the silly song she sang to him in an oddly endearing, rusty little voice. It was only when the children left them to their own devices that she returned to her wary ways.

Now, determined to make her admit he was not the ogre she supposed, but a perfectly normal, even lovable man, he halted his team and ordered his groom to take charge of the rig. Lifting Theo down, he suggested they walk down to a pond he could see through the trees that bordered the road.

"It is hot today, isn't it? Perhaps it will be cooler by the water," he said as he tucked her hand in his arm.

"I don't know who owns this property," she protested. "We will be trespassing."

"I'll protect you from an irate landowner, never fear," he said easily. "Do watch that branch, ma'am."

Theo began to feel uneasy, and a little pulse began to beat in her throat. She did not mind driving out with Canford, for with the groom clinging to the perch behind, he was forced to be circumspect and she could relax. Although she had to admit that since that day in the library, the earl had never attempted to discuss anything the whole world might not have listened to, nor had he acted the lover. Sometimes she had felt as if she were waiting for him to do so. After all, it was his right. They were an engaged couple and he had never even kissed her. She told herself bleakly it was just as she had thought. He might be marrying her, but he did not desire her nor care enough about her to pretend that he did.

"Your mother spoke to me this morning," he went on conversationally and she forced herself to listen. "She informed me she thought it would be a splendid idea if not only Marietta but your sister Violet accompanied us to Canford after the wedding."

Theo turned to look at him but before she could say anything, he went on at his most civil. "She reminded me it was often the custom for a bride to be accompanied by either a sister or a friend to bear her company in the first months of her marriage. She also said your brother Teddy would be delighted to, er, drop in on us at Canford since it is so close to Oxford. Did you know anything about this, Miss Meredith?"

"Of course not," Theo said in a rush. "What can Mama have been thinking to suggest such a thing?"

"I imagine she is trying to rid herself of the pair, if only for a short time. And you see how it would answer. Marietta would be removed from the younger footman's charms and Violet would have a new set of backsliders to reform. However, I must admit I reacted coolly to the suggestion. Canford has its own handsome footmen, grooms, and neighboring lads, and to be truthful, of all your brothers and sisters, Violet is my least favorite. No doubt it indicates some desperate failing in my character, but I cannot like her."

"I don't think anyone does," Theo said absently. "We all hope she will outgrow her excessive religious fervor. I think it is only her age. At twelve, you know, a girl can feel deeply about a number of things."

"So I may trust you to stand firm if your dear mama begs you to take your sisters along when you leave the Abbey?"

Theo ignored his teasing tone. "Certainly you may," she said.

They had arrived at the shore of the pond and a little breeze blowing over the water ruffled Theo's skirts and the ribbons that adorned the brim of her chipped straw hat.

"I can assure you you will not be lonesome at Canford," the earl said, slipping his arm around her. As his hand tightened at her waist and pulled her close to his side, Theo felt as if she were suffocating. Her heart was pounding in earnest now and she knew she must get away from him before he heard it. But before she could move, he turned her to face him and tipped her chin up. She stared at him, her lips opening in unconscious surrender. His back was to the sun and his tall top hat concealed it, and she had trouble seeing his face. It seemed an age to her—or only a second—before he bent his head and kissed her. The touch of his mouth did not frighten her, for it was warm and gentle in its exploration, even tentative, as if it were as unused to kisses as hers was. Theo knew such a thing was ridiculous. Lucas Whitney was in his late twenties, sophisticated, urbane. No doubt he had had many lovers. She concentrated on standing very still. She was glad he had his arms around her. If he let her go, she would be sure to fall in a faint, she felt so weak. She could feel her heart pounding still, and she was ashamed. He was being kind to her, but she knew the kiss they shared could mean nothing to him. She must not let him know how it was affecting her.

Aware that if she did not escape him she would begin to respond with the utmost abandon and therefore disgust him, she put her hands on his shoulders and pushed as hard as she could. He released her in an instant and she had to reach out blindly and grasp the branch of a tree nearby to keep her balance.

As she did so, she stared up at him and cringed when she saw how white his face was, how coldly furious he looked. For what seemed a very long time they stood facing each other without speaking. Then the earl held out his arm.

"We shall return to the carriage now, Miss Meredith," he said in his usual polite way. Only someone listening as intently as Theo could have known how constricted his voice was.

She did not try to speak, but only nodded as she took his arm and turned away a little so he could not see her face.

Canford had little to say on the return journey. Theo said nothing. When she would have left him at the Abbey steps as the groom drove the phaeton and pair back to the stables, Canford grasped her arm to detain her.

"I am leaving here tomorrow morning," he told her, addressing the lowered brim of her bonnet that was all she permitted him to see. "I have business in London. I shall return just before our wedding day. May I suggest you spend the intervening time at least attempting to accustom yourself to that inevitable event and the future we'll share together?"

He paused, but when she did not speak or look up, he added, "You will forgive me if I speak plainly. We may be making a marriage of convenience here, but I want there to be no mistake. I intend to have my heir. That is not negotiable. Have I made myself clear, Miss Meredith?"

Theo nodded, then ashamed of her cowardice, she made herself look up and say, "You may be easy, m'lord. I shall fulfill my part of the bargain since you and my father have forced me to it."

As she turned to climb the stairs he said, "I shall do my best not to beat you, Miss Meredith. No doubt such forbearance will be good for my character, although it is sure to be trying.

"Give you good-bye, ma'am. Until October."

5

Fanny Meredith's mother, Angela Hutton, arrived from Bath a week before the wedding was to take place. With her she brought her constant companion, Lady Handerville, an acerbic widow who delighted her with her wit, and twin spinster nieces who seemed constantly about to swoon at the horrid but truthful things these ladies were wont to say.

Theo was delighted to see her grandmama and gave her a fervent hug and an even more fervent kiss, her eyes filling with tears as she did so.

Mrs. Hutton held her away from her and looked up into her face. Nodding at what she saw there, she said, "Yes, yes, and we shall have a long talk presently, my dear Theodora. Just let me get myself and Handy settled. You do remember Handy don't you? Never go anywhere without her. She keeps me sane in an insane world."

"Of course she remembers me, Angela. I've been told often enough it's impossible to forget me, although the gentleman who said that did not intend it as a compliment."

Both elderly ladies went off in a gale of laughter and it was several moments before Mrs. Hutton recalled herself long enough to introduce the other two ladies traveling with them. "Here are the Misses Quales. I am not sure in what way you are related, but never mind. I often think everyone in England *must* be related, we've spent so many years inbreedin'. No, no, girls, don't faint! No one has time to see to you now.

"Is that you, Fanny? Well, a nice thing it is for me to have to stand about here on the steps waiting for my own daughter to come and bid me welcome.

"Is *he* here?"

Mrs. Meredith admitted that yes, her husband was in residence, and her fond mama sniffed. Ordinarily, Theo would have smiled to see the militant light that came into her eyes as she girded herself for the battles to come, but she had no heart for it on this occasion. There were only six more days, she reminded herself. Only six.

She had no time to brood about it however, for her mother put her in charge of everything as she herself swept her guests off to her own private sitting room.

Theo dealt with the baggage and room assignments, showed the maids where they were to sleep and how to find the back stairs, and explained how the bell system worked. Free at last, she left them to their unpacking in the adjoining rooms of the ladies Hutton and Handerville. It was tacitly understood the elderly twins would rely on a Meredith housemaid for whatever assistance they could not render each other. As she ran down the stairs, Theo thought being a spinster must be truly awful. At least her approaching marriage saved her from that lot, and she would have to try to remember it more often, she reminded herself just as Gwyneth came shrieking into the hall, her brother Huntley in hot pursuit. Gwyneth took refuge behind her big sister's skirts, still crying so hard it was impossible to discover what the matter might be. Theo did not waste time attempting it.

"What have you got in your hand, Huntley?" she demanded. "Show me at once."

Huntley Meredith was a big boy for nine, with a head of dark blond hair and a rosy face sprinkled with freckles. He had both hands behind his back, and now he held one of them out, empty.

"The other one, come on now, lest I get angry," Theo ordered. As he started to comply, Gwyneth began to shriek again and Theo put a hand over her mouth.

The small black-and-green garter snake that the boy held out did not look a bit threatening. Of course, having been kept captive by an energetic nine-year-old and brandished in a little girl's face probably had not helped. Now it dangled limply from his fingers, only an occasional weak twitch showing it still lived.

"You should be ashamed of yourself, Huntley. You know Gwynnie doesn't like snakes. Do stop crying, Gwynnie! The snake is almost dead and Huntley is about to put it back in the woods. Aren't you, Huntley? Papa is in the library, you know. And Grandmother Hutton has just arrived."

Her brother's blue eyes widened and he nodded. Theo was not sure whether he was more in dread of his father or his grandmother. Unlike most elderly ladies, Mrs. Hutton did not admire the male of the species, no matter their age, and was quick to point out her grandsons' numerous faults. Not even Lester could charm her. She adored her granddaughters, however, lavishing them with gifts and hugs and praise. Gwyneth quieted down immediately on hearing her name and rushed off to wash her face and hands and have her frock changed.

Shaking her head at both of them, Theo went to her mother's sitting room. She found the five ladies refreshing themselves with cups of tea and little cakes, and in Lady Handerville's case, a large glass of sherry.

"Come and sit by me, Theodora, dear," Mrs. Hutton said, patting the sofa she was perched on. Theo was quick to obey as the elderly twins tittered and peeked at her from behind their hands. "The blushing bride," Pamela Quales breathed. "Oh, happy, happy girl," her sister Georgina added, the tip of her nose turning pink.

"Don't say it, Handy," Mrs. Hutton advised. "Can't have them faintin' away when we've just arrived.

"Met him in London durin' the Season, did you?" she asked, turning to Theo. "Well, there's no denyin' it's a great match. The Whitneys have good blood lines too. And

I've heard he's rich as well as titled. I'm pleased for you, my girl. Very pleased."

"I didn't meet him in London," Theo said, determined on honesty. "Papa brought him down to Pobryn this August. The contract had already been drawn up between them."

"Never say so!" Miss Georgina exclaimed, groping for her handkerchief. Her sister only moaned.

"To be sure, it was a surprise to us, Mama," Fanny Meredith was quick to say. "But the earl stayed almost three weeks and he and Theo were constant companions. Indeed, sometimes I wished he would take himself off, for you know how I depend on her. And with the wedding to get ready, I was all at sixes and sevens."

"Tell me, Fanny, who organized your weddin'?"

"Why—why, you did, of course. Can it be you have come to assist Theo now? How wonderful, Mama. There are still so many things . . ."

"I've no intention of doin' anything of the kind," her fond parent interrupted. "Once was enough. What I meant was, it's not Theodora's place. As her mother, Fanny, it's yours. Look at her. She's much too pale and I believe she's lost flesh. She was too thin to begin with. She should be seein' her friends, monogrammin' her linen, restin' and amusin' herself in the last days of freedom that remain to her."

"Why, Mama, you sound as if marriage is some kind of ordeal," Mrs. Meredith said.

Lady Handerville snorted as she set her empty glass down on the table beside her. "Well, of course it's an ordeal, woman. Look at you. You've been increasing just about every time we've seen you over the years. Thank heavens you're too old for it now."

"I am not so too old," Mrs. Meredith protested, her face red. "I'll have you know I expect another child next spring."

"Lord save us," her mother said grimly. "Hasn't that old goat learned to keep his breeches buttoned yet, at least in the family bedroom?"

Moaning in distress, both the Misses Quales slumped over, and to Theo fell the task of waving a vinaigrette under their noses.

She did not have her talk with her grandmother until late the following day. Mr. Meredith had chosen to dine out with friends the evening his mother-in-law arrived, but he did not escape a searing interview with that lady the following morning when she cornered him alone in the breakfast room. Kendall told the housekeeper it had been all he could do to preserve his countenance, some of the things she had said. Then she had spent time with each of her grandchildren. Following their sire's example, the older boys had escaped as quickly as they could. Even Lester had been told it was no use smiling and trying to make up to her, for she had his measure and knew he was no better than he should be.

Marietta was petted and admired, but she was also warned about liaisons with the lower classes in a way she did not suspect was a lecture. Mrs. Hutton had exclaimed over her beauty and said that surely she was lovely enough to attract a duke when the time came. If, of course, she was prettily behaved now, for dukes were known to be starchy. Even the hint of past misconduct was enough to send them off in search of some more chaste but just as lovely girl. And surely Marietta remembered that dukes outranked earls, didn't she? Just so.

Violet was told that piety was much to be admired, but to be constantly talking about it made people recall the Pharisee who stood at the temple gates bragging about how good he was in a loud voice so everyone could hear, which you may be sure put people off religion in general and Pharisees in particular. Theo was delighted Violet seemed much struck by this observation.

At last, however, she was summoned to her grandmother's room. As she curtsied to the lady, Mrs. Hutton said, "I've told Handy we wish to be private and sent the twins out for a walk in the shrubbery. They'll probably get lost. Do remind me to send a footman after them when it

begins to get dark. Now, sit down and tell me what besides
this marriage is troublin' you."

"Why should there have to be anything else? Isn't marrying the earl troubling enough?" Theo asked as she sat down
on the footstool near her grandmother's chair.

Mrs. Hutton soon had the whole story. Although she had
scorned to ask her son-in-law anything about it, she had
heard her daughter's version and now she listened carefully
to Theo's halting explanation.

"You do not love him, of course. It is much too soon for
that," she said at last. "But it appears to me you don't even
like him. Why is that? Even in Bath I have heard of Lucas
Whitney, his charming manners, his virile good looks. But
stay! Was he horrid to you? Did he try and force you?"

She looked so fierce, Theo was quick to shake her head.
"No, no! He only kissed me once. It is just, well, he is so
insufferably *proud*! He took it for granted that I must be
thrilled to be chosen by him, with no consideration for *my*
feelings at all."

"Of course he did," Mrs. Hutton said with a chuckle. "He
is a *man*. There isn't one of them who doesn't think themselves superior to any poor female. It was ever thus,
Theodora, and you must excuse the earl for what is typical
masculine logic."

"Yes, but he doesn't *love* me, Grandmama. Although we
were at many of the same parties this past spring, we
weren't introduced and he never spoke to me. Why did he
choose me then?"

Angela Hutton stared down at her granddaughter's thin
face framed in the cloud of dark hair she had inherited from
her father and pondered the question without reaching any
satisfactory conclusion. She thought it was a pity Theodora
took after her father's side of the family. She was not petite
or richly curved, with golden curls and melting, big blue
eyes, nor did she have a pink-and-white complexion. Still,
there were times Mrs. Hutton had considered her almost
handsome. To the girl's credit, she had a ready wit and a
neat turn of phrase, and she was well-read and well-

informed. But if the earl had never spoken to her before the contract was made, he wouldn't know that.

She could recall nothing derogatory about Lucas Whitney. He was not a rake or a gamester, his estates were not mortgaged, and he had conducted his love affairs with discretion. It was really a shame Theodora could not like him. It would be such a splendid match. Still, remembering how regretful the girl had sounded when she mentioned his one kiss, she decided to try again.

"You know, my dear, it is your duty to wed," she began. When she felt her granddaughter stiffen, she reached down and smoothed her hair. "Of course it would be wonderful if you had fallen in love with the earl, but sometimes it cannot be that simple. I did not know your grandfather very well on my wedding day, and to be honest, I did not learn to care for him for a long time. But eventually love grew between us. We had a good marriage. I miss him still. Now consider your mother. I made sure she approved her father's choice, much good it did her."

She snorted. "Others might say that of course they love each other, why, look at the number of children they have had. But I think you are intelligent and worldly enough to realize that has nothing to say to anything. Your father does not care for his offspring. He leaves Fanny alone here in the country while he amuses himself in town. He has done so for years.

"There now, I've spoken plainly. I am glad you are not shocked. I can't stand mealymouthed females. Oh yes, the twins. They have to be a cross I was sent to bear for my sins.

"But I must not change the subject. Tell me, dear, isn't it possible you might come to love the earl someday, as I did my husband?"

A curtain of dark hair hid Theo's face. After what seemed a long time, she shook her head slowly. Her grandmother sighed as she reached down to lift her chin so she could see her eyes.

"Well, it will be a terrible scandal and the *on dit* of the year. There's no avoidin' that. But if you truly cannot bear to marry him, I suppose I'll have to see to it you don't."

Theo's green eyes began to glow and she added quickly, "Don't make a firm decision now. This is far too important, not only for you, but for the family as well. You have to understand there is every likelihood no one else will ever ask for your hand, for to the *ton* you will be known as a hopeless jilt. If that happens you will never know the joy of holdin' your baby in your arms—somethin' I would not have you miss.

"Then too, your actions may affect your sisters' chances. There will be those who will question the Merediths' mental stability. Yes, yes, I know it is unfair! Life is unfair, my dear Theodora.

"You must also remember that as an unmarried woman you will be an object of pity. Consider the Misses Quales. They had beaux at one time, but neither one of them could bring herself to cast off the other for a man. Now all they have is each other. You will not even have that consolation, for I doubt very much Marietta will have any fondness for you if you interfere with her chances for making a good match.

"Run along, now. Think hard before you come to a final decision. Just let me know sometime tomorrow morning."

By the time Theo went to bed, she had a headache from weighing the advantages and disadvantages of marriage with the Earl of Canford. It seemed no sooner did she decide that she could not, for any reason, take such a drastic step, than she would change her mind in order to avoid the scandal for the sake of the family.

Finally, just as dawn was beginning to brighten the eastern sky, she looked up at the canopy over her head and said, "All right. All right, I'll be honest. I say I don't want to marry Lucas Whitney, but the truth is, I'm afraid if I do I'll fall in love with him. And I know he doesn't love me and he probably never will. No, because he's just like my

father, proud and conceited and self-serving. How could I
endure such a marriage?"

She paused for a moment, then whispered, "On the other
hand, how can I bear *not* to marry him?"

She sighed, remembering how wonderful it had been to
be held close in his arms. She knew she would never forget
his kiss.

Perhaps Grandmama is right, she thought. Perhaps I have
a chance to be happy. Or perhaps I can learn to be with
only the respect and courtesy Canford is sure to show his
countess. If only it weren't so hard to have to settle for just
that.

6

As soon as it was full light, Theo went along the hall to her grandmother's room. That lady was still in bed, but she smiled when Theo said, "I have decided I must marry the earl, ma'am. I cannot bear to bring scandal to our house."

"I am so glad, my dear," Mrs. Hutton said, accepting this nobility although she was sure she was not hearing the real reason. "I think you have been very wise and made the right choice. You will not be alone, you know. If the earl mistreats you in any way, you have only to send word to me. I may be old, but I'm not dead yet. I'll take care of him, never fear.

"Now I'm sure you didn't sleep much last night. You look terrible. Get back to bed and stay there. I'll deal with your mother."

Theo kissed her and ran back to her own room. As she snuggled down under the covers, she sighed and closed her eyes. In only a moment, she was fast asleep.

It was mid-afternoon when she woke and rang for a maid. She felt rested and completely peaceful, as if by making a final and firm decision and ceasing to fight what she had come to accept as inevitable, she had banished all her worries. She knew this feeling of goodwill would probably only be temporary, but she was determined to enjoy it while she could.

The Earl of Canford arrived at Pobryn Abbey the last day of September. With him came his friend, Maitland Grant, to serve as groomsman and witness. The earl's sister, the Duchess of Lansmere, had sent her regrets in a stiff little note that Mrs. Hutton and her crony laughed over, claiming it positively oozed disapproval. The duchess's absence did not matter. The Abbey was as full as it could hold with various Hutton and Meredith kin.

Theo knew it was undeniably improved. The gardens were in much better order, the gold draperies had been made and hung in the drawing room, and several other pressing repairs had been made. All the public rooms were decorated with flowers that for once Theo had not had to arrange. She knew her mother was harried with all the wedding details, but when she would have, out of habit, stepped in to assist her, her grandmother was quick to send her away.

"She'll have to cope after you are gone, Theodora, now won't she?" that old lady had explained in an aside. "Best she begin to learn how, now."

Theo was not required to see Lucas Whitney alone. Instead, she greeted him and his friend in a drawing room full of people. She was sure Canford was studying her closely, and she hid her trembling and smiled at him as warmly as she was able. She was glad she had done so when she saw his expression lighten.

She liked Maitland Grant at once. He was only of medium height with a head of carefully tousled auburn curls, and he wore his fashionable clothes casually in a way that reminded her of her cousin Charlie. So did his easy conversation, his compliments and little jests. Theo looked forward to seeing him at Canford Hall. She hoped the rest of the earl's friends would be just as pleasant.

And then it was her wedding day, a misty October morning with a warmth to it that recalled the summer just past. And her mother was there weeping as the maids did her hair and helped her into her gown, while little Gwyneth and Will stared wide-eyed from the doorway, their thumbs in their mouths. And her grandmother, come to embrace her and whisper "courage!" so only she would hear, as well as give her a brooch of emeralds and diamonds for a wedding gift. Marietta, dressed in a new blue silk gown as her maid of honor, exclaimed at the gift, as she had at the earl's double rope of creamy pearls. And then she was walking down the broad stairs on her father's arm, past the smiling, whispering guests, to join Lucas Whitney before the fireplace in the drawing room where the Reverend Mr. Covington waited to make them man and wife.

It seemed only a moment before it was done and the earl bent to kiss her. It was a token kiss, no more, but still it unnerved her. And then there was music and dancing and lighthearted conversation while the footmen passed glasses of wine and negus and punch, and she stood with her new husband to greet the guests and hear their good wishes and congratulations. It seemed much too short a time before she was being helped into the earl's traveling carriage after kissing all the children and her mother one more time, and she could not help crying a little as the carriage went down the drive and her life as she had known it up to now was left behind her. She could still hear baby Donald's howls, not that he could know she was leaving the Abbey forever, she told herself as the earl handed her his snowy handkerchief.

"Thank you," she said in a husky voice. "I did not mean to cry, but leaving the children was so affecting . . ."

"I applaud your sensitivity," he said. "I myself felt only the urge to escape. Especially, I admit, from your grandmother. What an alarming old lady she is. She spent a great deal of time telling me her views on marriage and what she expected of me. And, I gather, if I do not comply, she is not above coming to Canford to give me a piece of her mind. She was terrifying."

Theo listened closely, but she could detect no stiffness in his voice. Perhaps he had forgiven her for her behavior when last they had been together? Perhaps it might be possible to make a new start? She resolved to do everything in her power to make that happen.

They stopped that night in Bath, putting up at York

House, an inn known for its cuisine. Theo discovered the earl had sent orders ahead so everything would be prepared for them. She was glad to excuse herself and retire to her room for a short time alone before dinner would be served in their private parlor.

After the maid who brought her hot water had gone, Theo wandered over to the window and stared out at the busy inn yard and the street beyond. It was crowded and noisy with carriages coming and going, men calling for ostlers and dogs barking. Theo didn't hear a thing. She was reliving the afternoon. Canford had been pleasant and courteous, asking her often if she cared to stop, discussing the wedding and the guests, and telling her how sorry he was his sister had not been able to attend. He said she was with child and found traveling difficult. Theo immediately forgave the duchess what she had considered a terrible snub and managed to contribute her share to the conversation as well.

As the afternoon drew on, however, and the light began to change, she began to feel more and more uncomfortable there alone in the luxurious carriage with the earl at her side. He had not touched her but once when the carriage went into a hole and she almost slipped off the seat, and he had been quick to release her as soon as she had her balance again. She had only been able to feel relief when he let her go and sat back on his side again.

He is my husband, she reminded herself. There had never been a time when she hadn't been conscious of him when he was anywhere near her. He was such a commanding presence, so tall and well-built and powerful. She told herself she must stop thinking of him. It was far too dangerous.

She put up her chin and went to stare at her reflection in the large mirror over the dresser. Her eyes seemed huge in her pale face with her dark hair confined in an unfamiliar chignon. She held up her left hand. The earl's diamond and gold band felt very strange on her finger. She had never worn a ring there. She saw that her hand was steady and she nodded and turned to the door. She had made a bargain and she would keep it.

The elegant meal they sat down to seemed to go on for hours, and Theo was hard put to eat much of it, no matter how Canford coaxed her. He had excused the servants so they might serve themselves. Theo was certain her appetite would have been better if the servants had remained. Still she managed some salad, a slice of chicken breast in a mushroom Marsala sauce, a small piece of game pie, and part of a cream jelly. She also drank three glasses of wine, something she had never done before. She was sure Canford was looking at her askance when he poured her the last one but she ignored him. She felt the wine would give her courage.

Lucas Whitney sat back at last and raised his glass to her. In the candlelight the wine in it gleamed a deep, sensuous red.

"To you, Countess," he toasted her before he sipped it.

Theo clasped her hands together on the table and attempted a smile. Her mouth was suddenly very dry but her glass was empty.

"You needn't look so nervous," he continued. "I don't intend to come to you tonight. I can see you are tired—who would not be after such a day?"

"What did you say?" Theo asked although she had heard him clearly. His brows rose and she hurried on. "I do not understand. I thought for sure—well, isn't it customary—I mean generally don't—and I am not that tired!"

He did not attempt to decipher her tangled speech. "A busy inn is not always conducive to lovemaking, especially the first time," he told her, his eyes never leaving her face. As if to augment his opinion, a burst of raucous laughter floated up from the tap room and someone with a heavy step clattered down the hallway outside the parlor.

Theo felt as if she had been slapped. She had known of course that he didn't love her but she had not expected this. After all, he had told her plainly he wanted an heir. That was why he had married her. Now it was obvious he did

not feel it was important enough to consummate that marriage immediately. He must not find her at all enticing. The
realization scalded.

"Well!" she said, rising to lean her fists on the table. It
canted a little under the pressure and the cover of a serving
dish fell over on the white cloth. Theo paid no attention although the earl reached out to secure the decanter of port.

"I suppose you are waiting for me to thank you for being
so thoughtful," she told him in a voice rich with sarcasm.
She ignored the frown that came over his face as she went
on. "You shall get no thanks from me, sir. This is our wedding night. And I am *not* frightened, only as nervous as I
daresay any girl would be. But *you*! You have the audacity
to tell me you will not come to me tonight and then sit back
and wait to be applauded while I simper and blush. Well,
when do you suppose you will be able to bear to come? In a
week? Two? A month or so? That is, if Your Royal High-
ness has no more pressing engagements, of course."

Canford rose, but Theo did not retreat. She felt a heady
mix of power coursing through her veins, along with a tow-
ering rage, and she thrust her chin out at an even more chal-
lenging angle.

"How dare you speak to me like that? Stop it at once,"
the earl commanded as he came around the table to grasp
her by the arms and shake her a little.

"I will not," Theo said, glaring up at him. "How dare *you*
treat me this way, so casually, as if I were of no importance
and my feelings of no account? We may have a marriage of
convenience, but did you really expect me to be happy to
be put aside until you were ready to enjoy me at your
leisure?"

He seemed startled and it was a moment before he said,
"Come now, Countess. You really should not say such
things. 'Enjoy,' indeed! What do you know of the matter?"

"Nothing of course. How could I?" she said airily. "But
since men seem to engage in lovemaking every chance they
get, what am I to assume except that it must be pleasurable?
For them at least.

"But I refuse to be turned from the subject, sir. I have never been so insulted. Know I consider you proud and pompous and completely selfish."

It was so silent then in the parlor that Theo was able to recall the impassioned things she had just said, and she wondered if she had gone mad. To think she had dared reproach the mighty Earl of Canford as if he were no older than one of her little brothers. It had to be the wine speaking. Surely, brash as she could sometimes be, she had never been so blunt, and at such a time too.

"If that is how you feel, madam, then of course I will be happy to join you in your bed tonight," he said, his eyes glinting down into hers. "I suggest you go and prepare to receive me there shortly."

"No, I won't, not now!" Theo exclaimed, twisting away from him and backing up until she stumbled and fell into a chair. Jumping up and grasping the table again to steady herself, she said, "Don't you dare come anywhere near me. I don't want anything to do with you."

She marched unsteadily to the door of her room, passing him without so much as a glance, although she fully expected him to stop her or at least say something. When he did neither and she had the doorknob held safe in her hand, she turned and dropped him a shallow curtsy, wondering as she did so why she felt so dizzy. "Give you a good night, sir," she said frigidly.

To her disgust and annoyance, Canford's voice when he spoke sounded as if he were trying hard not to laugh. "I intend to be on the road as soon as it is light. That way we will be at the Hall by evening. The maid will wake you and bring you some breakfast at dawn."

Theo nodded regally before she went into her room and shut the door firmly behind her. Putting her ear to that door, she listened hard. She could have sworn she heard Canford chuckling. It did nothing at all for her temper.

7

When the maid woke her the next morning it was still dark. Theo hurried her dressing, barely touched her tray, and was belowstairs just as the earl's carriage was brought around from the stables. She did not look at him, to be truthful she had concentrated on not thinking about him from the time she had been awakened. She saw that in addition to the carriage, a handsome mare stood saddled and she tried to hide her relief when Canford announced he intended to ride.

Unlike her wedding day, it was a cool morning with a brisk breeze, and clouds stretched unbroken across the sky. Everything was bathed in a cold gray light which Theo felt most appropriate to her mood and the headache she had.

As they left the inn yard, Theo, sitting in solitary splendor, glanced sideways at Lucas Whitney as he trotted alongside. She admired his rugged profile, then how well he rode. It was as if he and the mare were one. Was there anything the dratted man could not do well? she wondered. Somehow that thought reminded her of her uneventful wedding night and she sniffed. I have not forgiven him, she told herself, biting her lower lip in her determination. He is entirely at fault. Still, it seemed an inauspicious beginning to a lifetime together and she was sorry for it. She almost wished, unsaid the things she had told him. But then she reminded herself she had no intention of becoming an imposed-upon wife, treated casually and with no regard for her feelings. Not if she could help it, that is.

It was a long, weary journey to Canford Hall, situated as it was a little way northeast of London near Shillingford on the River Thames. As before, the earl had been diligent in seeing to her comfort, providing a private room for her at the inns where they stopped to change the teams, sending her maids to wait on her, and providing food and hot tea. He did not join her. Glad of this at first, Theo began to resent it as the day went on.

But by the time they turned in between the tall stone columns that fronted the gravel drive that led to Canford Hall, Theo was as tired of being alone as she was of trying to find a part of her anatomy to sit on that had not been tortured by the jouncing of the carriage. She peered eagerly through the windows at the little she could see now that the sun had set. The Hall itself, tantalizingly revealed and then hidden by the groves of trees they passed through, shone brightly with welcoming lights. It seemed a massive place compared to the Abbey. She could tell there was a sizeable lake before it from the reflection of those lights in the wide, dark water.

Canford himself was there to lift her down. Theo thanked him and tried to conceal how sore she was as they went up the stairs to large double doors flanked by flaming torches. A groom had run up the stairs before them, but before he could sound the knocker, the door was opened by the earl's butler. He bowed before he ushered them in. Theo could see there were several footmen in the hall, but no other servants arranged in rows to meet her. She was glad. She had been steeling herself for that ordeal throughout the day. She felt dirty and untidy and she was still stiff although she had finally lost her headache. She wanted nothing more than to bathe, eat a light supper, and seek her bed.

"This is Oates, Countess," the earl said, introducing the butler. "He is invaluable to me and I daresay will become so to you as well. Ask him or the housekeeper, Mrs. Standish, for anything you need."

"M'lady," the butler said, bowing again. Theo saw he

had a light in his eyes as well as a smile for her, and she was quick to smile in response.

"You received my message, Oates?" Canford asked as he handed his hat and gloves to a footman.

"Certainly, m'lord. A light supper will be served in your rooms as soon as you ring. The countess's trunks came yesterday. They have been unpacked. All is in order."

"Excellent," Canford said over his shoulder as he tucked Theo's hand in his arm and led her to the stairs. A tall footman preceded them, holding a candelabrum high to light the way.

As they went up the stairs the earl said, "Would you care for a bath, ma'am? I intend to have one before we dine. The roads were dry but I know the dust comes through the crevices of any carriage, no matter how tightly built."

"Thank you, that would be wonderful," Theo told him, trying not to be too obvious about it as she looked around at her new home.

"I'll take you on a grand tour tomorrow," Canford said. "It's difficult to see everything at night, especially the paintings. Ah, here we are."

As the footman opened a door and went to light the candles there, the earl led her inside. "These are your rooms. They are on the front of the house overlooking the lake. They were my mother's. I hope you will like them."

Before Theo could reply, he added, "I'll send a maid to you, and order that bath. We'll have supper served here."

He bowed a little and went away, trailing the footman and leaving Theo standing in the middle of a large sitting room. It was tastefully furnished in royal blue and gold, but it looked old-fashioned to her and worn. She resolved to redecorate it. Exploring further, she found the bedroom also in need of attention.

Four maids arrived together to ready her bath. They bore large copper cans of steaming hot water to fill the tub in her dressing room. Theo dismissed them almost at once. She did not want anyone to help her tonight, and she had already decided to leave her hair up during supper. It would not look so—so intimate that way.

As she sat in the tub and washed herself with the scented soap provided, all the nervousness she had felt the previous evening returned with a vengeance. What would the earl say to her? How would he act? Would he treat her coldly, leave her to sleep alone in the sumptuous bed she had seen in the other room to repay her for her hot, hasty words? That would be awful, she told herself as she raised one leg high to scrub it. But wouldn't it be even worse if he pretended nothing had happened, and tried to make love to her?

"Why *tried*?" she muttered as she soaped her other leg. "Just looking at him, you can tell the dratted man is capable of the act, probably successful every time he attempts it."

She groaned a little, remembering the virility that emanated from him even when he was just sitting quietly, intent on nothing more than eating a good meal.

As she rose from the tub at last and reached for one of the heated towels the maids had left for her, she saw herself reflected in a long pier glass set against one wall of the dressing room. She was startled. She had never seen herself in the altogether, for at the Abbey she had only had a small looking glass at her disposal. Quickly, she turned her back and rubbed herself dry. But then, as if compelled, she turned back and dropped the towel. She studied herself critically. She was very thin and much too tall and she was glad she could not see herself too clearly since she was not wearing her spectacles. Her legs, although she supposed they were shapely enough, seemed endless. Her waist was too slender, her rose nipples seemed much too large in breasts that were barely curved. The black hair between her legs was surely overabundant, and much too dark against her white skin.

Blushing, she grabbed the towel and wrapped it around her before she opened the press to find a gown and robe she could wear to supper. She knew there was no sense dressing again, for to do so was to leave herself open to ridicule. She chose the most modest night rail she had. At last she tightened the sash of her robe and slipped her feet into satin slippers.

Just before she opened the door to the sitting room, she took a deep breath. I will be brave, she promised herself. And I won't have any wine and I'll keep a civil tongue in my head if it kills me.

Canford was there before her, but she barely noticed him, or the butler where he stood arranging dishes over spirit lamps on a sideboard, for what seemed to be a large pack of dogs rushed across the room to her, barking and leaping up in excitement.

"Molly! It's all right, girl," the earl called, and the largest dog stopped at once. The others, young puppies, Theo noticed, were not so obedient, and she knelt to pat them and have her face licked with ardor. How dear they were, she thought, her hands buried in their soft liver and white fur. Their long ears were so silky, their dark eyes so soft. She heard the earl speaking quietly behind her, and a footman materialized to take the puppies in charge.

As he left, followed by the silent Oates, Theo felt her nervousness come back. She wanted to talk about the spaniels, but words failed her.

"Won't you sit down and let me serve you, ma'am?" Canford said. "If you continue to take as little as you did last night I'm afraid you might disappear completely."

As he spoke, he held a chair for her and Theo slipped into it gratefully, glad of the warmth of the little fire that burned on the hearth to take away the chill. She was sorry he had mentioned her size, especially since she had just seen for herself how deficient she was.

"The dogs are lovely," she said at last as he filled her plate. "They are young yet, aren't they?"

"Yes, only four months or so. Molly's first litter."

The older spaniel, who had remained in the room and was now sniffing Theo's slippers, looked up at her master and wagged her tail before she settled down near Theo and rested her head on her foot.

"I see you have been accepted completely," Canford said

with a smile. "It is a great compliment. Molly doesn't take to everyone."

As he set her plate before her, he said, "I hope you like duck with sour cherry sauce. It is one of my favorite dishes and my chef serves it often. There is also some omelette as well as quail eggs in aspic. Do try the asparagus. It is from my succession houses."

He sat down across from her and looked at her quizzically for a moment before he added, "You are unpredictable, Countess. One evening—dare I mention it?—you have too much to say and the next hardly anything at all. I say? Are you there?"

"Certainly, sir," Theo managed to get out. The aroma of the food before her was making her feel dizzy again and she shook her head as he lifted the bottle of wine and held it toward her glass. Or was it his damp hair, the clean scent of him? she wondered.

"Perhaps it is just as well," he said, filling his own glass before he set the bottle down. "Did the headache I am sure you had wear off by noon?"

Theo was aware he was teasing her gently, but she could not summon any indignation tonight. This was not a noisy inn. There would be no sounds or smells from a taproom, no echoing footsteps making their way down the wide hall outside. And no late coach rumbling into an inn yard, its driver bellowing for a change.

"The duck is delicious," she made herself say as she took a small bite.

She looked up when he did not reply to see him looking off into space and smiling a little. Then he shook his head as he cut his duck small. "Yes, it is," he agreed. "I am tempted to scold Stepan for serving it, especially tonight. But perhaps it was done in all innocence?"

"I—I do not understand," Theo said, nibbling a tip of asparagus.

"You are a bride, remember?" He popped a cherry in his mouth and chewed it before he went on. "Surely you have heard that a cherry in cant, or slang if you will, is another name for a young girl."

Theo grasped her fork tighter lest she drop it in her nervousness. "I was not aware of that, sir," she said with as much composure as she was able to summon. She took a sip of water, then another, before she forced herself to go on eating. If the earl noticed she left all the cherries in the sauce, at least he said nothing of it and for that she was grateful.

To her relief, he spoke from then on of innocuous subjects, and she was able to contribute occasionally. Still, she was glad when supper was over and she could bend and pat the spaniel at her feet.

"Are you very tired?" she heard him ask, but she would not raise her head. Instead she said in a muffled voice, "Yes, I am tired. I am sure I will sleep well tonight."

"I hope so," he said courteously. "I hope we will both sleep well tonight, Countess."

Theo had had enough. She rose quickly and backed away from the table, her gaze never leaving his face. "If you will excuse me, sir? I would retire."

He got up leisurely and stretched before he came to her side and took her hand in his. Theo held her breath, waiting, but after a moment he only raised that hand to his lips to kiss it. "I suppose if I were to remark that I hope you are going to bed to speed the time until I come to you, I would be accused of being conceited and pompous again," he said before he chuckled at her horrified expression. "No, no, I must not tease you. You are excused, ma'am."

Recovering her hand, Theo dropped a quick curtsy and tried for a sedate pace as she walked to the door of the bedroom. As she closed that door behind her, she heard the dog bark a little. It almost sounded as if Molly were questioning her master about the strange undercurrents even she could feel in the room.

Theo did not summon a maid. Instead, she quickly washed and cleaned her teeth, and she took her hair down herself, brushing it as best she could, and tying it back with a ribbon. After blowing out the candle, she fled across the room as if all the hounds of hell were after her, removing her robe as she did so, to kick off her slippers and climb into the big bed. Pulling the covers over her head, she cowered there like a small child intent on hiding from a bugbear.

But her particular bugbear did not appear and at last she rearranged the covers, straightened the pillows, and lay back with a sigh. There was a little moonlight coming through a crack in the draperies; the cloudy day had given way to better weather. Theo sighed again. He was not coming tonight either. It was maddening, no, it was terrible. She told herself if she knew where his room was she would have gone to *him*, just to get the thing done and the endless, awful suspense over.

She yawned and closed her eyes. Tomorrow, she told herself. I'll have it out with him, tomorrow sometime when he is showing me the Hall. This can't go on. I shall go mad if it does.

She did not know what woke her later, for surely there had been no sound. Still, she lay on her back, her eyes tightly closed while she wondered at the hurrying beat of her heart.

"Are you awake? I sense you are," she heard him say and she opened her eyes. He was standing halfway across the room, holding a candle. As he came forward and lit the lamp on the table beside the bed, she saw he was wearing a silk robe. She did not move or speak. She felt she could not blink even if she had wanted to. It was as if she were mesmerized.

She watched as Canford untied his robe and dropped it to the floor. He stood there naked in the golden lamplight and she thought surely he was as beautiful as any of the Elgin marbles of Greek gods she had seen in London. The lamplight emphasized the muscles in his broad shoulders and powerful chest, casting them in chiaroscuro, part in light, part in shadow. His torso narrowed to a surprisingly small waist and compact hips.

Swallowing hard, Theo closed her eyes, as if by doing so she could make him go away. He frightened her now. She did not want him to make love to her. No, for it was obvious he was too big for her, and she, too small.

But he did not go away. Instead, as he pulled the covers back and slid in beside her to take her in his arms, he said, his voice serious, "Now, Countess. *Now.*"

8

When Theo woke the following morning, Lucas Whitney was not beside her. She did not know when he had left her, indeed, she could remember little of the previous night in any sequence or with any clarity. Instead, parts of it came and went in her mind like pictures complete with sensations that made her blush even now. She shifted in the big bed, and the discomfort she felt still reminded her of what she had lost. He had been gentle and endlessly patient. She almost wept remembering how he had gone to get a wet cloth and as he washed her, told her how lovely she was, how sweet. Of course he had been lying, but Theo had been thankful he had been kind enough to tell that lie. He had not left her then, no, he had climbed back into bed to hold her close and cover her face with kisses while his hands caressed her. It had been all she could do to keep an iron control over herself, lest she disgust him with her ardor and give the game away.

Still, it had been the most wonderful, glorious, sensational, fulfilling . . . oh, she could not think of words enough to describe it, this, the most exciting night of her life. And what was even better was that there would be more nights like it. Often. Maybe every night. She smiled in anticipation at the very thought of it.

The bedroom door opened and the earl came in bearing a tray. He smiled down at her as he set it on the table before he went to throw the draperies open to let the morning sun stream through the windows.

Suddenly Theo felt very shy and she pulled the covers

high. She had no idea where her nightrail had gone, and she was very much aware of her nudity.

"There's no need to hide from me, Theo," Canford said as he sat down on the bed and poured her a cup of chocolate. "I thought you might not care to call a maid this morning, so I came instead. There's hot water in the dressing room. Come now, sit up. You can't drink lying down, you know."

Gingerly, Theo swept her hair away from her face and tried to do as he ordered without exposing herself. He chuckled at her attempts but she was glad he did not pull the sheets aside. Perhaps it wasn't only the bright sunlight. Perhaps she felt shy because he himself was fully dressed.

"I thought we would have breakfast together downstairs," he said. "Then I want to show you the Hall from attics to cellars. You must tell me when you've had enough. There's no denying it's a huge old pile."

"But beautiful," Theo said, for she could tell how he loved it by the pride in his voice.

"Oh, yes, it is beautiful." He looked around and frowned. "But this room is not. Strange, I never noticed how shabby things were in here. We must have the painters in, and the upholsterers—tell me, what are your favorite colors?"

Theo sipped her chocolate and pretended to think. All she really wanted to do was kiss him, he looked so handsome, and yes, so dear. So she had done what she had feared, had she? Fallen in love with him and in only two days' time? She knew that didn't change a thing except to make everything more difficult for her later, but today she didn't care. She was prepared to grab whatever happiness there might be in store for her, even if Lucas never learned to love her as she loved him. Lucas, she thought dreamily. Dear Lucas. My dearest, my darling Lucas.

"What are you thinking?" he asked, his voice amused. "You look like a kitten let loose in the cream."

"I'm not going to tell you," she said as she handed him her empty cup. "I hope I am allowed to have some private thoughts."

"Perhaps a few," he said as he threw the covers back and went to fetch her robe. Theo looked down at the drops of blood on the sheet beneath her, but when she would have pulled up the covers, Canford laughed at her.

"No, don't bother. It will be all over the estate in an hour no matter what you do," he told her. She covered her face with her hands and he pried them gently away. "Don't be ashamed. It is proof you came to me a virgin and it will please my people that you did. Come now, get dressed. I want my breakfast."

Theo did as she was bade, even letting him help her fasten her gown, and kneel to put on her stockings and sandals. She would not let him try his hand at hairdressing, however, and she brushed it herself in the old style she had always worn at home.

The Hall was as large as Lucas had claimed. Theo was sure it would be a long time before she was able to wander it alone without getting lost. She even asked the earl if she might not have one of Molly's puppies to serve as a guide after they had inspected yet another corridor full of bed-chambers, withdrawing rooms, sitting rooms, and stairways. She studied the family portraits carefully, searching for clues, but she found no one like him until they stood before his parents' double portrait. Looking from it to his face beside her, she nodded.

"Yes, there is some of your father in you, and more of your mother," she told him seriously.

"What? You say I am feminine, ma'am?" He growled in mock anger.

"Not at all, as if you didn't know that very well, you conceited man," she said tartly. "But you certainly do not have your sire's nose. I am grateful for that. And you have your mother's coloring and eyes and smile, even if you did get your father's height."

They stopped finally in the library so the earl could read the post that had accumulated in his absence. Theo sat down in a window seat filled with pillows to stare out at the bright gardens beyond. The sun was warm on her shoulders, and her eyes were heavy. In only a moment or so, she had slipped down, turned on her side, and fallen asleep.

She woke when Lucas kissed her cheek, to find his hand under her skirts, warm on her thigh as he caressed it. As that hand moved upward, Theo darted a quick glance out the window beside her, then at the door that led to the hall where she knew the butler and some footmen were stationed.

"Don't, oh, you mustn't," she whispered. "Anyone outside can see us here. And someone might come in."

He stopped and raised his head. She was surprised by the ardor she saw in his face. Could it be he was a consummate actor as well as the expert he appeared to be in every other part of his life?

"No one will come in," he assured her at his most lofty. "I have told Oates we do not care to be disturbed. It would take the Hall to be ablaze from end to end for him to disobey my order."

He saw she was still looking fearfully at the door, and he added, "I can, of course, lock it if that would make you feel easier. However, the key is old and it creaks in the lock. I daresay Oates might be insulted. I wouldn't blame him if he were. And as for what the footmen would be thinking . . ."

Theo sat up, pushing his hand away so she could put her skirts in order. "Surely the simplest thing would be to behave circumspectly," she said.

"I don't feel circumspect," he said, kissing her ear and then trailing kisses down her throat till his lips reached the neck of her gown. One arm slid around her to hold her close. His other hand caressed her breasts. "I want you," he said.

Theo wanted him too, but she did not say so. "Please, Lucas," she begged. "Please leave me alone."

Without another word he sat up and went back to his desk. Theo watched as he seated himself and pulled a sheaf of papers toward him. His face was cold now; obviously she had offended him. But really, she told herself as she turned to face the window, wouldn't you think he would have better sense? There was a gardener now, preparing some flower beds for the winter. Of course he was quite a distance away, but still, it shows I was right. It is too bad Lucas is upset, but he cannot always have his own way. It occurred to her that he probably always had, and that was why he took her refusal so much to heart.

After a few minutes, she went over to the shelves to see if she could find something to read. She saw Canford had several of Scott's novels and would have teased him about them if she had not felt so awkward still. He had not said a word to her since she had rebuffed him. It was as if he were a little boy, sulking because he could not have another sweet. Annoyed, Theo took down one of the novels she had not read and excused herself. He only waved a careless hand. As she went up to her rooms, she hoped he did not intend to keep this up indefinitely.

But of course he did not. She did not see him until dinnertime, and by then he was pleasant and smiling. She had read her book, taken extra care with her dressing, and allowed the maid who came at her summons to brush and rearrange her hair. The girl seemed deft enough. Theo decided to make her a personal abigail, a luxury she had never enjoyed before.

I am a countess now, she told herself as she went downstairs at the first dinner bell. A rich countess at that. Surely there can be no objection.

She told the earl of her decision while he enjoyed a glass of sherry before the fireplace. He nodded, but he could not resist saying, "I had hoped you might wait until we went up to London. The maids here are country girls, not at all up to scratch. You will need someone more skilled, someone who can turn you out superbly."

"Perhaps Betsy can learn how."

"And if she cannot, and later you have to engage another maid, are you prepared to deal with her hurt feelings?"

Theo nodded. "Of course. I never did suffer my mother's soft heart. Servants are meant to serve, are they not? I am sure they prefer knowing whether you are pleased or displeased with them. That way they can mend their ways, or, if necessary, be turned off."

"You are cool," he said, looking at her with interest. "I never suspected it."

"I have given the orders in my father's house for many years," she said. "Not from choice, you understand. Because I had to or nothing would ever have been done."

"Your mother did not take offense at being usurped?"

He seemed incredulous, and Theo smiled. "Hardly. She urged me to do even more. I love her dearly, but I have always known she was indolent."

"Perhaps that is why she had so many children," he mused.

"I don't understand."

"I meant if she had not been so lazy and careless, she might have avoided at least some of her pregnancies." Seeing she still looked puzzled, he added, "There are ways, besides denying your husband his rights."

"What ways?" Theo demanded, ignoring the latter part of his statement.

He chuckled then. "You have no need to know of them, Theo. Not for a long time anyway, since the object of this marriage is to provide Canford with an heir."

Once again Theo felt as if she had been slapped. Fortunately Oates announced dinner then and she was able to hide her chagrin as they went to the dining room. As she did so, she tried to forget his words, spoken as they had been in such a calm, ordinary way. She did not even think he had said them to insult her, or hurt her. No, he had only been stating the facts.

Why should those facts upset you, she asked herself. Because he acted as if he loved you last night? Because you now love him? *He* does not feel as you do and he never will. Give over!

He came to her that night and the next, and the next, but he never again suggested they make love anywhere but in

her bed. In a way, Theo was sorry. There were some wonderful opportunities during the days that followed and October waned, giving way to November. The days grew chill
and fires burned constantly in all the rooms in use in the
Hall. Theo was busy running the household, much as she
had done at Pobryn Abbey. She enjoyed it and it pleased
her to see everything go smoothly. She had established a
rapport with Mr. Oates and Mrs. Standish, who at first had
made the mistake of considering her an ignorant slip of a
girl who could be easily led. It took less than a week for her
to change her mind. The earl was busy as well, back to his
old routines. Sometimes it seemed to Theo that they had
become a staid old couple before they had even played their
roles as bride and groom.

The hardest part of all for her to play was having to pretend indifference when Canford made love to her. She
knew she could not let him know how his lovemaking af-
fected her. If she did, she might just as well declare her
love for him openly. And surely that would give him a disgust of her, since he did not reciprocate her feelings.

When he was with her in bed, she tried thinking of other
things. It was impossible. She promised herself she would
not move or make any sound at all. Even more impossible.
It got so she could not wait for him to leave her and go to
his own rooms so she might relax her rigid body and let the
waves of feeling he evoked sweep over her at last.

He had told her many times it would be better if she
could relax, learn to enjoy the act. She pretended that was
impossible too. Instead, she feigned indifference, as if
whether he came or not did not matter to her.

When she had her first menses at the end of October,
Theo could tell how disappointed Canford was. She could
not help being offended again although she knew such feelings were stupid. But even living day by day with nothing
but common courtesy to sustain her, she could not help
dreaming of more. Much more. Sometimes she was sure he
was growing fond of her. When the next day brought a moment of coldness, or impatience, she despaired anew.

She wished they might have company. Perhaps if he had his friends around him, he would be happier, and she, easier. When she mentioned a house party, he shook his head. It was after dinner one evening and they were sitting together in the library, their favorite room. Theo held a book she was not reading while the Canford studied a London journal, Molly at his feet. The puppies, worn out from a day at play, sprawled in a heap nearby.

"No, no house party," he said without a trace of a smile. "I would never embarrass you that way, ma'am."

"What do you mean?"

"We are too newly married. The world expects us to want nothing more than to be left alone. You see how an invitation to Canford at this time would be interpreted, don't you? Lord, all those vicious old tabbies would really have something to gossip about."

"I did not think of that," she whispered.

He shrugged. "I dislike gossip. Perhaps you should have brought your sisters here, as your mother suggested. If you want them, you have only to write. I'll send a carriage for them and their maids."

"But I don't want them here!" Theo exclaimed. "I only thought some company might please you, sir."

"I am content," he said shortly, disappearing behind his paper again.

Theo picked up her book although her eyes were so full of tears she could barely make out the print even with her spectacles on. As she did so, she wondered if she had only imagined that pregnant little pause before the earl told her he was content.

Near the end of November, an early post brought a letter from Canford's sister, the Duchess of Lansmere. She addressed this missive to him alone. She never acknowledged Theo except to send her good wishes to her at the end of one of her infrequent communications. Theo could picture her scowl as she penned the words. Now the earl tossed her letter across the breakfast table.

"Eugenia is asking us to spend Christmas at Lansmere Park. She cannot come here, that is certain. She expects to be confined the end of April. Would you care for the visit, ma'am? Since it is only to be family, it cannot be re-marked."

Theo was not at all sure she would care for it. She did not like the distant, proper duchess. Still, it would be a change. No doubt there would be other gentlemen there, and hunting and riding expeditions to entertain her husband. She could certainly put up with her unpleasant sister-in-law for his sake. And of course they would have to see each other sometime. It might be better to get that over with now.

"Why, that sounds very nice," she said. "I believe you told me Lansmere was located in Hampshire, did you not? Is it a long journey from here?"

"No. It can be done in a day if the weather is good and we get an early start."

"I know your 'early starts' and 'one day journeys,' " Theo said, trying to tease him. "I was never so sore as the night we arrived here."

"Very well, we shall do the thing in two days, then, ma'am. I had not realized you were uncomfortable. My apologies."

"Lucas, I was only teasing!" Theo said as she saw him picking up another letter. "Of course we shall travel from here to there in a day. Can't you take a jest?"

He stared at her from his side of the table. "It appears I cannot," he said, his voice cold.

Theo rose and threw her napkin on the table. "This is too much," she said. "I have borne with it all as well as I could, but I am tired to death of it now."

"Tired of what?" he asked, rising as well.

"Tired of your stupid indifference and your cold de-meanor, all carried out under the guise of courtesy," Theo snapped. "Sometimes I want to scream I get so angry with you. Speak plainly, sir. You cannot possibly offend me more than you have done already."

"I haven't the least idea what you're talking about," he said, and Theo, even in her anger, saw from the puzzled look on his face, he spoke the truth. "It seems to me you are being unreasonable, ma'am. Are you sure you are feeling well?"

"Aha! So you think I might be with child and it is making me emotional and sensitive, do you? I am sorry then to have to tell you I got my menses again this morning."

"No doubt that is the reason you are behaving so badly. You are excused, ma'am. I suggest you go and lie down. And perhaps it would be best for you to keep to yourself until you can act as my countess should. I shudder to think how a scene like this would be perceived at Lansmere Park."

Theo stared at him across the table, her face pale. It was so quiet in the breakfast room she could hear the lash of cold rain against the windowpanes.

"You are the most impossible, most imperceptive creature I have ever known," she told him. Not waiting for any reply, she left the room. As she went to the stairs, she told herself she had escaped just in time, for just one more minute in his company, and surely she would have thrown the teapot at him.

Of course, not an hour later, she was sorry she had precipitated an argument, but when she went to find Canford to deliver the handsome apology she had prepared, she discovered he had gone out and was not expected back until late afternoon. Theo longed to ask where he had gone on such a raw, rainy November day, but knowing such a question was impossible, she only smiled and went to the library. Alone in the hall, the butler shook his head, his generally impassive face mournful. Things were not going well for his master and the new bride and Oates was sorry for it.

Theo delivered her apology the moment she joined Canford in the drawing room before dinner, after spending a long day by herself.

"I do not know what came over me, sir," she said, making herself look him straight in the eye. "I was rude and I hope you will forgive me. I am so very sorry."

"Of course," he said, his voice easy. "I am sorry too for . . ."

"Then we may forget it?" Theo asked eagerly, not at all anxious to hear a lecture on the proper behavior required of countesses. "Pretend it never happened? Oh, how silly I am. Of course we cannot do that. Still, I do wish I did not have this unruly tongue. Ever since I was a child I have been given to blurting out the most terrible things. I shall try to do better, especially at Lansmere."

"Most especially at Lansmere," he agreed, coming to take her hand and stare down into her eyes intently. What he was searching for there, Theo could not tell, but before she could question him, Oates announced dinner and the opportunity was gone.

9

They arrived at Lansmere Park the second week of December. The weather had held, for it had not snowed yet. It was cold and crisp, the ground as hard as iron. There would be no hunting at Lansmere until the cold and frost eased. As the carriage trundled up the drive, Theo looked about with interest. The park was well laid out and meticulously maintained; she had expected nothing less. Still, she could not like it as well as Canford and said so. "I don't know why," she tried to explain. "It is a very handsome property, but somehow . . ."

The earl smiled. "Just look there," he said, pointing out the window as the carriage turned a corner.

"Oh, my," Theo said, her voice an odd mixture of awe and dismay. Canford laughed.

"Yes, it is a bit much, I agree. All that dreary red brick. And it is so symmetrical. I never come here but I long to suggest the duke put up a tower on one end, or throw out a wing somewhere. You won't feel called upon to suggest that, I hope, Theo."

"I have vowed to be on my very best behavior," she told him with a warm smile. They had walked carefully around each other since her outburst in November. It was breaking her heart but she did not let it show.

The earl lifted her down before a pair of massive black doors and she stole a surreptitious glance at him. He looked handsome with the cold air bringing color to his face, and his dark eyes were intent as he spoke to the servants.

They were shown to the duchess's private sitting room. She was reclining on a chaise longue covered by a light wool throw. She made no move to rise, only extending her hand to her brother before she nodded to Theo.

I am *so* delighted and happy you have come, Theo said to herself for her. How *wonderful* to see you both, you dear, *dear* people.

"So indolent, Genie?" Lucas inquired as he bent to kiss her lightly. "I trust we find you well?"

"Very well, thank you. It is unfortunate you came just now. I always rest at this time of day."

"Well, we have no intention of going away so you may take that disapproving look from your face," her fond brother told her. "However, we will leave you to your rest. There's plenty of time to visit."

The duchess did not appear to be pleased by this magnanimous offer. "Don't be so silly, Lucas," she said. "You're here now so you might as well sit down. I'll order tea."

"I'd prefer brandy," he said. "This frigid weather. Theo, my dear, what would you like?"

As he spoke, he held out his hand and she put her own into it and let him draw her closer. "Tea would be delightful," she said, smiling at the duchess as warmly as she could.

"We are not the first to arrive, I hope," the earl said as he led Theo to a sofa and took the seat beside her, still retaining her hand. For all the world like the happiest of bridegrooms, Theo thought bleakly. Oh dear, this is going to be even worse than I imagined.

"The Derbyshire Forrestals are here; Lady Blake and others." As she rang the bell she added, "And of course the dowager duchess comes up from the dower house on every occasion. She always does."

"Patience, Genie," her brother murmured.

"I have certainly learned that these past two years," his sister snapped, rearranging her covering with hands that shook a little. She sounded petulant. Theo could hardly wait to meet the dowager duchess.

"Then Maitland Grant is here. I invited him because I was sure you would enjoy his company, Lucas."

Turning her attention to Theo, the duchess continued. "How unfortunate I was unable to attend your wedding, Theodora. Especially since I understand Lucas did not see fit to invite any of the rest of the family. He will have some explaining to do this Christmas. Some of the aunts are very miffed. They are sure there must have been something unsavory about the whole affair."

"It was a quiet wedding," Lucas said before Theo could reply. "I did not want it turned into a circus."

"Still, we did have a great many guests from my family and the neighborhood," Theo said. She was tired of sitting there mutely, wearing a little smile. After all, she could think and converse. She was not a doll.

"Indeed?" the duchess murmured, patently uninterested. "You are settling in at Canford? It is a lovely place, is it not? Not that it can compare to Lansmere."

"Oh, no, it is very unlike Lansmere," Theo agreed. She felt a little pressure on her hand and glanced up at the earl before she went on. "I have seldom seen such grandeur as Lansmere presents. Surely it must be quite a cultural landmark."

"Yes, it is an extremely popular destination for people on procession," the duchess agreed, a shade more cordially. "I find it wearisome, but His Grace encourages all who come to investigate the grounds and the public rooms in the mansion itself. The King's Chamber is always a great success. Henry VIII slept there for a week."

"Alone?" Theo asked, truly interested now. "Or was one of his wives with him? Which one?"

Her hostess stared at her. "I have no idea. *That* is never mentioned."

And never will be again, Theo promised herself. She wondered if the duke was as stuffy as his wife, although she knew in all probability he was sure to be, for what warm, cordial man would choose such a cold stick?

"Genie, Genie, you'll never guess who has come . . . oh! I did not know you were *here,* m'lord. Er, ma'am. Please excuse me."

"Sweet Patsy," Canford said, rising and holding out his arms. The young girl at the door ran into them and hugged him, her eyes shining. Her love for him was so obvious, Theo stiffened. Of course, the girl couldn't be more than fifteen if she was that, but she could not like the way the earl kissed her so heartily and swung her around before he set her back on her feet. He was so *easy* with her. He is not that way with me, Theo thought bleakly. He never was.

"Here is my favorite cousin, Theo," Canford said. "She is Miss Patricia Ann Whitney, but everyone calls her Patsy. I hope you will like each other."

Miss Whitney looked as doubtful as Theo felt, but she curtsied. "How do you do, Countess?" she said, and Theo smiled. The child was certainly lovely with her soft brown curls and slightly tip-tilted hazel eyes. She was of medium height with a lovely figure and a waist so small it must tempt a lot of men to see if they could span it. Beside her, Theo felt awkward—tall and ungainly.

"Do forgive me for intruding, Eugenia, when I know you are resting. I was looking for Patsy," an older woman said as she came forward and inspected the three near the chaise. "So, you have come, have you, Lucas? Well."

"Aunt Florence, how delightful to see you," he said easily. "May I introduce my bride? Theo, Lady Dalseny."

Curtsies were exchanged. Theo was intrigued by this formidable dame. She was not even as tall as her daughter, but she was very broad. She reminded Theo of a ship under full sail, fully capable of plowing under anything that got in her way.

"I am sorry this is the first occasion I have had to welcome you into the family, Countess," she said. "Since I was not invited to your wedding, I was unable to do so before."

"No one was invited but the duke and duchess, Mama," Patsy reminded her.

"I am aware," her mother said with a sniff. In the background, the duchess could be heard giving her maid instructions for a tea tray and some brandy for the earl.

"Please sit down," she said as the maid hurried away. "It is so tiresome looking up at you all. And I can see my rest is at an end for this afternoon."

"For myself, I refuse to feel guilty," Canford remarked as he took his seat beside Theo on the sofa again. "I am sure the first dressing bell will ring shortly. You do still keep country hours at Lansmere?"

"I've tried to change things, but the duke prefers the old-fashioned ways of his mother," the duchess said. "However, I do not despair."

"Indeed not," her brother agreed. "Only present him with his heir and I guarantee you will be able to request as many changes as you like."

"Canford, if you please," Lady Dalseny said stiffly. "There is a young, unmarried girl here . . ."

"Well, if she is unaware Genie is increasing, she must be simple," he retorted. Patsy, who had not taken her eyes from his face, giggled.

By the time the refreshments arrived, Theo was having trouble containing a bubble of laughter that threatened to disgrace her. She had never seen the earl like this. He seemed set on being deliberately provoking, throwing out baiting remarks and barely waiting for Lady Dalseny to rise to rebut them before he said something even more disconcerting.

Alone in their suite later, Theo asked him about it.

"I've disliked my Aunt Florence from the time I was a boy," he said, his expression disgusted. "She sets herself apart, playing the grand lady. Yet she herself was nobody until she married my father's younger brother. Horace Whitney is Viscount Dalseny. You'd think he was Prinny himself the way Aunt Florence carries on. Pay her no mind, except to keep on her good side if you can. She has a vicious tongue and she can cut up nasty when she chooses.

"What gown are you wearing this evening?" he asked next.

"Why, I thought perhaps the rose muslin, if Betsy has had a chance to press it," Theo told him. She was a little confused. Lucas had never questioned what she was wearing before this.

"Ah, yes, that gown," he said, waving his hand as he went into the adjoining bedchamber to summon his valet.

Theo studied the gown carefully when she was dressed. She could find no fault with it. It was one of her London gowns, a soft rose, the three flounces at the hem trimmed in lace and tied with deeper rose satin bows. More lace adorned the little puffed sleeves and edged the round neckline. With it she wore the earl's pearls. She was wearing her hair up this evening, and her maid had set a spray of lace and ribbons in it that her mother had bought for her. For some reason the spray displeased Theo and she had the maid remove it.

Later that evening, Theo told herself she had been oversensitive. Surely not all conversation had died when she and Lucas entered the drawing room. Surely not everyone had assembled there early for the express purpose of looking her over. And surely she had only imagined the intent glances, the lifted eyebrows, the little surprised expressions so carefully hidden, when Lucas introduced her. And how could she possibly have heard the murmurs that began as soon as they moved on? Theo had felt her face growing stiffer and it was all she could do to keep her hand lightly on his sleeve when she wanted so badly to clutch it for protection.

She was only able to relax when they came to Maitland Grant. His long, honest face, his genuine grin, and warm hand revived her spirits. "Good to see you again, Countess," he said. "Lucas, old son, you're looking well. Married life must agree with you after all."

"As you say, Mait. Tell me, were you able to get to Tattersall's in time to bid on that horse you wanted?"

"Kingsley's breakdown? I did. Got him too. He's magnificent but we're not going to bore your countess by talking of horseflesh. Ah, Miss Berrington. You've met the Countess of Canford?"

"Indeed," the lady said, wasting only a quick glance at Theo before she returned her attention to Mr. Grant. "I could not help hearing you mention your new horse. I would be thrilled if you would tell me all about it. My papa says you have such an eye for a good mount."

As she led the gentleman away, Theo murmured, "If I am not mistaken, Mr. Grant had better watch his step. Do you, as I, detect the slight aroma of orange blossoms, m'lord?"

"Oh, she is only one of a pack of females who've been after Mait for years. Hopefully there will be some other unattached females here so he may escape her now and again."

"Or other unmarried gentlemen for them to try their wiles on now that you've been removed from the eligibles list."

Theo thought he looked startled. "Why—why, so I have," he said at last, as if the idea had only just occurred to him and he was not particularly pleased with it.

Patsy Whitney joined them then, and Theo was so glad to have her chattering away she did not even mind that she was all but excluded from the conversation, dealing as it did with Patsy's governess and Lady Dalseny's decision to send her daughter to a proper young lady's academy next year. By the time dinner was announced, Theo had a headache. Alas, the evening was only beginning.

She went into that dinner on Viscount Dalseny's arm. She did not find him a stimulating partner. He spoke only of his lands and his wealth and he often stole a glance at his wife seated some distance away, as if seeking her approval. On Theo's other side was an elderly gentleman whose main interest appeared to be Roman ruins. Theo often found her

eyes straying to the head of the table where the Dowager
Duchess of Lansmere sat at her son's right hand and held
court. The dowager had been a revelation to her. Slim and
white-haired, she had a merry expression, and she laughed
often. To Theo's surprise, the duke was very like her.
Frowning, Eugenia tried often to catch his eye, but once,
when she succeeded, he merely blew her a kiss before he
fell to conversing and jesting again. Well, Theo thought as
she took some sole in a lemon sauce from a platter the footman was presenting, it is true Eugenia is a beauty. Perhaps
that is why he wanted her.

When at last the ladies retired to the drawing room, Theo
was delighted to see the dowager beckoning to her, and she
went quickly to her side.

"No, no, Florence, you shall not capture the child. I saw
her first. Besides, I outrank you," the dowager said to an
eager Lady Dalseny. "Run along now. Your turn will
come."

She patted the sofa beside her. "Sit down, my dear. We
must become better acquainted. And I am sure you need a
respite, now don't you? These family affairs. So tedious.
And you are a new bride too, and so a source of great interest. Try not to mind. We have some very impolite, common
sorts on the family tree and the best thing you can do is ignore 'em."

Theo chuckled as she spread her skirts.

"Not that they mean any harm," the irrepressible dowager went on. "At least not *all* of them. I name no names.
You will discover who are the worst in short order, for you
have the look of an intelligent girl. Really, I am quite
pleased with Lucas that he chose so well."

"Thank you, ma'am," Theo said. "But perhaps you
should withhold judgment until you know me better? I
might be any number of unsuitable things . . ."

"No, you're not," Her Grace interrupted. "Lucas
wouldn't have had you if you were. He's very conscious of
what he owes his name. His mother, whom, incidentally,
his sister takes after, made sure of that. Enough of them.

Tell me of yourself, if you please. I believe I met your mother once the year she came up to London for her Season. She was such a pretty little thing."

Theo was happy to oblige. Anything to take her mind from the little sideways glances sent her way, the heads bent close together so secrets could be exchanged—the titters of laughter she could hear.

By the time the gentlemen came in half an hour later, she and the dowager were well on the way to becoming fast friends. "Now, my dear," that lady said, "you must come down to the dower house whenever you please. Or whenever the rarified atmosphere of the Park becomes too much for you. It is only a short walk. You will not need a carriage."

"Thank you, ma'am. You are very kind," Theo managed to say. For once in her life she was tongue-tied, and on the verge of tears. The dowager seemed to understand; she patted her hand and smiled so kindly.

Maitland Grant joined Theo when the earl was detained by Lady Blake. Of all the women in the room, Lucy Blake was the most beautiful by far. She had midnight black hair and brows and the whitest, purest complexion Theo had ever seen. This evening she was dressed in a deep blue silk gown that although it covered her voluptuous breasts modestly, seemed in some strange way to emphasize them.

Theo told herself the pangs of jealousy she was feeling were ridiculous. No doubt Lucas and Lucy Blake were old friends, and of course they had to be related in some way or she would not have been invited. Turning her back on the pair, she began a spirited conversation with Mr. Grant.

Later when the duchess asked her to play for the guests, Theo was quick to demur, saying she had little talent for the piano and her singing voice was dismal. Her Grace raised her brows. Theo wondered if it was because she was disappointed or because she seldom was refused anything she expressed a wish for. Somehow Theo was sure it was the latter as Lucas's "Sweet Patsy" obliged. She had a lovely soprano and a light accomplished touch, and she looked so winsome at the keyboard it was hard not to smile. As she was being undressed later, Theo wondered how she could have looked forward to this visit so. Now it appeared to stretch endlessly before her, since they were engaged to remain until mid-January. All those days and days of insipid conversation and gossip with the other ladies, night after night of three-hour dinners partnered by strange bores. She did not smile until later in bed when she remembered the dowager's invitation. She told herself she must take care lest she become a nuisance, calling on the older lady every other minute.

Lucas did not come to her that night, something Theo found vaguely unsettling when she woke the next morning. Could it be that now he had seen her with other women and compared her to them, to her detriment, she had lost any appeal she might have had for him? It was depressing to think of that; she began to wonder instead if it would be remarked if she took her breakfast in bed. If she lingered over it, and her toilette, it would shorten the day considerably.

She was just finishing her amply supplied tray when the earl came in and dismissed the maid. "You are not feeling well?" he asked brusquely as soon as the girl had left.

"Why, of course I am," Theo replied, wondering why she felt so defensive.

"Then why didn't you come down to breakfast? The duchess sent for me to discover where you might be. As I understand it, the ladies all gather in Eugenia's drawing room to do needlework and converse in the mornings. You may be sure your absence has been noted by one and all."

"Tell me, Lucas, is it necessary for me to do *everything* everyone else does?" Theo asked. "Endlessly conform?"

He paused and thought before he said, "Not everything, of course. But it would be very impolite not to join them sometimes, you know. And you cannot be hanging about me. It just isn't done."

"I'm not at all sure I'm happy we came," Theo muttered as she threw back the covers and rose.

"But since we are here, you will try to be an agreeable guest, won't you?" he persisted.

"Of course I will! Don't look so worried. I'll not disgrace you. Perhaps you might tell your sister I often have my breakfast in bed. She won't know it's a lie."

"I can do that, I suppose. Hopefully it may quell the rumors that are already circulating that you are with child, and feeling so unwell you must keep to your bed."

"For heaven's sake!" Theo snapped as she put on her robe. "Is there no end to this—this preoccupation with babies? We've been married less than three months!"

He laughed as he went to the door. Theo noted he had not kissed her. He had not touched her at all, and her stomach did a funny little hip-hop as the door closed behind him leaving her alone.

10

From then on Theo tried to be the perfect guest, entering into all the ladies' activities with smiling good humor. Doing so, she was forced to listen to all sorts of unpleasant conversations. She did not know what was worse, the positively scurrilous gossip or the detailed discussions of women's misfortunes and their terrible bodily ailments. Only when Patsy Whitney was with them did such conversations end. The duchess often asked Theo to read aloud then from some improving novel, for she had observed Theo did not appear to care for handwork.

But sometimes, her patience worn thin, Theo would run away down the well-worn path between Lansmere Park and its Dower House, to spend a pleasant hour relaxing with her new friend.

"More tiresome than usual today?" the dowager asked as she rang for tea after Theo had given her a fervent hug.

"I do not think I can bear to hear about Mrs. Forrestal's unfortunate digestion or Miss Olivia Whitney's problems with flatulence one more time or I'll be forced to put back my head and howl," Theo told her as she removed her warm pelisse and unwound the scarf from around her neck. "Or Eugenia's miserable morning sickness either. Oh, dear," she added as she sat down next to her hostess on a striped sofa near the fire, "I should not have said that. Please forgive my wretched tongue."

Faith Abbott smiled. "You need not consider what you say when we are alone, my dear. I am sure if Eugenia knew how tiresome I find her conversation, consisting as it does of all the tiniest details of her pregnancy, she would engage in it more often, for then I would stay here and not persist in invading what she now considers her exclusive domain."

"You know that she does not like you?" Theo asked, her eyes wide.

"Of course I do. It was obvious right from the start that she did not approve of me. I was nowhere near *grand* enough, you see, to be Duchess of Lansmere; she has thought so since our first meeting. I am too gay, too informal, and much too quick to laugh. And where is the cold dignity a woman of my exalted station and great age should have? Why, nowhere to be seen. That is why she is so diligent in trying to restore that dignity herself, poor misguided child."

"The duke is very like you," Theo ventured. She was relieved when the dowager smiled brilliantly.

"Thank you," she said. "It pleases me to hear you say so. I tried very hard to bring him up in such a way he did not take his honors too seriously as I fear Eugenia has done since becoming his wife. I have great hopes however that she will relent someday and unbend. Being a duchess is a grand thing to be sure, but it does not set you apart from the rest of humanity.

"Tell me, dear, how are you surviving the party?"

Theo did not answer immediately, for the dowager's elderly maid came in behind the butler and the tea tray, to fuss over its placement. There was a great rivalry between these two old retainers, but Theo was sure their loyalty to their mistress was entire and unbreakable.

At last, holding a steaming cup, she said, "I am managing fairly well, I think. It is just there is no one I feel could be a friend."

"You mean no one your age?" the dowager asked as she stirred her tea.

"Age wouldn't matter. I meant no one who shares my views, or feels as I do. Except you, ma'am. I cannot tell you how grateful I am you are here and that you like me, for without you Lansmere would be dreary indeed."

"That handsome scamp of a husband of yours is treating you well, I hope?" the dowager asked, careful not to look at Theo as she spoke.

"Oh, yes," Theo said enthusiastically. "He is so kind. Of course he is busy with his own pursuits, the other men, and his friend, Maitland Grant."

"You love him, don't you?" the dowager asked quietly.

Theo bent her head over her cup to hide the sudden tears. "Yes, I do. Dreadfully," she confessed in little more than a whisper.

"Well, then, there is nothing to cry about, dear child. To love one's husband is a great advantage. It makes life so much easier, to say nothing of more exciting, now doesn't it?"

Although Theo nodded, Faith Abbott noted how quick she was to change the subject.

"How is Lady Blake related to everyone?" she asked. "She is so beautiful, isn't she? So assured and cool."

"Lucy? She was the wife of one of my husband's cousins. He died shortly after their marriage. I'm surprised you have never heard of it. It was the *on dit* of that year's Season—the young bride of seventeen, the old man of sixty. The print shops had a field day, you may be sure. But Lucy did not seem to notice. She went into deep mourning and behaved just as if she felt enormous sadness at his passing. Which I, for one, knew was a lie. Her family forced her to the match for the man's title and wealth. Now she has it all and I find it singularly fitting she has cut all ties with that family and refuses to have anything to do with them. She is something of an enigma, Lucy Blake. And not a woman to confide in others."

Theo had listened with some apprehension. Had Lucas been thinking about that situation when he had talked to her back at the Abbey about all the unsuitable men her father might have chosen for her? Was he now regretting he had not thought to ask Lady Blake to wed? And why hadn't he? she wondered as she took a muffin from the plate the dowager held out.

"Preparations for Christmas are going well?" Faith Abbott asked next. "I know the Kissing Ball is in place; have they brought in the Yule log yet?"

"We are to do that later this afternoon if the snow does not prevent it," Theo told her, looking anxiously out the window. It was cold and crisp, but only a few soft flakes drifted down and she was relieved. There had been snow a few days previously, enough so dragging the log would be easier. But another storm would postpone the fun, and she had been looking forward to it for days. Lucas would be with her, perhaps even hauling on the rope directly ahead of her as the younger guests and some sturdy servants pulled a large section of the fallen oak trunk from the woods to the mansion.

"I suppose Eugenia has stood firm regarding the matter of greenery, hasn't she?" the dowager asked next. Then she chuckled. "She told me she thought it *undignified,* all those pine branches and fir cones and candles. And messy too. Ah well, I have to admit she is the perfect chatelaine for Lansmere Park, for she is as formal and stuffy as it is itself.

"Tell me again about Canford. I have never seen it, you know. You must take care lest I start importuning you for an invitation."

Theo assured her she would be welcomed any time she chose to come, and for the next hour the two sat and chatted together as if they had known each other all their lives. Theo was smiling as she made her way back to the mansion later, but that smile disappeared when she entered the front hall and saw the duchess about to ascend the stairs for her usual afternoon rest.

"You have been to the Dower House?" the duchess asked.

Her voice held no expression, but Theo felt a shiver run down her back.

"Yes. The dowager is very well this afternoon," Theo told her as she came to join her.

The two began to walk up the stairs together. The duchess held tightly to the banister. Behind her, a footman hovered to offer assistance if it should be required, a precaution Theo considered ridiculous, this early in the pregnancy.

"Of course one must be delighted to hear it," Eugenia said in the same even voice. "Lady Dalseny remarked your absence."

She paused as if to catch her breath and Theo was forced to stop beside her.

"I tell you this for your own good, Theodora," the duchess said. "It will do you no good at all to antagonize Lady Dalseny. She is one of London's leading tittle-tattles."

"Lucas has told me much the same," Theo admitted as they went upward again. "But tell me, why should it matter to her where I am or what I do?"

"I suppose because she considers your defection from our ranks a slight. I must admit I do myself," the duchess said coldly.

"I—I am very sorry. I—I did not think . . ." Theo stammered. "But after all, you have many people to keep you company, and your mother-in-law has none."

"Except you. Practically every day."

Theo put up her chin. She was being badgered and she did not like it one bit. "Yes, except me," she said as evenly as the other woman had spoken. "And I intend to keep visiting her. I am fond of her. But I must not detain you, ma'am. You will be wanting your rest and I must get ready to help bring in the Yule log.

"Till later then?"

She smiled to temper this display of independence before she hurried up the stairs, leaving the duchess standing there with her mouth a little ajar to be dismissed by the chit of a girl that her brother had had the misfortune to choose to marry.

Ten of the younger guests assembled in the front hall half an hour later. They were to be led by the duke himself, and His Grace was in an exuberant mood that soon had everyone including the servants chosen to do most of the work, smiling and laughing.

Even Lady Blake sported a delicate color in her cheeks when the duke chided her for not dressing warmly enough and came to wrap her scarf more securely around her throat. Theo saw that Patsy Whitney stayed very close to Lucas, almost hanging on his arm as they went toward the wood, and she fell behind them to join Maitland Grant. This was no hardship of course; she enjoyed Mr. Grant's company enormously. Still, she could not seem to keep her eyes from the young girl artlessly chatting with Lucas. After all, he was *her* husband, wasn't he?

The plumes of their breath were white in the cold winter air and when the sound of Lucas's laughter drifted back to her, she did not think the ache in her throat was due to her breathing that same arctic air.

An early winter dusk was falling now and the lazy snowflakes seemed to be intensifying. In the light of the torches the servants held, that snow whirled in crazy circles, borne here and there by the whim of the wind.

The log had been brought from deep in the wood to its outskirts by the duke's woodsmen a day or so ago to ease things for the guests. Still, it was a huge thing, and Theo could see they would have a time of it. She was aware Miss Whitney took her place beside her cousin the earl, and she was angry but there was nothing at all she could do about it without risking a scene. A scene she knew Lucas would hate, so she was forced to watch the duke position Lucas and his "sweet Patsy" to one rope and assign her and Maitland Grant to another. At his cry to heave ho! they all bent to the task. It was not too difficult. The servants were in the vanguard, and they did most of the work. Still, by the time the log was hauled up before the steps of the Park, everyone was a little out of breath.

The duke hurried them inside to warm up before a fire and enjoy glasses of mulled wine and cider. To the servants remained the unenviable task of lopping the log down to size, bringing it inside, and installing it in the huge old fireplace that graced the main hall. There it would be set alight later by the duke, and footmen would keep it under observation day and night. It was thought that very bad luck would come in the New Year if the fire went out. This year, with the birth of the duke's first child imminent, it was twice as important to keep it burning steadily.

Theo was hurt when Lucas still remained beside his cousin, teasing her about a broken fingernail Patsy claimed had been acquired during their labor. She felt the ready tears about to spring to her eyes, and she turned her back on them to talk to Lucy Blake. The duke joined them, exclaiming when he saw how blue Lady Blake's hands were after she removed her mittens.

"I told you you did not dress warmly enough, m'lady," he scolded. "Have you never brought in a Yule log before?"

"I—I assure you, sir, I will soon be warm again," the lady said. Even in her own distress, Theo heard the catch in her voice, and she wondered at it. Was there some association with this old holiday custom that had upset the lady? If so, why had she bothered to come?

It was after dinner that evening that Theo realized she had not had a chance to speak to her husband all day. She had had her breakfast in bed again, and when she came downstairs, she discovered Canford had gone out with some of the other men for a ride along the snowy roads. Of course that afternoon she had visited the dowager; her husband was involved in a billiards game. Later they had all brought in the Yule log. She was annoyed Lucas had not seen fit to come to her side, or even speak to her, not only then but later, waiting for dinner to be announced. And now that the gentlemen had rejoined the ladies after their port, he still did not seek her out. Her heart was heavy, but she was determined he would not know of it, and so her smile was brilliant for Maitland Grant, once more her faithful escort. One time when she looked up, she saw Canford staring at her and his friend, so close together on a small sofa.

His face was so stern that for a moment she felt encouraged, but then he turned away, and her gloom returned.

Theo would have cried herself to sleep that night, except the earl came to her as soon as she had been undressed. She even wondered for a wild moment if he had been listening for her to dismiss her maid. His lovemaking was impetuous, intense, and Theo had the greatest difficulty to keep from crying out. He did not speak, but his hands and his lips spoke for him as they teased her, tempted her, brought her to heights she had never before imagined. When it was over at last, she was gasping, and the earl's breath was uneven too. Shaking, Theo reached up to touch his cheek before she brushed his hair back from his face. Then, aware she was dangerously close to telling him how she adored him, she dropped that hand and turned her face away.

Leave me, oh, leave me now, she pleaded silently. Just go! As if he had divined her sentiments, Canford rose and stooped to pick up the robe he had thrown to the floor when he first came in. Theo held her breath as she watched him go to the door that connected their rooms. With her eyes half closed, she saw him hesitate there and half turn as if he meant to come back. But he did not return. Instead he seemed to shrug before he closed the door softly but firmly behind him.

Theo's sigh of relief mingled with regret was ragged. Slowly she relaxed her tense muscles and easy tears flowed down her face. Tears of regret and longing for what she knew she would never have. For although she had gained a great deal by marrying the Earl of Canford, she had forfeited as much again.

It was a long time before she slept.

Theo did not feel well when she went down to breakfast the next morning. Her head ached and she was lethargic. All the emotions she had been hiding seemed to rise up inside her and threaten to undo her completely. As she went past the footmen standing stiffly in the hall, she told herself the duchess had better not say anything to her today. Anything at all, for if she did, she was not at all sure she would be able to control her temper.

She ate her breakfast with Lady Blake and two elderly gentlemen, none of whom appeared to care for conversation this early in the morning. Theo was glad. She took an egg and a piece of toast and sat staring out the window at the gray day, wondering where Lucas was this morning. She wished she might seek him out; spend some time alone with him having a long talk. But what would I talk about? she wondered. I cannot be honest with him. I have never been honest except at the very beginning when I expressed my doubts about our marriage and tried to get him to cry off.

After a dreary morning spent with the other ladies in the party, Theo escaped to the library. She was glad there was no one there. Eventually she found a charming little book written about a journey to Italy some long departed Abbott had taken with his tutor in the 1700s, and she settled down in a big wing chair close to a window in one of the alcoves to read. When a footman came in to see to the fire Theo did not even notice him. She was deep in a description of a rustic inn on the shores of Lake Maggiore at Domodossola and she was completely absorbed.

Sometime later, she heard the library door open and the duchess's cool voice, and she stiffened.

"I see there is no one here. How fortunate. Now, Patsy, what is it you wish to discuss with me in private?"

"It is very hard to begin," the younger girl said. "You see, it is about Lucas, er, I mean Canford—your brother."

"What about him?" the duchess asked, her voice sharper now.

"I have been wondering, that is, where did he meet the countess? And why did he marry her so quickly? I can't understand it. Mama can't either. The countess does not appear to be increasing, which I heard Mama tell one of her friends must have been the reason for the hasty marriage. And she is not the sort of girl I thought Lucas would marry."

"No, I agree. As the Earl of Canford, he might have had anyone."

Theo had meant to speak up and announce her presence, but now she sat frozen in the wing chair, pressing against the back of it and hardly daring to breathe lest she give herself away.

"But *why* did he marry her? I could just cry. I had so hoped he would wait for me to grow up. After all, it is only two more years before I make my come-out."

"My dear, I do not mean to be unkind, but Canford would never have married you."

"Why not? He likes me, I know he likes me."

"Of course he does. You are his little cousin. He thinks of you as a child. But he could not wait for you, or anyone."

"Whyever not?"

"Because of a promise he made to our mother. You know she died five years ago when Lucas was twenty-five. Before she died, she made him promise he would marry before his thirtieth birthday. He was wild then with his gambling and mistresses and unsuitable friends and she was concerned he would not do his duty for Canford. I fear he might not have indeed had I not reminded him of that promise this past Season in London. He married Theodora Meredith on October the first. His birthday is the second."

"But why her?" Patsy persisted. "She is not beautiful, she has no accomplishments—she does not even dress well. And she is so strange. So outspoken and different. She even wears spectacles."

"Yes, she is not conformable, I agree. And she is entirely too willful. But time was growing short. I know my brother thought to have Lady Mary Williams, but I suspect she refused to be part of such a hurried affair, and Lucas could not wait. Ah well, it serves him right. If he had set about the thing in the usual way, he would not be in this fix now. He would have had the lovely Lady Mary to wife. Instead, he is saddled with a thin, plain girl of no distinction, having no talents, and with an upbringing that must be suspect, she has so few graces or manners."

She sighed audibly. "I am sorry for him, indeed I am. But there. I have spoken much too freely to you, Patsy. You are such an easy person to confide in. Pray you will keep what I have told you to yourself. Do not even tell your mother, you hear?"

Patsy promised faithfully she would be as silent as the grave, although Theo knew it would be amazing if the entire company did not have the duchess's views on her brother's marriage by nightfall. The whole thing was too delicious to be kept secret. She wondered at the spite she had heard in Eugenia's voice. Was it there because she was angry her new sister-in-law preferred her mother-in-law? Could she be that petty?

When she heard the library doors close behind the two intruders, Theo made herself relax. She saw she had clutched the book she was holding so tightly she had bent some of the pages, and carefully she smoothed them out with a hand that shook a little.

So, Canford had married her because she was available and her parents would not quarrel with the date he had chosen for the ceremony to take place. Indeed, she knew they had been so thrilled by the fine match she was making, they would have let him marry her on the spot, the day he first arrived. She had known he was making a marriage of convenience, but learning he had been forced to it by a deathbed promise, and had chosen her because he could not have the woman he really wanted, made it twice as hard to bear. Theo stared out the window. She saw it was snowing hard again. It looked as if it would continue for hours. It was gray and cold, depressing and drab—exactly the way she felt.

She swallowed hard, trying to get rid of the large lump in her throat, telling herself it was far too late for regrets. She had made her bed. Now she must lie in it.

11

The Earl of Canford was confused. Confused and angry as a result. He had slept no better than his wife had done, risen early, eaten breakfast alone except for the servants arranging the meal on the sideboard, and restless, gone out for a walk in the cold, crisp air. As he went along the drive, he thought about the situation he found himself in, and he shook his head.

He had not known what marriage would be like, of course, but he had not expected anything so annoying—so disconcerting. Theo was not a loving, dependent girl always demanding his attention. He had not wanted her to be. But he had not expected her to hold him at arm's length, either.

She did not seem to care whether he spent time with her or not. Only consider how she had suggested they have a house party just a short time ago. Was she that bored by his company? How *dare* she be bored. He was not an insipid fop, he did not lack conversation, he was not disagreeable. At least he had never thought he was, he told himself grimly. And now that they were at Lansmere Park, she almost seemed to be avoiding him. Why, she had kept her distance when they were bringing in the Yule log, and later as well. He frowned when he recalled how friendly she had become with Maitland Grant. All smiles and vivacious conversation she was whenever *he* was around. Could it be she found Grant more appealing than her husband? He growled a little as he swung his arms before he turned back. It was cold, and more snow threatened.

But, he told himself, the thing that bothered him the most was the way she behaved when he made love to her. She was so stiff and lifeless. At first he had considered this a challenge, put it down to her youth and inexperience. But as time went by, nothing improved. Although her body was always ready for him, she was not. In fact, she acted as if she did not give a groat whether he loved her or not. For the first time in his life, Lucas Whitney had seriously questioned his prowess, especially since he bent every effort toward seeing to her fulfillment, even before his own. Of course, eventually he could not restrain himself any longer so he always lost that battle.

Was it possible Theo was cold? He knew there were women like that; how ironic it would be if he should have had the misfortune to marry one of them. True, he had thought only of a marriage of convenience, but he had expected it to be pleasant, both in and out of bed.

Theo had not refused him, except that one time in the library, and he knew he had been at fault there. She had still been shy with him, as any girl would be the day after she had lost her virginity. And it had been broad daylight too, something it would take a while for her to get used to. But somehow, even knowing these things, he had not been able to stop himself from going to her and caressing her. She had looked so sweet fast asleep in the window seat with the sun playing in her hair and her breast rising and falling with her breath. He had been amazed at how much he had wanted her. She was not his usual choice. Generally he preferred beautiful, voluptuous women. But this slip of a girl excited him more than they had ever been able to. It was not all his desire for an heir that kept him coming so often to her bed, and he admitted it.

He stopped then and stood still, and a slow smile spread over his face as he remembered. There was that strange little sound she always made deep in her throat during their lovemaking and he had come to listen for that sound, wait for it. It was the only clue that showed she was not perhaps as indifferent as she pretended.

Last night . . . he had almost lost it last night. Angered by what he saw as her preference for Maitland Grant, he had taken her almost roughly, and in the silence that had become the norm for them. Certainly she never spoke, lying there so coldly with her hands clenched by her sides. He had been determined then to bring her to release, to *make* her cry out, *make* her want him as much as he wanted her. But he had not succeeded even though he had used every wile he could think of. Damn the woman. Why didn't she sigh in delight as every other woman he had ever held in his arms had done?

Still, when it was over, she had reached up and touched his cheek before she brushed his hair back. It was only a little thing, but he was astounded at how it had encouraged him, how, when he was leaving, it had been all he could do not to go back to her, take her in his arms again. He wondered what she would be like if she were to let down her guard, relax, enter into the act with enthusiasm and abandon. Just picturing her that way made him groan.

He had reached the mansion again and he took the steps two at a time. He felt better for the walk physically, but he could not in truth say it had brought him any mental relief. He was still as confused about Theo as he had been when he set out. Surely the woman was maddening.

Christmas came and went with all the usual festivities. Canford gave Theo a pair of pearl ear bobs to match his wedding gift and a lovely blue cloak trimmed with fur, and when she protested the extravagance, he made light of his gifts. She felt ashamed. She had only a pair of velvet slippers she had made and embroidered for him as a gift. But as he tried them on, he told her his sister had told him how his wife disliked handwork, so he knew what the gift had cost her. This tiny bit of rapport did not last the day, however, for that afternoon, Maitland Grant caught Theo under the Kissing Ball and embraced her heartily. The earl was not amused. He did not seem to recall that half an hour before, he had kissed his cousin Patsy just as thoroughly, and two days previously, Lady Blake. Theo remembered both occasions all too well, and the remembrance, added as it was to what she had heard in the library, festered and burned like salt on a wound. She knew it was wrong to brood about the results of her eavesdropping, but she did not seem to be able to forget it. It made her stiff with the other guests, whom she was positive were laughing at her behind her back, and as surly and graceless as the duchess had claimed she was.

After the holidays and a ball the duke gave for his guests and the neighbors, the party seemed to turn flat. Theo wondered at the custom for having such long parties. Surely a month in the company of the same people, all of them confined by the cold inclement weather, was entirely too long. She herself had developed a positive antipathy for Lady Dalseny, and she told herself the earl's sister would never be a sister to her, and not only because of her disapproval. The duchess was so stiff, so cold. She managed to turn any occasion sour with her haughty demeanor and attention to form. Sometimes Theo surprised a confused look on the duke's face, as if he were wondering where the smiling, adorable girl he had courted and won had gone. Only the dowager duchess continued dear although she saw much less of her than she had previously. Afraid that in her absence the ladies would have a grand time discussing her and her inadequacy for the exalted post of Countess of Canford, she stayed very much to home. Still, she knew when it came time to bid the dowager good-bye, she would regret it.

The weather eased early in January, and some days the younger guests managed either an expedition on horseback or a sleigh ride. Theo almost enjoyed those days. It was so good to get away from the red brick mansion. Since the duchess had given up all exercise for the duration of her term, she was not there to frown on high spirits. Although she was relieved it was so, Theo did not approve of her coddling herself at this time. Her mother, although indolent, had never rested as often as the young duchess did.

She had carried on her usual routine sometimes right up to the day of the birth. But of course as a newly married girl, Theo was not expected to know such things, and certainly no one asked her opinion. Which was just as well, she thought grimly, for probably she would have told them, and surely such a shocking revelation would only prove her gaucheness.

But even with the diversion of outdoor exercise she was still relieved when early one morning she and the earl bade the duke good-bye, to begin the daylong journey home. They had said their farewells to the duchess and the dowager as well as the other guests the evening before. When Theo saw Patsy's sad face and the way she clung to Canford when she kissed him good-bye, she told herself they couldn't leave soon enough for her. And the expression of regret Lady Dalseny wore, her deep sigh, told her only too plainly what that lady had hoped for her daughter.

To Theo's relief, the earl had elected to ride. She was aware that all too soon they would be alone at Canford, just the two of them. She did not know how she would manage, knowing what she did now. How could she talk to him as if nothing had changed? How could she even look at him, never mind smile? Still, as they went along the snow-covered roads, she often found herself peering from the window of the carriage, hoping to catch a glimpse of him. Surely she was perverse.

Fortunately, the first week home they were both busy. A number of things had arisen demanding the earl's attention, not the least of which was a leak in the roof of the northwest wing, and a nasty quarrel between two of his tenant farmers that had ended in a fight that left one of them maimed. All Canford was in a furor, taking sides and discussing the matter endlessly. The earl worked hard to calm tempers, calling them both before him to hear their stories. He told Theo feuds were common among families on estates, but he wanted none of them at Canford. Eventually he found for the maimed victim, and ordered the other to leave. Theo was sorry for the man's family, although she agreed he had brought the trouble on himself.

By the middle of February, things returned to normal. The earl often came to her at night, and his lovemaking was as wonderful as ever but what little closeness they had shared early in their marriage had disappeared. Theo did not think it would ever return.

Then one evening after dinner, when the two of them were seated before the fire in the library, the earl spoke up at last.

"What is wrong, Theo?" he asked, his voice almost gentle.

"Wrong? Why—why nothing," she said, considerably startled. "What could be wrong?"

"That is what I am asking. You have changed. Did something happen on our visit to Lansmere Park that you haven't told me about? Something that distressed you?"

Theo knew she would be hard put to stop if she were ever to begin. Instead she shook her head, her lips compressed.

Lucas Whitney stared across the hearth to where his wife sat, her eyes downcast, and her hands clasped tightly in her lap. There was something wrong, he knew it. But if she would not tell him, there was nothing he could do. Still, he had felt he had to try. He was becoming more and more dissatisfied with his marriage—more frustrated. And thinking of the years and years that stretched out before them to be spent together was horrifying. How could he live like this, with a cold, contained woman? What had happened to the girl he had overheard at a London party, jesting with her cousin, Charles Talbott, so gay and witty and wry? In her place had come this solemn girl who never laughed anymore, rarely smiled, and lately had nothing to say for herself, witty or otherwise. He couldn't think of anything he might have done to offend her, but then, with women it was hard to tell. Enigmas, all of 'em.

He came to a decision then. Heir or no heir, he was going to go to London to end this fiasco and preserve his sanity. He hardly thought Theo would miss him. She didn't seem to care whether he was there or not. Later, when the Season was in full swing, she could join him in town. And Parliament was in session now; it was the perfect excuse. Not that he needed an excuse, of course. He did not need to account to her, or anyone, how he spent his time or where he was.

Perhaps she would miss him, he thought, brooding into the fire. Perhaps absence did make the heart grow fonder. He told himself it wouldn't hurt to try it anyway.

Two mornings later when she came late to the breakfast table, Theo was surprised to see Canford still there. He was quick to dismiss the butler and footmen. She felt her heart begin to beat faster, for this was so unusual, and her husband looked so stern.

He waited until the servants' footsteps died away before he said, "I am off to London this morning, ma'am. There are things I must see to in town, and Parliament is sitting now. It is more than time I took my place there."

Theo stared at him. She sat so still, she seemed a statue. A little unnerved by this, and the expression of disbelief she wore, he went on. "There is no need for you to put yourself to the trouble of coming as well. There is little to do in town at this particular time. Of course I shall expect you to join me in a month or perhaps two. In the meantime I trust you to see to the estate for me. Call on my agent if you need anything. But I am sure that in your competent hands, all will be well."

No, Theo screamed in her head. No, don't patronize me! Don't give me a worthless compliment to ease your going! But she did not say it aloud. Instead she cleared her throat and said, "The staff can easily manage Canford, as they did while we were at Lansmere Park. It would be no trouble for me to come too."

He shook his head. "No, I want you to stay here. I will be far too busy in town to attend to you, and you would be bored."

"I assure you I would understand," Theo persisted, hat-ing herself for begging. She saw he was shaking his head, and angry, she added, "And what of your heir, sir? How are we to provide one for Canford if I am here and you are there?"

He folded the newspaper he was holding carefully, giving the act his full attention while she waited, breathless at her daring.

"We don't seem to be having much success no matter where we are, do we?" he said at last. "But never mind. I have come to believe that happy event will take place when it is most propitious for it to do so, and placing such emphasis on it as we have been doing, may well be delaying it.

"Now you must excuse me. The carriage is waiting and I would not keep the team standing on this cold day. Keep well, madam."

As he spoke, he rose and bowed to her. For a moment he hesitated, and Theo wondered if he would kiss her goodbye. But he never kissed her except in bed, and he did not do so now. Only a moment later the door closed behind him and she was left alone.

She never did eat her breakfast that day. For a while she sat on at the table. Her tea grew cold, her porridge congealed, and the toast hardened in the rack. At last, aware the servants must be talking, she rose and went blindly to her sitting room, telling Oates she did not wish to be disturbed.

Lucas was gone. She would not see him for at least a month, no, two. He had left her—just like that—happy no doubt to be free of her, the burden he had assumed for his name, not the woman he had married because he loved her. But she had always known this. Why did it upset her so much now? Because, she told herself, I am missing him already. With every mile he travels, he is getting farther and farther away from me.

Suddenly she was reminded of her father and she sat up straighter in her chair. So, Canford was going to be like him, was he? Leaving her to see to things as her father had always done with her mother? Amusing himself in town while his wife rusticated in the country?

Theo rose abruptly to pace the room. In her mind's eye she could see Lucas now, so handsome and tall and virile. Yes, virile. She did not think it possible he would remain celibate all the weeks she was at Canford. No, for he was used to making love to her almost every night. Who would he choose in London? Or was it possible he already had a mistress there? A mistress who was no doubt angry he had deserted her for such a period of time. Would he bring her jewels to appease her? Would he, perhaps, spend this very night in her bed?

She clenched her fists. Pretty Patsy and the elegant Lady Blake had been bad enough, but she had never really been concerned about them. She was Canford's wife. No matter how much they might have wanted him, they could not have him. But a mistress, now that was another matter entirely. And she would not, she *could* not share Lucas, she told herself fiercely. Somehow she must find a way to prevent him from such liaisons. If only she had the faintest idea how she was supposed to do that.

12

The Dowager Duchess of Lansmere arrived at Canford a week later. She was accompanied by Lady Blake. Theo was astonished and none too pleased to see her companion, for she had certainly not extended an invitation to *her*. But once she was alone with Theo, the dowager explained she had thought it best to come immediately rather than waste time exchanging letters to explain the additional guest.

"I could tell something was wrong from your letter, my dear," she said. "Not that you told me anything, oh, no. But I suspected the same at Lansmere. Things have not been going well for you and Canford? Do not tell me, if you do not care to.

"I brought Lucy along because she has been staying with me for a few weeks. It is lonely for her in London in that big house in Portman Square she inherited from her husband. It would be a kindness if you would have her here. There is something wrong with her as well. Something very wrong, but she won't tell me about it, any more than you care to speak of your problems."

She shook her head and her white curls bounced. "I shall just have to discover your mysteries for myself. Never fear! I'm good at mysteries. And it is not that I pry, as Eugenia claims I do. I am *concerned* for you both."

"You won't have to wonder about me at least," Theo told her. They were in her sitting room. Lucy Blake had excused herself to help her maid unpack and, Theo suspected, give them a chance to be alone. She was grateful for it.

"It is not that I am unhappy to see Lady Blake," she explained. "But I need your help, and I don't think I can discuss all this openly with her. She is so beautiful, so poised and elegant."

"It is Canford, of course," the dowager said briskly. "My dear, believe me, the early days of a marriage are not all bliss. Sometimes they are hell, and that's plain speaking for you. Come now, tell me. What has he done?"

"Nothing," Theo said, her mouth drooping. "Except to go to London to take his seat in Parliament. And he as much as ordered me to stay here. He—he did not want me with him."

She rose then and went to the window. With her back turned, she said, "I overheard things at Lansmere. I learned everyone was wondering why such a paragon as Lucas Whitney could marry a nobody with no grace or distinction, a nobody who was plain and ill-dressed besides. And everyone knew we made a marriage of convenience. They questioned why even that circumstance would make him choose me."

"Who dared to say such things?" the dowager asked, sounding quite harsh.

Theo turned back to her and attempted a smile. "No need to take up the cudgels in my defense, ma'am. They were quite right. I've asked myself the very same questions.

"At first I thought to ask my mother to come and bear me company. But she is with child, and she would probably bring most of the family with her. That would not help me. And if I went home to Pobryn Abbey, I would become the eldest daughter again, at her beck and call. Besides, even though I love her, I don't think Mama *can* help me in this instance.

"Then there is my Grandmother Hutton. She lives in Bath with her best friend, Lady Handerville. Do you know them perhaps?"

When the dowager nodded and smiled, she went on. "But Grandmama has rheumatism, and she knows little of fashion and society."

"And I do," the dowager added, looking thoughtful.

"Yes, yes, you do. I would be so grateful for any advice you can give me. You see, I came to understand after thinking it over, that there is nothing I can do but make the best of what I have. I'm not beautiful or even passing pretty, but I'm not *ugly*. And although I don't have much of a figure, there might be ways I could improve it . . ."

The dowager was sitting up straight now, looking indignant. "Ugly? Too thin? You're all about in your head, child. I grant you your gowns are unfortunate, but I suspect your mother had the choosing of them, did she not?"

At Theo's nod, she went on. "Well, then. If I remember, your mother is a little woman, and, er, plump? Are your sisters like her? Blond, with round pretty faces and pouting lips? I see. Now you take after your father. What a handsome man he is even now. You have his height and his facial features, his slender build. No, you are not pretty, thank heavens. Prettiness fades, but a woman with your bones will grow more and more handsome as the years pass. Those cheekbones! I admired them on first meeting."

"Do you mean it?" Theo asked, coming back to sit beside the lady and stare into her eyes as if to try and catch her in a falsehood.

"Of course I do. With the right clothes and a more fashionable crop—did no one ever suggest you have your hair cut, child?—you will be amazed.

"And, Theo, now that I know what this is about, I am so glad Lucy is with us. She will be the perfect one to help for she is young and knows fashion better than I. You'll see. And she is a dear girl. She only seems cold because she is troubled and so involved with her own problems. You will be doing her a kindness, giving her mind a new direction."

"What trouble do you think she might be having, ma'am?" Theo could not help asking.

The dowager only looked sad. "It is a man, of course. It has to be a man. But we must not ask. If Lucy wants us to know, she'll tell us."

Feeling a little better about her unexpected guest, Theo

decided she had no choice but to throw herself on her mercies. To her surprise, Lucy Blake seemed only too happy to assist her, and after dinner that evening, sat with Theo discussing morning gowns, carriage gowns, ball gowns, and pelisses, as well as bonnets and shawls. The dowager sat by the fire, nodding and adding a comment every now and again.

"I know a wonderful modiste in London," Lady Blake said at last. "She is a French emigré, and particular about whom she dresses. I am sure she will take you.

"Now, tomorrow, I have some gowns I do not wear any longer that I would like you to try on. One of them is a gorgeous jonquil color. The other is azure silk. I think they will be stunning."

"But, m'lady," Theo protested, "you must not be giving me your gowns."

Lucy Blake smiled and patted her hand. "I no longer wear these particular ones. I have gained some weight over this past year and they do not fit me well anymore. Truly. And please, won't you call me Lucy? Lady Blake is so formal for conspirators."

"I would be glad to," Theo said softly.

"Tell Lucy what you told me this afternoon, Theo," the dowager demanded. "About what you overheard at Lansmere."

Theo obeyed although she felt a little shy still. To her delight, Lucy Blake told her she had been wrong to listen to such slander for it was all a lie.

"I think we must consider removing to London sometime soon, however," the dowager said as she folded the baby gown she was smocking for her first grandchild and put it in her workbasket.

"You would be most welcome to stay at my house," Lucy said. "But I warn you I live secluded, for I have been having problems with my health."

"Then you should be there, for that is where the best doctors are to be found," the dowager said. "Do not worry about seclusion, Lucy. When the Season begins in earnest will be time enough to surprise Canford with Theo's trans-formation. Yes, let us do that. I shall have such fun looking forward to seeing his face when he sees that the grub he thinks he married has turned into a butterfly."

Theo tried to keep her composure at being compared to a grub, but her sense of the ridiculous got the best of her and she collapsed in laughter. After a moment, Lucy Blake joined her, as did the dowager when the joke was explained to her.

Her Grace, Lady Blake as well, declared the first order of business was Theo's posture.

"I noticed it at Lansmere Park the evening we first met," the older lady declared at the breakfast table the next morning. "You have a way of bending slightly and pulling your shoulders in. I suspect you acquired the habit because you are so much taller than the rest of your family, and you sought to fit in. But it will not do, Theo."

"No, indeed," Lady Blake said as she poured herself another cup of tea. "You must hold yourself proudly. Otherwise you seem to be begging people not to notice you for you consider yourself beneath their touch."

"I didn't know I did that," Theo said in amazement. Making an effort, she sat up straighter in her chair and squared her shoulders. It seemed to her as if she were thrusting her breasts out in a most immodest way, but when she mentioned this, the dowager told her not to be such a ninny.

"You've got 'em, haven't you?" she asked as she slathered marmalade on a scone. "Can't hide 'em. Besides, when you huddle as you did, it only calls more attention to 'em."

After breakfast the ladies retired to the largest drawing room, and for the rest of the morning, Theo practiced sitting and rising gracefully, curtsying with her head held high, and walking up and down with a book on her head.

"I am surprised your mother did not make you do so when you were a child," Lucy Blake said. "My mother was very strict with me. And if she thought I was beginning to

relax or slouch, I was forced to wear a wooden backboard."
She sighed. "It was very uncomfortable."

"Pray you will not feel it necessary to fit me to one,"
Theo said, careful not to turn her head lest she lose the
book perched on top of it. Her neck was beginning to hurt
from the strain of holding it up, but she did not complain.

Released at last from her exercises, Theo went with the
others to Lucy Blake's room to try on the promised gowns.
Her maid, a middle-aged woman of few words and fewer
smiles, assisted. The jonquil muslin was perfect, but the
azure silk needed a few adjustments. Theo sighed in delight
at both of them, they were so lovely. She had not known
what a difference flattering gowns could make, especially
when she stood tall with her shoulders squared and her
head up.

"Of course you will need many more gowns," the dowager remarked. "Morning, garden, promenade, carriage, dinner, evening, full evening, opera, theater, and perhaps a
court dress. Were you presented at Court last Season?"

Theo shook her head. "My father was supposed to make
the arrangements, but for some reason, nothing came of it."

"Then your husband shall have the honor of presenting
you. We must make sure you have only the best. I do believe you will be stunning in the wide hoops that are worn
at Court, with ostrich feathers in your hair and only your
pearls for jewelry."

"All this sounds as if it will be very expensive," Theo
said. She hesitated, then decided that since she had thrown
her lot in with the dowager duchess and Lucy Blake, she
must not be reticent now. "I do not know how I am to pay
for any of it. The earl did not leave me any money, you
see."

The dowager snorted. "That man," she said darkly.
"Never mind the cost, my dear. You may apply to your
husband's agent here for such monies as you will need to
travel to town and for your expenses for a month or so afterwards. As for payment of your gowns, you have only to

announce you are the Countess of Canford. I do assure you, you will not be dunned."

"But won't the dressmakers and shopkeepers send the bills to Lucas, then?" Theo asked. "If they do, he will know I am in town, not rusticating here as he supposes."

Her Grace thought for a moment. "Very true. You are quick, Theo, very quick. I shall be your banker then. And when the game is up, it will give me a great deal of pleasure to bring such an enormous sheaf of bills as we are going to have to the earl for payment. He should be ashamed of himself, not giving you your pin money as every husband is expected to do."

"There was no need for it," Theo said, stung into defending Canford. "We were only here and then at Lansmere, and I had my bride clothes."

"Such as they were," the dowager said tartly. "Lucy, dear, do you think a pair of chicken-skin gloves to be worn at night would improve Theo's hands? I detect a slight redness, due no doubt to the cold weather."

"I'm sorry," Theo apologized. "I know I should not be seen without gloves, but I do dislike them so. They always seem to be in my way."

"I have a pair she may have, and some cream," Lucy volunteered. Then, turning to her maid, she added, "Would you fetch those for me, please, Franklin? And then give us your opinion of Lady Canford's hair?"

Theo sat down at the dressing table while the maid brushed out her hair and studied it. At last she said, "It must be cut, of course, but in London, not here. Some curls clustered on the forehead, I think. Perhaps a chignon high on her head behind? And some curls for fullness on the sides. M'lady has good thick hair. It will hold a curl nicely."

"Do you have a competent abigail, child?" the dowager asked next. "A good dresser is so important."

"Just a girl from the staff, ma'am," Theo admitted. "But Betsy is willing. Perhaps she can learn."

Only too clearly, she heard Miss Franklin's sniff of derision, and she added, "Of course when we go to town, I might see about hiring another maid, if you will help me do so. I wouldn't know what to ask."

Lucy Blake smiled at her own maid. "We'll have Franklin help you," she said. "She knows exactly what skills an abigail should possess.

"Now this afternoon I think we must begin a most important part of your education, Theo. No, no, do not look so concerned. It is nowhere near as taxing as posture lessons, but it is just as significant. Perhaps more so. I refer, of course, to flirting."

"But—but I am a married woman," Theo protested, much shocked.

"So? You should still learn to flirt, first with your husband, then with other men. They expect it, and it is a delightful pastime."

As the dowager chuckled and nodded, she went on. "We must also be sure you know the language of the fan. How to beckon, how to deny, how to show pique, or tenderness. And you must learn to smile too."

Theo laughed then. "I've been smiling all my life," she protested. Then she paused and stared as Lucy Blake smiled just a little, lowered her eyes and turned her head slightly away.

"You see?" she said. "I did not have to say a word, but a gentleman would know I found him fascinating, even though I was shy with him. Then there is the gay, teasing smile you toss over your shoulder as you run away—oh, a million ways of flirting. And it is harmless, you know," she added when she saw Theo was beginning to look dubious. "Done lightly with a deft hand, no one can take offense."

"I did, at Lansmere Park," Theo said baldly. "I resented it when you flirted with Lucas."

Lucy Blake laughed softly. "It meant nothing, my dear. You have a handsome husband, but believe me, I never wanted him."

Her face seemed to darken a little then, and the dowager interrupted. " Theo," she admonished, "you're slouching again."

Obediently, Theo straightened up, but she sighed as she did so. This transformation she was embarked upon was not going to be easy. Why, she had never dreamed it would entail so much work and effort. But, she told herself, all I have to do is remember it is all for Lucas and then it will be easy. And when I get tired or discouraged, I'll try and picture his expression when we meet again for the first time. Will it be astonished? Delighted? Admiring? Perhaps even *awed*?

Oh, please, let him be awed.

13

When the Earl of Canford saw his wife next, he did not look astonished or admiring, and he certainly did not seem awed. Instead he wore a mighty scowl, which fortunately Theo did not notice. It was three weeks later in London and she and the dowager were being driven down Bond Street in Lady Blake's dashing open landau, on their way to a fitting at the dressmaker's.

"I say, isn't that your wife?" Maitland Grant asked Canford as the carriage rolled by them where they stood on the pavement waiting to cross the street. "I thought you said she was remaining in the country."

Lucas Whitney stared for a moment at the profile that was all he was treated to, for the dowager had pointed out a bonnet in a shop window that Theo was admiring. He did not need more than her profile to identify her however, and it was then he scowled. It was Theo all right. What was she doing here? Where was she staying? Not at Canford House, that was sure. What a charming bit of gossip this would make for the tabbies, he thought viciously as the landau disappeared in traffic and he and Grant moved on. Oh, they would have a fine time discussing this delicious item over their teacups and macaroons, the new bride separated from her husband already. Was Theo deliberately trying to make him a laughingstock?

"I must say she looked well," Grant went on, unaware of his friend's black mood. "That was quite a dashing hat she wore, wasn't it? Has she come to town to shop?"

"I've no idea," the earl admitted. "I didn't even know she was here, but I'll thank you to keep that information to yourself."

"Silent as the grave, old boy, silent as the grave," Grant said cheerfully. Then he frowned a little. "Where do you suppose she's staying? Not at a hotel, I hope."

"She was with the Dowager Duchess of Lansmere so it shouldn't be hard to find out," Canford said.

Nor was it. A letter went out by special messenger to the Duchess of Lansmere an hour later. The man was ordered to wait for a reply, so the earl had his answer the following day. His sister wrote her mother-in-law had traveled to Canford less than a month ago, in company with Lady Blake. She had not heard from the lady, but if she had removed to London, she, for one, was not the least bit surprised. The dowager, Eugenia wrote, was entirely too flighty for a woman of her advanced years. She probably had set off on a whim to visit the metropolis, with only her maid and a small portmanteau. It was not at all dignified and furthermore . . .

Canford did not bother to read any more. So, Theo had invited Faith Abbott to Canford, had she? And then traveled to town with her and Lucy Blake? Then surely the three of them would be found at Lady Blake's house in Portman Square, for the dowager had properly turned over the Lansmere town house to her son when he came into the title. Nodding to himself, the earl set off on foot with fire in his eyes and a scathing lecture all ready to deliver.

To his disappointment and chagrin, Theo was not at home when the butler admitted him. Informed that only the Dowager Duchess of Lansmere was there, he asked that lady to receive him. Moments later, he was ushered into a drawing room full of dark, old-fashioned furniture and heavy, burgundy velvet draperies. The atmosphere was depressing, which perfectly fit Canford's mood.

"Where is she?" he demanded as soon as the butler had bowed himself away.

The dowager managed to look affronted, and as regal as

her daughter-in-law could ever have wished. Unfortunately, she could not maintain the pose.

"Oh, do take that scowl from your face, Canford, and sit down," she ordered. "I've no mind to break my neck gazing up at you while you stand over me, glowering. Sit!"

Thus admonished, the earl did as he was bade, feeling somewhat like a nine-year-old boy about to be chastised for some prank.

"I've been expecting you," the dowager told him. "Yes, I saw you the other day on Bond Street and I knew it wouldn't take you long to discover our whereabouts.

"Theo is busy this afternoon at the dressmaker's. Not that I consider it any business of yours where she is or what she is doing. The very idea, man, leaving her alone at Canford when you'd only been married four months. You should be ashamed of yourself."

The earl decided he had had quite enough. "What I do, and when and how, is not your concern, ma'am, although I suppose I must thank you for accompanying Theo. Heaven only knows what mischief she might not have got up to by herself. Yes, I did suggest she remain in the country. I knew I would be busy at Parliament most of the time, and she would be bored. Didn't she tell you she was to join me for the Season? I take it hard that she has been maligning me to you behind my back."

He looked very black and the dowager took pity on him. "She has done no such thing," she said tartly. "When she speaks of you, which is not very often, she is complimentary. I don't know where you got the idea that your wife—such a dear, thoughtful girl—would say anything to your detriment. Unless, of course, you have given her some very good reasons to do so?"

She paused then as if considering what she was about to say. Finally she shook her head a little, closed her lips, and folded her hands in her lap, as if she was determined not to say more, lest she tell him exactly what she thought of him.

"When will she return home? When may I see her?" he demanded.

The dowager shrugged. "I've no idea. You know how long fittings can take, especially since Theo is ordering so many gowns. Then I believe she said something about shopping for some accessories as well. Lady Blake's maid bears her company. We have had no time as yet to engage an abigail for Theo."

The earl leaned back in his chair for the first time and crossed one tightly breeched leg over the other. He wore an air of amusement now. "I think you have been very busy, have you not, ma'am?" he asked. "But if you think to anger me by telling me how much of my money Theo is squandering, you will be disappointed. I am aware she needed gowns—a great many things. I intended to buy them for her when she came up to town. When *I* told her she might."

"Hoity-toity," the dowager said, tossing her head of white curls. "She is your wife, man, not your slave. She can come and go as she pleases. I always did."

"The last Duke of Lansmere must have been a man more tolerant than most," he remarked. The glint in his eye told her he would not have stood for such foolishness.

"As for seeing Theo," the dowager went on grandly, "I suppose it wouldn't do any harm for you to call on her. Not often, of course. Shall we say once a week?"

"What?" the earl thundered, rising to his feet and clenching his fists. "*Call* on her? I am not courting her, ma'am! I am her husband!"

"Well, if you'd had any sense, you would have courted her, marriage of convenience or not," his hostess scolded. "However, it is never too late to begin, and so you shall. I shall arrange for Theo to be home this coming Friday. Shall we say at four o'clock?"

She rose then and went to the door before a bewildered earl could gather his wits to protest again. "Till then, m'lord," she said sweetly, holding the drawing room door open for him.

Canford had no choice but to leave. If he had not there would have been a scene, and he knew he had no chance of winning an encounter with the elderly duchess. This time she held all the cards. Still, he told himself as he took his hat, gloves, and stick from the butler, he would not consider his dismissal losing the battle. This first meeting was more in the nature of a brief skirmish. He would do better later, he told himself, his face grim as he headed back to Canford House on Park Lane.

How dare she treat me this way? How *dare* she? he thought, and it was not the Dowager Duchess of Lansmere who was on his mind.

The front door had barely closed behind the earl before Theo ran into the drawing room from the library next door where she had been hiding, her ear pressed to the door.

"Oh, ma'am, you were very harsh with him," she cried, looking distressed.

"Not as harsh as I might have been if you had really been out," her friend told her with a sunny smile. "Do sit down, Theo, and try not to fret. What I told Canford was for his own good. You'll see. He has been used to getting his own way for far too long—what man this day and age has not? They think the sun rises and sets because they are on the earth, every one of 'em. It is necessary for women to give them a set-down on occasion to keep them at all fit to live with.

"Canford will be here Friday, hat in hand and considerably more amenable. By then I hope to have been able to instill a suitable aura of disapproval and haughtiness in you.

"No, no, do not protest! It will do you no good in the long run if you give in to him now. He'll just take it for granted he can run roughshod over you whenever he pleases. Is that what you want in a husband?"

Theo was reminded of her father. She had seen him from one of the front windows a few days ago, strolling through the square with a pretty redhead who did not appear to be much older than she was herself. The girl had hung on his arm, looking up at him adoringly, and Theo—a picture of her mother, all her siblings, left alone in the country in her mind—had had all she could do not to run from the house and confront him with his iniquity.

"I certainly do not want a husband like that," she told the dowager. "But it will be so hard, ma'am. And to tell him he may only come once a week!"

"It will be easier for you if you do not have to see him often," the dowager said. She ended the discussion by excusing herself for a short nap.

After she was left alone, Theo went to the window to stare out into the street. She did not understand what the dowager had meant, saying it would be easier if she seldom saw Lucas. She did not believe it, she was missing him so. Just hearing his voice, even though it had been full of rage, had caused her heart to act strangely. She wished she might have seen him this afternoon—alone. She wished she might have run into his arms and kissed him, as she had never dared to do before. And after that? She blushed as she wished she might have taken him by the hand and led him up the dark stairs to her room. She missed being his wife. She wished they were there now, in her bed.

She shook her head. In Lady Blake's house that would be impossible, so there was no sense in dwelling on it. And surely she was being ungrateful after all the dowager and Lucy were going for her. She looked down at her smart afternoon gown. It was made of ecru silk, cut severely with little trim, and it fit her superbly. She smoothed it over her hips, smiling a little.

Lucas Whitney was on the doorstep of Lady Blake's town house just as London's church bells rang the hour the following Friday. He had found himself looking in vain for his wife everywhere he went that week but she was nowhere to be seen. Nor did she and her friends appear at any of the parties that were beginning again, now that the fashionables were trickling back to town. For that he had to be grateful. Perhaps no one would have to know of their estrangement. Not that they were estranged, he corrected himself as he gave his card to the butler. Of course not. It had simply been a little misunderstanding that would soon be set right.

He found Theo alone in the same depressing drawing room, and for a moment he paused by the door to study her. She looked different to him, and it was not that she no longer wore an insipid pastel gown all flounces and ribbons that her mother had chosen for her, but a lovely white silk trimmed in matching braid. No, it was more than her gown. She seemed taller somehow, and her face was fuller. His glance went over her body. He did not remember her breasts being quite so prominent, and he felt his desire for her grow.

"I am glad to see you, Lucas," his wife said, smiling a little and peeking up at him as she curtsied. Was she wearing cosmetics? he wondered. And what had she done with her hair?

"Won't you sit down?" she added, indicating a sofa. "Allow me to pour you a glass of wine."

"Cutting up sweet, are you, my girl?" he asked as he took his seat. "I am very angry with you, you know."

"But why?" she asked, looking puzzled as she handed him a glass of Canary. "Because I came to town? I do not know why that should annoy you. I came with Lady Blake and the dowager duchess, both of them impeccable companions."

"I distinctly remember telling you you were to stay at Canford for a month or two," he said, still looking severe.

"And I distinctly remember you saying you did not care to bring me to London with *you*. Surely that did not rule out my traveling with someone else. And you see how well it has worked. You do not have to bother with me while you are busy about your own affairs, for Lucy asked me to stay with her."

"You don't bother me!" the earl snapped, feeling somehow outflanked. "And that's another thing. What will people say when they learn I am at Canford House and you are here? Are you determined to make us food for gossip with everything you do?"

Theo put her head to one side, as if seriously considering what he had said. "I am sure I can't remember another thing I might have done that could cause people to talk," she said at last. "But surely, Lucas, you are overreacting. We live very secluded here, for Lucy has not been feeling well. We do not go out to the theater or the opera, drive or stroll in the parks, or attend any parties. It is only March. Not many of the *ton* are about."

"A few of them are," he persisted. "And you do spend a great deal of time shopping, do you not? Isn't it entirely possible you might run into other ladies intent on refurbishing their wardrobes?"

"I suppose I might, but how would they know where I was living?" Theo answered, sweetly reasonable. The earl did not know whether he wanted most to kiss her or strangle her.

"And when do you think you might consider removing to Canford House, ma'am?" he asked next. His words were polite, but Theo shivered.

"I don't know," she said. "I have been so busy since my arrival. The dowager and Lucy have been the greatest help and support. I could not manage without them. Just consider this gown. Isn't it smart? Lucy chose it for me. And have you noticed my new haircut? The dowager suggested it, and I am sure it gives me a certain cachet I was lacking before. Don't you agree?"

He waved a careless hand, not to be turned aside from his main purpose. "You look very well, but I intended to help you choose your gowns myself. I am sure my taste is as good as your new friends'. Anyway, you could still see them, shop with them, even if you were sleeping at Canford House. Where, I am sorry I have to remind you, madam, you belong."

"Did you miss me, Lucas?" Theo asked. Then, not waiting for a reply, she added, "Or did you set up a mistress in town?"

He looked stunned. "What did you say?" he demanded.

"Have you no delicacy of mind? You don't ask a man that!"

"I wouldn't ask anyone else," Theo said, defending herself. "But you're my husband. Surely I have a right to know."

"First, I am delighted you have remembered you have a husband," he retorted. "Second, you have no right to know anything of the sort. Still, I'll tell you anyway. No, I don't have a mistress."

"I am so glad," Theo said, reaching out to touch his hand for a moment. He set his untouched glass of Canary down on a table beside the sofa and moved closer. Alarmed, she retreated. Before she could protest, the earl captured both her hands and held them close to his heart. "What? So shy?" he asked, bending over her.

Theo did not know where to look. Her heart was pounding and her breath came quickly. He was far too close to her, overwhelming her with that vibrant sensuality he had in such abundance. Even now she wanted him, but she knew it would not do. The dowager had been very explicit about which intimacies she was to deny him, and those few she might allow.

"Have you forgotten all those nights we were together?" he asked, his voice husky. "The love we've shared?"

"No, of course not," she managed to say, still trying to free her hands.

He let her go briefly, but only so he could gather her in his arms. For a moment he stared down into her face, then he bent and kissed her. His mouth was warm on hers, warm and demanding and just the way she remembered it—heavenly. She tried to keep her lips together, but Lucas was having none of that and at last she gave up a very unequal battle, a battle she had not cared to win in any case.

It seemed an age before he released her, and she was able to take a deep breath. His arm still held her tightly, his other hand explored her breasts.

"Please," she whispered. "You must not."

"But I must," he replied. "We have been apart much too long."

"And whose fault is that?" she demanded, pulling free and moving to the end of the sofa. She had suddenly remembered the dowager's instructions. *She* was the injured party. She must behave like it.

For a moment, she thought he would not reply. He looked haughty now, his eyes mere slits, as if he found being called to account most unappealing. "Very well," he said at last, sounding as if the words were being dragged from him. "Very well, madam. It was my fault. My fault alone. That admitted, you will send for your maid and have her begin your packing. You are coming to Canford House with me right now."

"You go too fast, sir! I cannot just *leave*. That would be a terrible way to repay both Lady Blake's and the dowager's kindnesses to me."

"Very well, call them in and explain; thank them as well," he said, as gently reasonable as she had been.

"They—they are not home this afternoon," Theo lied.

"Write them a fervent letter. Write two. I'll wait," he replied, picking up his glass of wine and settling back as if prepared to do just that.

"I can't. I simply can't be that rude," Theo told him. "No. It would be terrible to behave that way. And, Lucas, I won't. There is no need to sit there scowling at me. I won't do it and there's nothing you can do to make me!"

Her impassioned speech seemed to hang in the air of the drawing room long after she finished speaking. She felt herself trembling, but she did not look away from him. She could tell he was furious, both with her and with the situation. At last he said, "Very well. You may remain here until the ladies come home. Say your thanks, exchange all the hugs and kisses and tears you care to, but then come immediately to Canford House. Have I made myself clear, madam?"

Theo nodded and he rose and bowed to her. "I shall expect you no later than six. We dine in. Do not worry if your trunks are not ready by then. You won't need anything tonight."

Theo decided it would be better not to examine that last statement too closely. A moment later he was gone. She heard him speak to the butler, heard the front door close behind him, but still she did not move. It was several minutes before she was able to go and tell her friends everything that had happened, and what she had been ordered to do.

Once again Lucas Whitney strode along the pavement, heading for Park Lane. Today, however, he wore a little smile of contentment for what he had accomplished. Of course it would have been better if Theo were beside him, but even though he thought her refusal to leave with him slightly ridiculous, he had decided to humor her. He was aware it was a good thing he had, for otherwise he was sure he would have had to carry her, kicking and screaming, from the house. What a formidable girl she was! He did not think he had even begun to find out everything there was to know about her.

On reaching home, he conferred with his London butler, ordering a festive meal and special wines. He ordered the housekeeper to make the countess's suite ready and sent a footman out for flowers to fill it. He told himself he was being ridiculous. After all, he was an old married man now. There was no need to play the nervous suitor, no matter what the Dowager Duchess of Lansmere had told him. Still, he did not seem to be able to stop.

By six o'clock, all was in readiness, but Theo did not come. He waited in the drawing room, the draperies pulled to hide the rain the dark evening had brought. Perhaps the weather had delayed her. He wondered if he should order his carriage for her? Then he sat down where he would be able to keep the mantel clock under his supervision and prepared to wait. She would come. He must not read too much into a slight delay.

When the clock struck seven-thirty and there was still no sign of his wife, he rose to his feet and prepared to do battle.

14

"I hope you are right, ma'am," Theo said as she sat on at the table with the dowager and Lady Blake. Dinner was over, the servants had been dismissed, and the dowager was drinking her customary snifter of brandy.

"Of course I am," Faith Abbott told her. "You are not to curtsy meekly the first time he gives you an order. We are agreed on that, are we not, Lucy?"

Lady Blake nodded. "Of course. Men are difficult enough, Theo, without allowing them to become even more impossible. You'll see. When you finally agree and move to Canford House, the earl will be in a properly chastised state of mind."

"I hope you are right," Theo said again, frowning now. "But you do not know Lucas that well. He does not like to be crossed. I don't know what he might not do, now he has been."

"Of course, legally, he would be well within his rights to insist you live with him," the dowager said. "We must hope that does not occur to him. Or, if it does, that he will not want what has happened to become common knowledge. I am sure that is what will happen. He will be forced to be circumspect, lest he set off a wildfire of prattle and conjecture. Men do so hate to be made to look like fools."

She chuckled, and then as the sound of voices in the hall became louder and louder, she set her glass down and looked expectant.

"What on earth can be happening?" Lady Blake asked, her hand going to the bell beside her.

"It's Lucas," Theo whispered, grasping her napkin tightly in her hands. "Oh, dear, I knew I should not have defied him."

The dining room doors opened to admit the earl. Behind him, Lady Blake's butler was bemoaning the intrusion although he could do nothing about it since he was held tight in a groom's arms. A groom, Theo noted, wearing the familiar dark green and gold Canford livery. Two other servants similarly clad stood on watch behind him, their pistols covering the hall and front door.

"Do forgive me for intruding in this manner, Your Grace, m'lady," the earl said smoothly. "I've come for my wife."

"My word," the elder lady said, sounding shocked. "Are you an *animal*, Canford?"

"No, madam. I'm just your ordinary John Bull Englishman and as such I demand my rights. Get up, Theo."

Theo did not move. She didn't feel she could.

"Have you forgotten you were to dine at Canford House this evening, wife?" he asked, moving around the table toward her as he spoke. She stared at him, mesmerized.

"Such a festive dinner as I had planned too. All your favorite dishes. And your rooms are ready, freshly aired and dusted. I can't tell you how disappointed I was when you did not come as we had agreed. It was then I saw there was nothing for it but to fetch you myself. By whatever means were necessary."

"See here, Canford," the dowager blustered, restored to her usual commanding self. "You simply can't come in here, *grab* Theo, and spirit her away. You can't!"

"Just watch me do it, ma'am," he said. He had reached Theo's chair and in one motion he pulled it back from the table and scooped her up in his arms. Striding back to the door, he said over his shoulder, "Give you good evening, ladies. And my thanks again for all your care of my wife."

He swept past the now quiet butler, and nodded to his men.

As the front door slammed behind the intruders and their prize, Lady Blake said, "It seems we were wrong, ma'am.

Bringing Lucas Whitney to a chastised state of mind has proved to be impossible."

The dowager poured herself another brandy and gestured with the decanter. When Lucy shook her head, she said, "I did not think it necessary to have armed men to protect us. Still, I suppose I should have carried a pistol myself, as a safeguard, for you see, I *do* know Canford."

Her hostess stared. "Oh, much better not, ma'am," she said. "I really could not have had you shooting him in my dining room."

The two chuckled before she added, "Will Theo be all right? He'll not harm her, will he?"

"No, no. He is not that kind of man. He'll bluster and stride about, shake his finger at her and perhaps even threaten her with punishment, but he won't touch her. Not *that* way, anyway," she added with a saucy grin.

Outside it was raining hard. Fortunately Canford had brought his carriage. Theo found herself deposited on the seat, and as the earl climbed in behind her, she was quick to move to the opposite corner, as far from him as she could get. She felt so strange. She knew she should be apprehensive, yes, and frightened as well, but instead she had the most peculiar urge to laugh.

Telling herself he would think her truly insane if she succumbed to the temptation, she looked at him with wide eyes. The flickering candles set in holders on each side of the carriage gave only a dim light, but she could see there was a glint in his eyes and a firm set to his mouth that boded ill for her immediate future.

"What on earth do you have there?" he asked, pointing to her hands.

Theo looked down and saw she still clutched her dinner napkin and she set it on her knee and smoothed it.

"Did you think you might be in need of a bandage, wife?" he asked, coldly polite. "I don't beat women. No matter how much they deserve it," he added darkly.

"I know that," Theo said, swallowing the laughter that still threatened to disgrace her.

"We will not discuss anything now," he said, holding up his hand. "There is no need to have everyone in town listening, for I intend to speak plainly, ma'am. Very plainly indeed."

Theo glanced out at the street. Under the hissing gas lamps they were passing, the rainy street was empty. But better not point out the obvious, she told herself. She was on very thin ice at the moment.

They arrived at Canford House moments later. One of the grooms held the carriage door for them, looking meek as a lamb now with his eyes downcast and his pistol nowhere in sight.

"I won't need the carriage again tonight. Stable 'em," Canford told his coachman. Turning back to her, he said, "Will you step down, ma'am, and walk, or must I carry you?"

"Don't be ridiculous, Lucas," she dared to say. "Of course I'll walk."

The earl's town house was a vast improvement over Lady Blake's. The foyer and hall were inviting, painted in cream and gold and not cluttered with dark furniture and dingy carpets. Two graceful staircases rose on opposing curved walls, meeting above in a gallery. The earl led her up to a drawing room where a fire burned brightly.

"Some wine?" he asked as she shook out her crushed skirts and tried to brush the damp away.

"No, thank you," she said just as formally. "I have only just finished dinner."

His face darkened again, and she cursed her unruly tongue. Why had she felt she had to remind him of that?

"Sit down then," he said. He waited until she obeyed before he took a deep breath. Theo steeled herself.

"Now you will have the goodness to tell me exactly why you did not come here as you promised you would, and put me to the trouble of having to fetch you like a parcel. The truth now!" he ordered, shaking his finger at her just as the dowager had said he might.

"I didn't want to, not just yet," she told him. "And I never promised you anything. You just thought I did because you gave an order."

Ignoring that provocative statement, he said, "Did you rebel to pay me back for what you considered my neglect? Or perhaps the dowager duchess put that idea in your head? I wouldn't put it past her, old meddler that she is."

"She didn't have to," Theo blurted out. "I felt neglected enough without her reminding me of it."

"As I've told you before, wives do not hang on their husbands' sleeves, but we won't discuss that now.

"You disobeyed me, madam. Not only disobeyed, you defied me. And yes, perhaps I did give you an order this afternoon, but as my wife, I certainly expected you to comply with my wishes. Instead you defied me again. What am I to do about such flagrant willfulness?" he asked, bending close and looking belligerent.

Theo saw he was waiting for her response, and with her voice shaking a little, she said seriously, "Well, you could have me shipped off to a penal colony as a hardened criminal, I suppose, or you might consider the old-fashioned punishment of the stocks or a ducking stool. But I don't think the Crown would let you have me beheaded, or even flogged for that matter—oh, dear, I'm sorry! I can't control myself any longer."

To Canford's amazement, she put her face in her hands, sounding as if she were choking. When he would have lifted her into his arms to stop the tears of remorse he was sure were flowing, he heard her laughing. In a moment, she dropped her hands and he saw that although her eyes were full of tears, they were tears of merriment. At his look of confusion, she laughed even harder, so hard she had to hold her stomach and bend over from the pain of it. He stood there absolutely still for what seemed an age, wondering if the servants were thinking he had married a madwoman. At last her laughter died away into weak chuckles, and she collapsed back in her chair.

"I haven't laughed like that in ages," she said unevenly. "Do you have a handkerchief I might borrow? Oh, never mind. I see I still have Lady Blake's dinner napkin, and it will serve."

She seemed about to go off again, but with a visible effort she controlled herself and set to mopping her tear-streaked face.

The heavy silence in the drawing room brought her back to reality and she paused to look up at him. Seeing his scowl, she said, "Come now, Lucas. You're not still angry with me, are you? Surely you can see what a farce this has been."

"I find I resent being made a figure of fun," he said stiffly, turning away so she would not see how hurt he was.

"But I wasn't laughing at you, Lucas," she said to his rigid back. "I was laughing at this whole ridiculous situation we've managed to get ourselves embroiled in."

"You find it ridiculous I would want you beside me?" he asked, still sounding injured.

"Yes, I do, considering that you didn't want me there only a short time ago," she retorted.

He spun around. "Will you be continually throwing that up in my face?" he asked. "Am I never to be forgiven?"

She rose then and went to him and put her hand on his arm. "I promise I'll never mention it again, sir," she said. "There, that's a handsome offer for you."

He smiled at her then, a smile that turned her insides to butter. "Shall we start again, Theo?" he said. "Surely we can do better than this. I'll try if you will and here's my hand on it."

She put her hand in his big strong one and he pressed it gently. A glance at the mantel clock told her it was not even nine o'clock. What were they to do with themselves until bedtime? Sit and chat? About what? Family news or the estate? She did not think he would find an account of her London shopping that enthralling, and she could not honestly say she was at all interested in what Parliament had been doing.

He hesitated, then he dropped her hand and said, "Would you like to see the house? It would probably be better done in the daytime, but you can get some idea even so."

"Yes, I'd like that," she said, smiling in relief. "I could tell when we came in it is a vast improvement over Lucy's mansion in Portman Square. How dark and dreary that is. I wonder she does not redecorate now her husband has been dead five years."

"I know. It is hard to picture her living there, wouldn't you agree? She is so beautiful and the house is so ugly."

Theo told herself she must stop taking every compliment Lucas gave another woman personally. No doubt they would meet Lady Mary Williams sometime this Season, and she must be in command of herself when that occurred. But she knew that even though they were going to try and make a fresh start, she would never forget what she had overheard at Lansmere Park, about being the earl's second choice. And even though she knew her new gowns and hairdo and all the things she had learned from Lucy and the dowager had vastly improved her, she was still not beautiful, and she never would be, let the dowager prate about cheekbones till the cows came home. It was all very well for her to say Theo looked like her father, but what made a man handsome could not be said to enhance a woman's appearance. Still, she told herself as she took the candle Lucas handed her, she had done the best she could.

The drawing rooms were duly admired, and dining room, morning room, and library as well, although they left the kitchens, storerooms, and servants' rooms in the basement for the morrow. Going up another flight, Lucas showed her the guest chambers and sitting rooms before he ushered her into her own suite at the back of the house.

"You overlook a small garden which is rare in this part of London, and it is quieter here," he said, carefully not looking at her. "We face Hyde Park, which is an excellent location, but it can be noisy on Park Lane."

"I am sure it will be lovely," Theo said shyly. "The flowers are beautiful. Thank you."

"Are you tired? Would you like to go to bed now?" he asked. "Er, I mean, did you have a strenuous day?"

Theo told herself she must be imagining the slight tinge of color in her husband's lean cheeks. Surely suave, sophisticated Lucas Whitney would not blush. Still, it gave her the courage to say, "Yes, I did, rather. I would be glad to sleep now."

He bowed. "I took the liberty of buying you a few things as soon as I left you this afternoon. I hope you find everything you need."

He made no move to touch her, and it seemed an age before the hall door closed behind him. Theo sighed. Her muscles were so tense it took a conscious effort to relax. And never mind my posture, she told herself as she rubbed her stiff neck.

She went into the bedroom again and inspected it more carefully than she had done with him beside her. More roses in silver vases were placed on tables on either side of the bed, a large four-poster draped in pale blue dimity. Tidy as it was, the room had the same air of genteel neglect her rooms at Canford had had. No doubt no one had used them since the earl's mother had died.

She saw the bed had been turned down, and a nightrail placed there with a pair of satin slippers on the floor beneath. Curious, she went and picked it up. It was only a wisp of sheer white fabric, and she found herself blushing. She wondered if Lucas was looking forward to seeing her in it. Out of it, more like, she told herself.

When she went into the dressing room, she discovered a maid must have come and gone, for a large pitcher of hot water steamed gently on the dresser. She recalled Lucas having a few quiet words with the butler before they began their tour of the house. There was a comb and brush as well, and, she was happy to see, a toothbrush. He had thought of everything.

After she had undressed and brushed her hair, she

opened a window in the bedroom. The rainy spring night smelled fresh and cool—a perfect night for sleeping. But when she climbed into bed, she lay staring up at the canopy above her, her body tense again. Waiting. Waiting.

He found her there minutes later, and in his hunger for her, managed to forget how tightly in control she still was, no matter how he caressed and kissed her. It did not matter, he told himself. I want her, and she is lovely, lovelier even than I remembered. Her body seemed softer somehow, rounder. He cried out at last and for some minutes lay beside her, catching his breath. He did not leave her right away as had become his custom. Instead, he took her in his arms again and kissed her lips, her cheeks, her closed eyes and her throat, waiting for that little growl deep in her throat that he remembered so well. When it came, following a ragged gasp, he said, "Sleep well, Countess. And welcome home."

15

All Theo's belongings were delivered to Canford House by ten the following morning. She had ordered her breakfast to be served in bed, since she had nothing to wear but an unsuitable evening gown and a more unsuitable nightrail. As she ate, she could hear two maids chatting softly as they hung her gowns in the dressing room armoire, and put her shifts and stockings in the dresser drawers. At last they finished, and after asking if there was anything else she required, they curtsied and went away.

Theo lay still for a moment, wondering where Lucas was. Somehow she had thought he might visit her this morning, but he had not. Was it possible he had gone off to Parliament as must have become his custom, not giving her another thought now he had her back where he wanted her?

She told herself she must stop being so foolish. New start or not, nothing had changed between them, in spite of rooms full of roses, filmy gifts, and an impetuous kidnapping. She was still the wife he had married "conveniently" to fulfill a promise to his mother—no more, no less. It would be entirely out of character for him to suddenly begin dancing attendance on her. And, the way she felt about their marriage, it would be most unpleasant for her if he did. She was able to preserve her composure only because she did not have to do it that often. If he were constantly in her company, that would become impossible.

Half an hour later when she was conducting an interview, the butler brought her two calling cards.

As she read them, Theo smiled and dismissed the housekeeper. When the Dowager Duchess of Lansmere and Lady Blake entered the drawing room, they both looked at her closely, and Theo told herself she must not blush.

"Well, I see he didn't beat you," the dowager said tartly as she took a seat. "Not any place that's noticeable anyway."

"Of course he didn't beat me," Theo told them.

"But has he learned his lesson?" Lucy Blake asked. As usual, she wore a quiet expression, almost one of sadness. Theo realized how few times she had seen her smile.

"He seems different, yes," she told her. "I think he did miss me, and I think he knows he was wrong to leave me in the country. But if you mean, has he changed completely, no, he hasn't. And he was very angry last evening, till we resolved our problems."

"The dratted man." The dowager snorted. "Still, one has to admire his fortitude, storming the gates with armed men and snatching you away. Pity we can't tell anyone. It would make a wonderful *on dit*."

"But are you content, Theo?" Lucy persisted.

"Yes, yes I am," Theo said, lowering her eyes and blushing in earnest now.

"I am glad," Lucy said softly.

"Shall we be on our way, then?" the dowager asked, rising and smoothing her gloves. "You haven't forgotten we were to inspect some silks this morning, have you, Theo? And isn't this the day all your new sandals will be ready?"

Theo had forgotten, but she only asked to be excused so she might fetch her hat and reticule. She was careful to tell Canford's butler where she was going, saying she expected to return in the early afternoon.

The man bowed. "M'lord mentioned something about a stroll in the park later, m'lady," he said. "If it would be convenient, that is."

The time passed quickly, and if Theo was preoccupied, she tried hard not to show it. Which of her promenade dresses would she wear, she wondered even as she exclaimed over a silk so richly embroidered it seemed fit only for royalty. Perhaps the pale gray twill with the black velvet trim? And that smart matching bonnet with its shiny black feathers and dashing brim? Although the rain had stopped, it was a cool day.

When she took her leave of the dowager and Lady Blake, she promised to send word when they might meet again, and she hurried into Canford House to get ready for her outing with the earl.

When they crossed Park Lane later, following an energetic little boy sweeping the road for them to get a penny, she asked Lucas how he had spent his day.

"I had an engagement this morning that I almost forgot," he confessed. "Then I met Mait Grant at White's. Do you really want to hear about our sparring match at Gentleman Jackson's? The wagers we made on the outcome of a certain sporting event? No? Well, I don't blame you. Boring stuff for ladies.

"Ah, good afternoon, m'lord, Lady Grafton. May I present my bride, Theodora Whitney?"

Theo curtsied and accepted the lady's best wishes and tried to ignore the gentleman's knowing eye. They met several other members of the *ton* that cool afternoon as they strolled the paths of Hyde Park and admired the Serpentine from its banks. Once again, Theo was always conscious of the man beside her, so masculine and virile. So dear.

It was growing late and they had turned toward home when an open carriage stopped beside them and Theo found herself looking up into the Lady Mary Williams's face. The young lady was with her mother and two brothers, and seeing her up close, Theo's heart sank. She was more than beautiful, she was glorious. She had chestnut hair and a perfect complexion, set off by a pair of smokey blue eyes, thickly framed in dark lashes. Suddenly Theo seemed to hear the dowager hissing at her, and she straightened her back and held her head high.

"Canford, well met. We heard you were in town," Lady Williams exclaimed. "We have only just arrived ourselves."

"M'ladies. Sirs," Lucas said before he introduced Theo to them all. She spoke easily to the two ladies, and nodded to the two young men, lowering her eyes and smiling a little as Lucy had taught her to do.

"How delightful to meet you, Countess," Lady Williams said. Theo thought her a very good actress. She could hear nothing in her voice that was not cordial and welcoming.

"I am sure you're aware there will be many a mama who will not be pleased to see you, however," she went on, gently teasing. "Stealing a march on the rest as you did, marrying Canford right out from under their noses."

Theo sensed Lucas was uncomfortable with this banter but she continued to smile at them all, including the gorgeous young lady he had really wanted. "But isn't it true that all is fair in love and war, ma'am?" she asked before she turned to Lucas and gave him a look of hopeless devotion. She saw his mouth twitch slightly, and encouraged, she went on. "And also, that to the victor belongs the spoils?

"I hope we will see you all at Canford House in the near future. We were just discussing an evening party, weren't we, my dear?"

Canford made a noncommittal remark and they went their separate ways. Theo thought she had come out of the encounter very well. Only she knew what it had cost her.

"And what was that all about?" Lucas growled as they reached the Stanhope Gates. "Relegating me to 'spoils' I mean. I find that rather offensive. And what evening party? I had no intention of giving one this Season. As newlyweds, we are entitled to be entertained by one and all."

"It was just something to say," Theo told him, pushing her hurt deep. She wondered he could speak so casually when he had just seen the girl he loved whom now he could never have.

"The Williamses are good *ton* but I see no need for us to

become intimate," he went on, stabbing her again, for she was sure he spoke as he did because he could not bear to be in Mary Williams's company.

"I did not care for the way you flirted with the Williams brothers, either," he continued, looking at her sternly. "Nominally they are gentlemen but they're no better than they should be. I prefer we keep our distance."

"Whatever you say," Theo said so meekly he looked at her sharply.

The minute the butler admitted them to Canford House, Theo was aware something was wrong. The whole place seemed to be holding its breath, and the butler, generally the most impassive of men, wore a harried, flustered expression. Then, far above them came the wail of an unhappy infant. Theo turned to Canford and found him staring back at her. "But it can't be," she whispered. "They are all at Pobryn Abbey."

"A Mrs. Meredith and her family have arrived, m'lord, m'lady," the butler hastened to say. "I—I put them all in the gold drawing room, sir, for I did not know what else to do with them."

"Quite right of you. I never did care for the decor there, and now it has no doubt been ruined we will have the perfect excuse to redecorate. Shall we go and see, Theo?"

"That is not at all kind," she said tartly, picking up the skirt of her gown to climb the stairs. "They are only children, you know."

"Excuse me, m'lady. The housekeeper was wanting to know if they would be staying and which rooms should be prepared."

"I have no idea. I must see them first," Theo flung over her shoulder. She was followed up the flight by a thoughtful Canford.

Theo was attacked as soon as she entered the drawing room. Gwyneth clasped her legs, screaming her greetings, and two little boys ran around her, both talking loudly about a broken vase and each putting the blame for it on the other. The earl could see the pieces of it on the carpet. It had been one of the Sevres too, he noted.

Mrs. Meredith, very heavy now in her pregnancy, half lay on a sofa, a handkerchief to her face. He noted the pious daughter was busy fanning her, while the other one sat quietly, eyes downcast, in a straight chair a little distance away. Canford was aware there were fewer children than he had first encountered at the Abbey, and for that he could only be thankful, for he had had the most horrible thought that the entire tribe was about to be thrust upon his shoulders.

"Mama, what is the matter?" Theo asked, pitching her voice to be heard over the little boys' fevered explanations. "Gwynnie, dear, yes, I am glad to see you too, but let me go now. I must see to Mama. Lester, William, stop talking! I can't hear a word you say when you both speak together."

The three youngest fell silent, and Mrs. Meredith's sobs were clearly heard by all.

"Perhaps it would be better if we were to speak privately, without the children," Canford said, startling them all, for even Theo had forgotten he was there.

Mrs. Meredith's sobs increased, and she said disjointedly, "But I must have them around me to sustain me, sir. I can't have them torn from my side in this time of affliction."

"I find it difficult to believe that anyone would care to tear them from your side, madam. However, let me arrange for a footman and a maid to take them to the park." He saw Theo was about to speak, and he added, "They'll come to no harm, and they will return shortly."

As he left the room, Theo went and kissed her mother, holding her tightly. Violet looked so righteous, her heart sank. It was most unlike Marietta to sit so quietly, not even attempting to flirt with Canford. Something was wrong, very wrong indeed.

In only a few minutes, the room had emptied of children, and as the front door slammed behind them all, Canford pulled a chair up close to his mother-in-law.

"Now, ma'am, won't you tell us what has brought you to London, and here in particular? Why didn't you go to your husband's house?"

"We do not have a house in town," Fanny Meredith said, trying to compose herself. "Theodore considered it a needless expense. He takes rooms. But I did go there first and—and, oh, I cannot tell you!"

Theo was reminded of the pretty young redhead she had seen on her father's arm, and her lips tightened.

"Well, never mind that now," Canford said easily. "Why did you come to town in the first place?"

"I simply couldn't cope alone another minute. Oh, Theo darling, I have missed you so. Everything has been horrid since your wedding, all sixes and sevens. The housekeeper and two of the nursery maids gave their notice and Miss Harpence left as well. She said such terrible things about the girls! I told her I wouldn't give her a reference, and do you know what the woman said to me in reply? She said any reference from the Merediths would make it impossible for her to get another position, and she wouldn't take it if it were offered. I was much mistaken in Miss Harpence, Theo."

She took a deep breath and hurried on. "And Marietta, well! She has disgraced herself with the youngest footman. You remember Harry, don't you? Well, I am sorry to say he forgot himself. I was never more shocked to discover they were having trysts out behind the stable, and he was kissing her and heaven only knows what else. I had Kendall send him packing, you may be sure."

"How did you find out?" Canford asked, sounding genuinely interested. "Did that holy girl tell you, er, what's her name?"

"Yes, Violet told me. She knew it was her duty, even though she shrank from paining me with the news."

"I am sure she did," Canford agreed smoothly.

"But, Mama, surely you did not travel all the way to London just because of that," Theo interjected. "Not in your condition."

"No, of course not," her mother agreed, groping for her sodden handkerchief again. The earl handed her his own snowy square and she blew her nose in it with gusto. He managed to remain impassive.

"It's Teddy," Mrs. Meredith went on. "He has been sent down from Oxford, if you please, and for only a prank."

Theo seemed puzzled. "I know I did not see him. Did he come too?" she asked, wondering where they were to put everyone.

"No, no, he went off to a friend's home. He was also sent down. I am sure they did not mean to burn the porter's lodge and they did not know he was in it at the time. Besides, he was only burned a very little. Boys, you know, are so high-spirited.

"But that is not all. Reginald and Huntley are home from Eton with the measles. It was when they arrived that I thought to remove to London before all the children caught the disease. And I really must take baby Donald to a good physician. Surely it is not right for him to cry so much. None of my other babies did."

"Of course you must," Canford agreed. "Theo, my dear, why don't you and the housekeeper between you settle sleeping arrangements? I'm afraid the children will have to share rooms. We are not spacious enough here for everyone to be private. You have brought servants too, ma'am?"

"Only my maid and the baby's nursemaid. I gave the boys' tutor leave."

"Lucky man," Canford muttered as Theo passed him. She could not resist putting her hand on his shoulder and pressing it. He was so good to do this. Especially since she knew he did not care for her family. She did not wonder at it. Her mother had whined and she looked blowzy. She should not have worn that pink gown. It was not suitable for traveling, and it was much too young for her, Theo decided. She realized, now she had been away from them for some months, that her sisters and brothers were unappealing children to say the least. They were undisciplined, noisy, careless, and rude, and they had no manners at all.

She closed the door of the drawing room softly, leaving Lucas to handle his weeping mother-in-law. That he would be able to do so, she did not doubt for a moment.

When she returned half an hour later, she found them both enjoying a cup of tea. If Fanny Meredith was not exactly wreathed in smiles, at least she had stopped crying.

"Ah, Theo, I am sure your mother would like to talk to you privately. I am going to see if I can find your father and apprise him of the situation.

"Since we are pledged to attend the theater with the Williamses this evening—you do remember, don't you?— your mother has agreed that it would be best after the rigors of traveling, for everyone else to have an early dinner and bedtime."

Theo only glanced at him for a moment before she nodded. "Of course, my dear," she said as he bowed to them both.

Left alone, she turned to her mother. "Now there, Mama," she said with a smile. "Canford will make it all right, you'll see. He is the most capable man."

"Yes, I am sure I must be grateful to him in my adversity," her mother said, picking up the earl's handkerchief again. "Oh, Theo, it was so terrible! When we arrived at your father's rooms, there was a young woman there, and no, she was not the maid. Dressed as fine as the Queen she was, preening herself in his parlor. I knew immediately what she was to Theodore so I swept the children away lest they become corrupted. But never, never did I think my darling Theodore would—and with a girl your age too— and to think I was carrying his child under my heart and he would act so—oh, I shall never be the same again, never!"

Theo patted her hand. "It is unfortunate," she said, wishing she had her dear, *dear* father alone here so she might give him a tongue lashing he would never forget. It was suddenly borne in on her that her Grandmother Hutton had been right about him all along. Still she could not waste time and energy thinking about him now. She wondered how long she and Lucas would be expected to house them all. The girls had been assigned one bedroom with Gwyneth on a trundle there, while the boys were to share another. That left the smallest guest chamber for the baby and his nurse. She had been forced to give up her own rooms to her mother, and with the housekeeper regarding her, had announced she would share the earl's room for the time being. She still felt uneasy about this, but there was no other place for her to sleep. Lucas would have to find the Merediths a suitable house, whatever her father thought of it.

They would have to see about servants too, to travel back to Pobryn Abbey with them when the measles had run their course.

"Mama, who is staying with Reginald and Huntley?" she thought to ask. "If they are ill they must have someone to care for them."

"But of course they do. Did you think I would leave them alone?" Fanny Meredith said indignantly. "I hired a nurse for them and Kendall has twin nieces who want to go into service. He assured me they could help in the sickroom, and the doctor is to call once a day."

"If the nieces are satisfactory, they can take the place of the two defectors in the nursery later," Theo said. "Then you must only replace the housekeeper and Miss Harpence. And perhaps, Mama, it would be wise to employ an older, stricter woman as the girls' governess? And give her more authority so she can punish any misdoing? You see what has happened to Marietta. You have too soft a heart, but you cannot want the girls growing up wild."

"No, no. But Marietta, how she grieves me. She is so very pretty and now her chances for a good match are ruined. Ruined, Theo! Oh, dear, why does everything have to happen to me?"

Theo bit back her quick retort, only patting her mother's hand again.

"You are looking very different," Mrs. Meredith said at last, after she had composed herself. "Wherever did you get that gown? It is so plain. Perhaps you could set your maid to sewing on some bright ribbons, or perhaps a double row of flounces to the hem would help. And the color, Theo. What were you thinking of to choose gray? It is so depressing. Now, a nice pink or a soft blue would be more becoming."

"This gown is all the crack, Mama," Theo told her. "And no, I'm not going to have it ruined by adding unnecessary trimming."

"Oh, dear, you have become a woman as well as a wife, haven't you, and you don't want your poor mama's opinions anymore," Fanny Meredith said. Then she sighed. "Well, I only hope it doesn't put Canford off, to see you dressed so queer. But I must say your hair looks very well. Maybe if I have Marietta's hair done that way it might save the day for her . . ."

Theo didn't dare ask how a new hairdo could be expected to save her sister's reputation, if, that is, she had soiled it beyond repair. She would have to talk to Marietta alone later and find out how bad things were. She realized her head was beginning to ache and she reached up to smooth her forehead. No one could say she did not love her family, but she wished with all her heart they were safely home at Pobryn Abbey, and she was once again alone with Lucas. And then she told herself she was nothing but a selfish wretch.

16

When Theo went up to dress for the evening, leaving her mother supervising the arrangements for the family dinner, she discovered that a slight change had been made. It appeared she was not to give up her rooms after all, for on Canford's orders his things had been brought to her dressing room. She changed quickly with Betsy's help so she would not delay him when he came in. She hoped he was not having trouble with her father, wherever he had found him. Then she smiled into the mirror as the maid did her hair. Canford have trouble with Theodore Meredith? Not likely.

She was ready when he came in at last. "I'll tell you all about it later," he said as he disappeared into the dressing room and rang for his man.

Theo went to the window to look down into the garden. Her little brothers were there, playing tag around the paths, watched by an impassive footman. She hoped the exercise would wear them out so they would do no more damage to Canford's treasures. She meant to speak to her mother about the Sevres vase the boys had broken, for it should be replaced, and by the Merediths too. Her mother had forgotten it, so concerned was she with her own problems, but it would not do. Theo felt enough shame that her family was so unattractive and difficult. She told herself it would be different if they were trying to do better, but they did not even bother to do that.

She went down to the hall on Canford's arm, glad she had said her farewells earlier. She could hear the racket in the dining room and she prayed no one would spill their milk or dribble sauce on the tablecloth, or break anything.

As the house door closed behind her, she resolved to put the Merediths from her mind. Whatever they did, she could do nothing about it, and she wanted to forget them, at least for the next few hours.

"Alone at last!" the earl whispered dramatically as he helped her into the carriage.

Theo was confused. He didn't seem angry or even annoyed that his carefully regulated life had been turned upside down. Of course it was early days yet, she thought gloomily.

"We won't have time to discuss the meeting I had with your father, Theo. Not in any depth," Lucas was saying and she made herself pay attention. "We'll do that later at the hotel where we're to have supper. For now, let me say only that he will set about finding his family a furnished house first thing tomorrow. I think we may look forward to resuming our customary routines within the week. Perhaps even sooner."

Theo smiled at him. He looked impossibly handsome tonight, all in black except for his crisp white linen and discreet gray waistcoat. His hair was combed in a careless style she knew required a deft hand to accomplish, and the smile in his eyes, his shapely mouth, made her feel weak all over.

"I'm so glad," she said. "I really cannot think why Mama chose to come to us, and with the children too."

"She has always depended on you, of course. And she was distraught by what she had discovered about her husband," he suggested.

"Well, yes, I suppose there is that."

"Did you know?"

"I saw him crossing Portman Square with a young woman some days ago," she admitted.

"There was no keeping it from you. Many of men have mistresses but even so, Theodore Meredith's weakness for pretty girls is well known in town. Every Season there is a new bit o' muslin."

"I despise him," Theo said, her voice shaking a litt**le**. Then she made a conscious effort and went on. "But I d**o** think Mama might go to my Aunt Gloria's. After all, **I** stayed with her all last Season."

"But that was only your mother and yourself, wasn't i**t**," he pointed out. "Perhaps Mrs. Meredith knew she wo**uld** not be welcome there with most of her family in tow."

Remembering her aunt, Theo was inclined to agree **with** him. Gloria Talbott was a very proper lady, cool and **col**lected, and she had not seemed fond of either her niec**e or** her sister-in-law.

She looked out the window beside her. The carriage **was** inching along in the press of traffic that was bound fo**r** Drury Lane. Theo had attended the theater twice the p**revi**ous year and had found it vastly entertaining. She ha**d no** idea what they were to see tonight, but it did not ma**tter.** She was with Lucas, they were alone, and she was sur**e she** would have smiled through the most affecting traged**y, she** was so happy.

"That was quite a bouncer you told about being prom**ised** to the Williamses," she said as the carriage lurche**d in**to motion again. "And right after you told me we were to **keep** our distance too."

"I knew you would understand. One of the things I **have** always admired about you, Countess, is your quick w**it," he** said, smiling down at her.

I'd rather be beautiful, she thought although she th**anked** him for the compliment.

The carriage pulled up before the theater and a **boy** hurried forward to let down the steps. The stre**et was** crowded with people and carriages, young bloods an**d cho**risters, orange sellers and ladies of easy virtue, alon**g with** the elite. Theo saw from a playbill, tonight they wer**e to** see yet another reprise of John Gay's *The Beggar's* **Opera,** the early eighteenth century lyric drama comple**te with** music. It never appeared on the London stage **without** drawing crowds, even now, a hundred years later.

Theo enjoyed the path that was cleared for her and

by his servants, and the box he had procured for them, so spacious and comfortable. The other boxes were beginning to fill, and Canford exchanged bows with the occupants. Theo saw everyone was studying her carefully, and she remembered to sit up straight and keep her shoulders back. She knew they could find no fault with her gown. It was a deceptively simple fall of emerald silk, the low bodice edged in fine lace and topped with a sleeveless half jacket of darker green velvet. With it she wore the customary long white gloves, and now she opened a cream and ivory fan decorated with paintings in the classical style, and waved it gently before her face, hoping she looked sophisticated and unconcerned about the scrutiny she was undergoing.

"Remind me to thank the dowager and Lady Blake again sometime," Lucas said as he took his seat beside her just as the candles at the sides of the theater were being extinguished. "Your gown is stunning. I could not have chosen better for you myself."

After the performance, Canford took her to Stephen's Hotel on Bond Street where he had engaged a private dining room. Theo had never been in a public hotel before and she was interested in everything and everybody she saw. While the earl conferred with the waiter, she inspected the room they occupied, amused by the couch she saw along one wall. Could it be gentlemen brought women here for other purposes than a good meal? she wondered. She had seen more men here than women, to be sure, but there had been some ladies passing through the lobby.

After they had been served and the waiter dismissed, Canford said, "I found your father in his rooms when I arrived there. There was no sign of the, er, young lady your mother mentioned."

"I hardly think he turned her off just because his wife discovered his wandering eye," Theo said gloomily as she toyed with her salad.

Canford ignored this comment. "We discussed the situation at great length and he agreed he would see about renting a furnished house tomorrow. Not at once, of course. He made some comments about how crowded London was becoming, bewailed the lack of suitable houses in the best part of town—you know. It was obvious he was not happy his family was here. He made that abundantly clear, but he quite understood, after I pointed it out to him, that we could not be expected to be responsible for them for—how long *is* one sick with the measles?"

"I've no idea," Theo admitted. "I never had them."

"No more have I," Canford said, taking another slice of beef. "Your father was quite the bon vivant, today. He spoke to me man-to-man, as if this matter were only a slight obstacle in his path. I say, you're looking pensive. What are you thinking?"

"I was wondering if any of his pretty little things ever had a baby. I mean, here's my mother almost constantly increasing, yet they are rarely together. Surely his light o' loves must be similarly afflicted. Dear me. To think there may be ten or twenty more little Merediths in the world is startling, isn't it?"

Her voice was wry and perfectly controlled but Canford heard the pain in it, and he reached across the table to touch her hand.

"You must not let him upset you, Theo," he said earnestly. "Some men are that way. But I hardly think his women suffer your mother's burden. They are more knowledgeable. They have to be.

"I'm afraid your sister Marietta takes after her father. You'll have to speak to her about her wantonness. Unless you'd like me to perform that unpleasant task."

"No, let me see her first. Not that I think it will do a bit of good. You know, Lucas, I just realized this afternoon that the Merediths are not particularly appealing people. They do what they want when they want to with no regard for anyone else. Look at Marietta. She knows full well a blemished reputation spells social ruin, yet what does she go and do? Meet a footman out behind the stable, and she's only fourteen too. How refined. How elegant."

"You are the only Meredith who has any claim to refinement and elegance, but you have those traits in abundance," he told her, holding her gaze.

"It is kind of you to say so," she murmured, not believing him in the slightest. Turning the conversation from herself, she said, "Tell me, sir, do men bring women here who are not their wives?"

"Why do you ask?" he said. To Theo it sounded as if he were stalling for time.

"That sofa there against the wall. It seems an odd piece of furniture for a room devoted to dining."

He raised his wineglass and sipped before he said, "I suppose it has been used on occasion."

"But not by someone fainting away because he or she did not make a good meal, I daresay."

"Would you care to try it?" he asked, leaning forward and capturing her hand.

"What on earth are you thinking?" she was quick to say, although of course she knew very well what was in his mind.

"We can lock *this* door," he persisted. "No one will come in."

"Certainly not," she said, considerably shocked. She told herself she must be imagining the fleeting disappointment that crossed his face.

"I only thought you might like to do something a bit unusual and daring," he said. "And we *are* married."

"May I suggest you have one of the cakes if you want a sweet after your supper, sir?" Theo said.

"No, thank you," he said, rising and coming to help her from her chair. "I find I suddenly have a burning desire to seek my bed. Oh, I do beg your pardon, ma'am. I should say, *your* bed."

Putting his hands on her bare shoulders, he drew her back to rest against him as he kissed her throat. "Do you know," he went on, "that is the one good thing I can think of, about your family's arrival at Canford House. I must remain with you all night. I hope you ate a fortifying meal, ma'am."

Lucas Whitney woke long before his bride. There was enough light coming through a crack in the draperies for him to be able to see her clearly. She lay on her side, facing him, and one arm was across his chest. It had been that slight pressure that had awakened him, and his mouth twisted wryly as he thought how much more approachable she was asleep. He could remember her touching him voluntarily only a few times in all the weeks they had been wed.

He studied her face in the dim light. It was serene and empty, an enigma. Or perhaps it would be better to say, she was a contradiction. Just consider last night. She had spoken freely of her father's mistresses, her mother's many pregnancies, and during the farce that had followed the performance at the theater, she had laughed as hard as he had at some very warm jests. She had even questioned him about the sofa in the private dining room, all subjects many another woman would have been loath to discuss with any man. But when he had suggested they make use of that sofa, she had turned icy and indignant—horrified, in fact. And what was he to make of that? he wondered, bending to kiss the one shoulder that was all that the sheet exposed. Theo grumbled and turned on her other side, pulling the covers up to her neck as she did so. Her deep breathing had not changed; he knew she was still fast asleep.

Ah, well, he thought with a reminiscent grin, as he lay back and crossed his arms under his head, I did love her hard last night, and often. At one point he had thought she was going to respond at last, but she had controlled herself, only fleeing to the dressing room as soon as he released her. After that, she had reverted to her normal behavior, much to his everlasting disappointment.

I must have it out with her, he thought once again, frowning now. We cannot go on this way. And surely after almost six months of marriage, she cannot still be shy with me.

Faintly, he heard the Meredith baby begin to cry, and he threw back his side of the covers and rose to stretch. It would be easier for Theo if he were not here when she woke, and easier for himself too, he realized. A good hard canter in the park would do him good. There was plenty of time to think about how he was to speak to his fascinating, seductive, icy enigma of a wife. For Lucas Whitney had no intention of giving up. No, he would make her care for him if it was the last thing he ever did.

Two hours later, Theo sent her maid to fetch her sister. She had had breakfast in bed before she dressed, for she did not feel she could bear to be with her noisy family this morning. Not first thing, anyway. Not after the wild experiences of the night before. Just remembering, she felt a warmth growing deep, and she groaned. Not now, she told herself sternly. She had other things to think about now.

Marietta looked sulky when she entered the room. She went at once to the dressing table to finger the silver brushes there and pick up a vial of perfume to sniff it. Theo hated having her touch her things, but she only said, "Please come and sit down over here, Marietta. We've a deal to discuss."

"You're not my mother, nor my father. I don't have to listen to you," the girl said even as she obeyed.

"Why did you do it?" Theo asked. "I know Grandmama warned you about the lower classes at my wedding. I heard her do so."

Her sister shrugged. "I don't know," she said at last.

"Did you think yourself in love with him?" Theo asked.

"In love with Harry?" Marietta asked, as if she could not believe her ears. "You must be daft. He's a *footman*."

She began to laugh at the very idea, and it was some time before she wiped her eyes and said, "Love! What's *love* got to do with it?"

Everything, Theo thought, but she did not say so.

"He was young and handsome and clean enough. I fancied him, I guess. You know what it's like, now you're married, don't you?" she said, bending forward. "There's nothing like it, is there? I say, what are you looking so sour for? Isn't Canford any good? Coo-ee, he certainly looks like he would be."

"That will be quite enough," Theo said as crisply as she could. "My relationship with the earl is none of your business. We are not discussing that. We are discussing what is to be done with you."

Marietta shrugged again and picked up a delicate porcelain figurine from the table beside her. She turned it this way and that and Theo longed to jump up and snatch it away, but she did not dare, lest Marietta drop it carelessly.

She asked several more questions that her sister refused to answer. At last, exasperated, she excused her. Marietta went to the door, her lush hips in fluid motion. Once there, she turned and said, "You've got it soft, haven't you, Theo? A title, a rich husband, all the gowns and jewels you could ever want. But all that's wasted on *you*. Because you know something? Marriage hasn't changed you. You've got no more life in you than that fancy figurine. Canford would have been better off to have had *me*. I'd have led him a merry dance I would, for all I'm only fourteen."

The door slammed behind her, and Theo waited for her anger to subside before she went to her mother. She thought that lady looked ridiculous sitting up in Lucas's big bed in his masculine room. She even felt a stab of resentment that she was there at all.

"I hope you slept well, Mama," she made herself say as she came to give her a kiss.

"Very nicely, my dear, thank you. Such a relief after those dreadful inns we encountered on the road.

"You'll think me slothful, but the earl sent word he had arranged for the little boys to be taken on a sightseeing tour of London this morning, and I've sent Gwyneth to the park with my maid. Marietta, of course, remains here. She can expect no treats, no, not a one."

"It is of Marietta that I would speak, Mama," Theo said, sitting down on the bed. "I tried to talk to her just now, but she is unrepentant. And I cannot see her changing her ways."

Fanny Meredith sighed and wiped her eyes on a corner of the sheet. "She must take after her father," she said, inadvertently echoing Canford's assessment of the girl. "What am I to do with her, Theo? I'm at my wit's end."

"I think it would be best for everyone if she were sent off to school. A very strict school that has little or no contact with the opposite sex. If she remains there until she is seventeen, and you can marry her off quickly, everything may work out after all. But you must choose an academy known for its severity, its careful guardianship of its charges, and the quality of its instruction. Perhaps Marietta might even like to read, do sums, and study history and languages."

"Why would she want to do that?" Mrs. Meredith asked, blue eyes wide. "She's going to marry, isn't she? Someone, anyway. She doesn't need all that education."

Theo did not try to explain. "Let me ask Canford what he thinks best," she said. "He may know of some suitable place."

"The very thing," Fanny Meredith said, wriggling her swollen body sideways until she reached the edge of the bed. "Hand me my robe, there's a dear girl. I can't tell you how I've missed you, Theo, or the times I've regretted your marriage. It's all very well to be able to brag your eldest daughter has married an earl who's a pink of the *ton,* but it certainly left me in a fix. And now there's this new baby. From the way I'm carrying it, I'm sure it's another boy. I expect I'll end up having it in London. It's almost my time."

"We must make arrangements for that too," Theo said. "I'll see about nurses, find a good accoucheur . . ."

"No need for that, as you know, dear. Not after all my babies. Just a competent midwife will do. Now, I suppose I'd best dress. The earl has set up an appointment for me to take baby Donald to the doctor. I am so glad you will be with me to sustain and help me."

Theo smiled weakly and went away to write a note canceling an afternoon engagement with the Dowager Duchess of Lansmere and Lady Blake. She could tell her time would now be completely bespoken, at least until the Merediths were settled into their own establishment. And, she thought, she was not at all sure she would be able to escape the yoke of her mother's servitude even then.

17

By the end of the week, Theo was holding on to her temper by only the thinnest of threads. It was not so much the children, although heaven knows they were aggravating enough with their racket and untidyness and endless demands on her time. No, it was her mother, who, having found her again, was once more giving orders and expecting her eldest daughter to see to everything for her. And try as she might, Theo could think of no way she could escape this subjection without giving offense. The coming birth made it even more difficult, for of course her mother needed assistance, even just to climb the stairs.

The one ray of hope that Theo clung to was the knowledge that on Wednesday next, all the Merediths were to remove to a furnished house on Upper Brook Street. Servants had been hired and supplies laid in, a nursemaid engaged for the new baby, and a reliable midwife found.

The earl had accomplished most of this with some nominal help from his father-in-law, who, although he agreed that yes, he did have a family in the country, seemed to feel they had ceased to be related to him the moment they entered London.

But by Wednesday evening I shall be free of them all, Theo thought as she started down the stairs. Free of Mama's incessant demands, free of Marietta's surly, impolite ways . . .

It was strange, she thought. Since yesterday Marietta had been much more amenable, even taking Theo's place with her mother and the children on occasion. She wondered why.

She had reached the flight that led to the ground floor and saw the earl down on one knee, Lester and Will lined up before him, their hands clasped behind their backs and their heads down.

Oh, dear, what have they done now? she wondered. But before she could call down and ask, Canford began to speak, and she paused to listen.

"I do not know how it is at the Abbey, but here at Canford House we have rules. Do you know what rules are?"

"Oh, yes, sir," Lester said with his beautiful smile.

"Be good enough to explain them to your little brother later," the earl said, not sounding at all softened by this knowledge.

"My rules are made to be obeyed. Did you hear me? Both of you? *Obeyed.*

"The first one is there will be no sliding down the banisters in this house."

Theo bit back a smile. Of course. Those twin staircases must have been much too tempting for the boys. But certainly Lucas was right. The stairs were steep and high, and either boy would be badly injured if he lost his balance and fell.

"Furthermore, we do not run in this house. Have you ever seen me running?"

"No, sir," came in unison.

"Or any of the servants? Or your sister Theo?"

"No, sir."

"You will not run either. If you want to run you must go out into the garden, or ask someone to take you to the park.

"The next rule is that you are never, ever, to leave this house without a grownup. It has come to my attention that you both did so this morning. You could have been killed crossing Park Lane. It is a busy thoroughfare, crowded with horses and carriages and heavy drays.

"No," he said, holding up a hand when Lester would have spoken, "this is not a subject that is open to discussion. You will not leave this house without permission, sir! Do you understand?"

He waited for their assent before he went on. "And the last rule is that there will be no throwing food at the table. We eat food. We throw balls.

"You are excused."

The two boys backed away from him, then turned. As they moved away, the earl called after them, "I said no running! Stop that at once!"

Theo started down the stairs again as he rose and ran a hand through his hair, ruining his valet's careful arrangement. He looked up and said ruefully, "Did you hear all that?"

"Yes, I did," she said, unable to stop smiling. "You were, mm, very forceful, sir."

"If I thought it had done any good, I'd be pleased, but I'm willing to wager it all went in one ear and out the other. Twice."

"Did they really go out this morning?"

"Yes. Young Will told the footman who was sent to fetch them that he wanted to look for frogs in the Serpentine."

"In March?" Theo asked. "And how could he remember frogs? He's not quite four."

"I suspect it was Lester who had the idea, then made Will claim it for his own to escape punishment. Perhaps Lester should consider politics or the diplomatic corps in a few years. He has a devious mind.

"Have you time for a cup of coffee with me?" he asked, indicating the library door. "I never see you anymore."

Theo nodded. It was true, the only time they seemed to be alone together was in bed. The rest of the time was taken up by the Merediths and all their turbulent, abundant problems.

When the coffee had been brought and the library door closed firmly with a footman stationed outside to forestall intruders, Theo relaxed.

"This is nice," she said. "Lucas, I do thank you for everything you've done for my family. You've been wonderful."

"It almost makes it worthwhile to hear you say so. If only I could stop counting the days till their departure."

"You too? I feel so guilty, wishing them all away."

"Only three more days. We can survive till then."

A crash came from the floor above, and he winced. "Thank you for putting the most delicate ornaments away, Theo. I think Gwyneth is worse than any of her brothers, she is so clumsy. And that voice. It could cut glass."

Theo sipped her coffee. "We all hope it will moderate as she grows older. But forget Gwynnie. I understand you spoke to Marietta yesterday. What did you say to her?"

He grinned at her over the rim of his cup. "Better you don't know, Countess. Much better. Oh, I forgot to tell you, I have heard about a school in the Midlands. It was recommended to me by a chap whose sister was very like Marietta. He claims the time she spent there did wonders for her, and now she's meek as a lamb."

"I cannot believe any place could have that salutary an effect on my sister, but any improvement will be welcome."

There was a sudden commotion outside the door, and Violet's voice came clearly as she explained to the footman she had no intention of bothering her sister and the earl, she merely wished to get another volume of sermons from the earl's bookshelves. She was firmly refused admittance and quiet descended again.

"She shows no sign of slackening her fervor, does she?" he asked idly.

Theo sighed. "No, but at least she is a quiet child and she doesn't chase footmen, break things, or cause problems. And she told me she has decided she will never marry. Instead she intends to be a shield and buckler for Mama."

"Well, that must please you. If she does, you won't have to be one anymore. Not that you would anyway, Theo. If your mother continues to make these incessant demands on your time, I am going to speak to her."

"Oh, please, Lucas," Theo said, setting down her coffee cup and stretching out her hands to him. "Please do not.

They will be gone soon, and although of course I will see them now and then, I do not intend to be caught up in all their doings. Please, for my sake, hold your tongue. It would hurt Mama so to be chastised when she has not the least idea she is so demanding."

"Very well, but I still think someone should set her straight. Now then, what do you say to a drive in the Park this afternoon? Before you agree too quickly, you should know I've asked Marietta to join us."

Theo stared at him. "Lucas, you *bribed* her, didn't you? That is shameless, making her good behavior a condition for an outing."

He looked a little sheepish. "It was all I could think of to do, at the time. Please say you'll come. I'm not at all sure I can control her alone. I mean, suppose she sees some handsome groom? What then?"

Theo almost told him it would be impossible for Marietta to see a more handsome man than he was himself. She caught herself just in time.

Wednesday was an exhausting day for all, but when the door finally closed on the Merediths for the last time—for in the move several items had been forgotten and had to be fetched—everyone from the earl to the scullery maid sighed in relief. Theo was relieved as well. Her mother had fully expected her to come to Upper Brook Street with them that day, to set all in order, but she had pleaded a prior engagement with the earl.

"Well," Mrs. Meredith had said sadly, wiping an imaginary tear away, "I suppose he does have first claim on your time. However, I do think it is heartless, with me so near my time, and so much to be done—for you know, Theo, rented houses are not always what they've been puffed up to be—and I do feel that weary."

Theo told herself she would not be made to feel guilty. Her mother had Marietta, Violet, and the housekeeper and maids to help her. Attired in one of her new promenade gowns, she enjoyed a stroll with Canford that afternoon, and later, an evening at the opera.

She was disturbed to find out later he had not moved back to his old room as yet. It was something she had been dreading in a way, even as she looked forward to it, for having him so close all night was playing havoc with her nerves. She had barely dismissed Betsy before he wandered in and came up to her dressing table to pull the ribbon from her hair so he could brush it.

"There's no need, sir," she said, their eyes meeting in the glass. "Betsy brushed it thoroughly."

"You can never brush your hair enough," he told her, winding a tress of it around his finger for a moment. "Perhaps I should have been a hairdresser. I seem to have an affinity for the profession, wouldn't you say?"

"It does feel good," Theo admitted, closing her eyes as much to shut out the sight of him in his open-necked shirt and tight breeches as to savor the sensations.

"I can't get used to the quiet," he remarked next.

Her eyes flew open. "That's not fair, Lucas. It was never noisy at this hour. The children were asleep."

"You forget the baby. Your mother said the medicine the doctor gave her for him made a great difference, but personally, I didn't notice it. He still seemed to squall night and day."

"It is peaceful, isn't it?"

"I trust it will remain so. We're to go down to Richmond tomorrow to visit Maitland Grant's grandmother. She has a place on the river there. And you haven't forgotten tomorrow night is the first gala of the Season? Trust Mrs. Griffin-Cole to lead the way. Still, her parties are notable for their music and lavish suppers."

He paused for a moment before he said, "Do you know, tomorrow night will be the first time I'll have the chance to waltz with you, since Genie didn't approve of it for the Christmas ball at Lansmere."

"I'll try not to disgrace you," she said, smiling up at him. He put the hairbrush down, then bent to gather her hair in one big hand and sweep it to one side so he could kiss the back of her neck. As shivers ran down her spine he said softly, "Come to bed, Theo. Come now."

Fortunately the next day was fair after a misty, rainy dawn. They went to Richmond in the earl's phaeton, which Theo thought very smart. Maitland Grant was before them with several other guests, and Theo admired the house, her elderly hostess, and the concert that lady had arranged to entertain them.

When they arrived back at Park Lane, she was already planning a bath before the evening gala, but as she moved toward the stairs, the butler cleared his throat and said, "Your pardon, m'lady. There have been several messages sent over from Upper Brook Street . . ."

"Give them to me," Canford said, holding out his hand for the sheaf of papers the butler was holding. "No, Theo, you are not to trouble yourself."

"You have also had a caller, m'lady," the butler said. "A Mr. Theodore Meredith."

"My father is here?" Theo asked, stiffening.

"This is a young gentleman, m'lady. I've put him in the library since he insisted on waiting for you."

"And how many aunts, uncles, and cousins came with him?" the earl drawled. "No, never mind." As he went with Theo toward the library, he said, "So, we have not seen the end of the Merediths after all. The second contingent has just arrived."

Teddy jumped to his feet when they came in. He had obviously been there for some time for he had removed his jacket, helped himself to the earl's Madeira, and spread the day's papers all over a sofa and the floor nearby.

"Another untidy Meredith too," Canford murmured, eyeing the large portmanteau set against the wall with an unfriendly eye.

"Teddy! What on earth are you doing here?" Theo asked.

"Well, that's a nice way to welcome me, I must say," the boy said, trying for an air of injured dignity.

"I thought you were visiting a friend somewhere," Theo persisted. "The one who had been sent down from Oxford with you, I believe Mama said."

Teddy kept shooting nervous little glances at his new brother-in-law, who so far had had nothing to say for himself. He was sure it was not because he did not care to interrupt this tender reunion.

"Oh, well, yes, so I was. Roy Hammond. Capital fellow, Roy. Capital! But his father seemed to feel, because of some silly letter the authorities at the college sent him, that we would be better separated, and I was forced to hare off. I did go to Pobryn Abbey but Lord, Theo! Deadly dull there with Reggie and Huntley both ill. Besides, I've never had the measles so I decided to follow Ma and the babes to town."

"Your mother has taken a house in Upper Brook Street," the earl said, speaking up for the first time. "Number thirty-eight."

"Has she? Yes, well, you see, I think I'd rather stay with you. I mean, all those children and a new one due any minute. Not the place for me. And besides, I'd only be in the way. I've pretty much decided I'm not going back to Oxford anyway. Had enough of books and such. Thought I'd live in London instead, see a bit of life. Perhaps you could introduce me to your tailor, m'lord. Take me round your clubs and get me started in the Four-in-Hand Club and such. I'd be much obliged and . . ."

"No."

"No?" Teddy echoed, stunned by this terse comment. "No to what?"

"No to everything," the earl said, moving forward into the room.

"Lucas," Theo said behind him, and without turning to her, he said, "No, Theo, we are not going to have your brother using us as a hotel. Nor do I have any intention of being his sponsor. The very idea."

Fixing a distinctly sulky Teddy with a baleful eye, he said, "If I remember correctly, sir, you are eighteen. Well, what on earth makes you think you'd be welcome at a gentleman's club, you young puppy? Furthermore, the Four-in-Hand consists of expert drivers, a skill I would wager any amount you cannot claim. As for that inexcusable prank you played at school, it only shows your immaturity. That porter might have died screaming while I suppose you and your *capital* fellow arsonist stood around wringing your hands and exclaiming you didn't mean to have done it.

"Someday you may amount to something, but I don't think I'll hold my breath till you do. At the moment you are nothing but a callow fellow with considerable gall and only a modicum of common sense.

"The number in Upper Brook Street is thirty-eight. Bid you good day."

Teddy's face was white now and even though she knew every word Lucas had said had been true, Theo's heart went out to him. She knew Teddy was selfish and he never thought of anyone but himself, but still she wished Lucas had been less scathing as her brother picked up his jacket and portmanteau, made her a shaky bow, and stumbled to the door.

"No doubt you think I was cruel," Canford said when Teddy was safely gone.

"A little," she said, not looking at him. "But you were right. He was very brash to just assume we would be glad to house him for an indefinite period of time. Still, I daresay my mother will not be pleased to see him either."

"If she's clever, she'll put him to work running errands for her, and make him take charge of Lester and Will. Some weeks of that should make him want to return to Oxford as fast as he can be reinstated.

"Go have your bath, Countess, and a rest too. I expect you to put everyone else in the shade tonight."

18

Theo wore white silk to the gala. The gown was cut low both front and back, and trimmed with delicate gold embroidery on the bodice, the puffed sleeves, and the hem. With it she wore gold sandals, and in her gloved hand carried a gold-and-white fan.

"Why, that's immodest," was Canford's first remark. He frowned as he said it and for a moment Theo felt doubtful. Then she remembered other evening dresses she had seen.

"Can it be you are becoming prudish, sir?" she asked. "This is the current style. I am sure you will see many others tonight even more revealing."

"If they are, their wearers should be ashamed of themselves," he persisted.

"If you really don't like it, I will change to something else," Theo said, although she was very disappointed.

"No, we don't have time. It grows late," he replied. "But perhaps if you were to drape a stole over your shoulders?"

But this Theo failed to do, inadvertently assuring the earl's almost constant attendance all evening, for he was determined that none of the gentlemen present would have a chance to enjoy what he had come to feel was his exclusive property.

Mrs. Griffin-Cole's house was spacious, which it certainly needed to be to accommodate everyone she had invited. Fortunately it sported a ballroom as well as the usual drawing rooms, and it was to the ballroom the Whitneys repaired after they had greeted their hostess. The dancing had just begun, and they stood to one side watching the couples on the floor as they went through the steps in the set.

As Theo fanned herself she saw her Aunt Gloria seated a little distance away. She went over to greet the lady with the earl close behind. After a few minutes' conversation, he was called away by one of his friends, but he felt safe leaving Theo with an aunt who appeared very proper indeed.

"An excellent man, the earl," Lady Gloria said approvingly. "You have made an enviable match, Theodora."

"Yes, I think I have," Theo agreed with a sunny smile.

"I am so glad to see you have abandoned those horrible *deedy* gowns you wore last year. I did try to speak to your mother about them, but she would not listen."

"Mama is in London, Aunt," Theo told her. "She has taken a house on Upper Brook Street, but I do not know how long she intends to stay. She is to give birth any day now."

"Yet *again*?" Lady Gloria said, her brows arched in horrified amazement. "Er, is my brother residing there as well?"

"No, he has taken his usual rooms," Theo said with as much composure as she could muster. "And Reggie and Huntley remain at Pobryn Abbey. They have the measles. But the other children are with Mama. They all stayed with the earl and me until the house could be made ready."

Her aunt sniffed. "I daresay you and Canford were glad to see the back of them. Fanny never did have the sense to discipline her children. It is a wonder you turned out as well as you did; I'm sure none of the rest of them will."

"How is Charlie? Have you heard from him?" Theo asked, deftly changing the subject.

Her aunt's face brightened. "Yes, we had a letter a month ago. It is too bad it takes three months for one to arrive. He is in good health and enjoying himself immensely."

"I'm so glad," Theo said. "He was a good friend to me last Season. If it had not been for Charlie, I would have had a miserable time of it."

It seemed to her Lady Gloria paused for a moment as if debating the wisdom of what she was about to say. Then she looked at her niece and said, "I was not kind to you then, my dear, and I am sorry for it. But when I saw how well you and Charlie dealt together, I was afraid."

"Afraid? I don't understand."

"I was afraid he would ask you to marry him, and I did not want any alliance between you. It was not only that you were first cousins, although I have never approved of unions where the parties were closely related. No, it was more. My brother—perhaps you are not aware of your father's life here, and I would not distress you . . ."

"I know about his mistresses," Theo told her, color tingeing her cheeks.

Her aunt nodded. "He is more than an embarrassment, with his endless parade of young girls while his wife keeps on producing." She paused to take a handkerchief from her reticule to pat her lips. "I thought you might have inherited some of his traits; he is your father after all. That is not what I wanted for Charlie. If I am overzealous where he is concerned, please remember he is my only child and very dear to me. But I do hope you will find it in your heart to forgive me."

Moved, Theo reached out and squeezed her hand.

Her aunt's eyes were suspiciously bright. She seemed to gather herself before she went on. "Now you have married the earl and I am so pleased for you."

"Well, well, if it isn't Canford's new bride," a familiar voice exclaimed loudly, causing several people in the vicinity to turn and stare. Theo looked up to see Florence Whitney regarding her with hauteur and she rose reluctantly.

"Lady Dalseny," she said, her voice without inflection. "Are you acquainted with my aunt, the Lady Gloria Talbott?"

The two elder ladies exchanged wordless nods.

"So, you are come to London for the Season, are you?" Lady Dalseny continued. "Now that is strange. I was sure I heard you had been left at Canford to rusticate while the earl came alone."

"But as you see, I am here indeed," Theo said lightly. It seemed the lady was belligerent for some reason, and she was determined not to lose her temper, especially after Lucas's warning about his aunt's virulent tongue.

"I hope Patsy is well? And your husband?"

"The viscount enjoys superlative health, as does my daughter. Tell me, did you come to town with Canford? Or did you, as I have heard, come up with someone else?"

"Why this sudden interest in my travel arrangements, ma'am?" Theo asked, sounding only confused. "Yes, it is true I was with the Dowager Duchess of Lansmere and Lady Blake," she admitted. "I was in desperate need of new gowns, and Lucas could not help me there. Men, for all their boasts about their impeccable taste are nowhere near as omnipotent as they would like to think. I am sure you will both agree," she said, including her puzzled aunt in the conversation. "Why, just this evening the earl tried to get me to change my gown, claiming it was not at all the thing, which of course it is."

"He did not want other men admiring you, child," Lady Gloria said, and Theo turned to her and winked a little as she smiled her thanks.

"I think he was entirely right," Lady Dalseny said. "That gown is much too revealing. I would never allow my sweet Patsy to appear so immodestly dressed, and *she* has a much better figure than *you* do."

Theo heard her aunt's sharp intake of breath and she laughed to forestall any intervention on her part. She had Lady Dalseny's measure now. She was annoyed, annoyed to see that what Faith Abbott had called a "grub" had indeed been transformed into a smartly dressed sophisticate.

"But of course you wouldn't," Theo said, amused. "Patsy is only a child of fifteen. *Most* unsuitable, except for married ladies. Like me.

"Ah, Lucas, there you are. I was beginning to think you had abandoned me. Here is your Aunt Florence. Could anything be more delightful than to meet her again?"

Theo saw her husband was looking at her as if she had lost her mind, but he bowed to the lady before he said, "I have been told on good authority that the next dance is a waltz. Please excuse me, ladies. It will be our first waltz, you see, and I would not miss a moment of it."

"Thank you, oh, thank you for saying that," Theo whispered as he led her to the floor. "Nasty old crow."

"Forget her," he ordered as he put his arm around her and took her hand.

The waltz was much too short for Theo. Just to be held in his arms while he smiled down at her as they turned in perfect harmony was happiness such as she had never known. When the last notes sounded and Lucas released her to bow and pretend to kiss her gloved hand, Theo had all she could do not to throw her arms around him and kiss him as she had been longing to do from their first night at Canford all those weeks ago.

When they finally reached home not long before dawn, Theo could hardly keep her eyes open long enough for Betsy to undress her, and she was fast asleep when the earl came to her. He only looked at her for a moment before he went to his own room.

She rose late the next morning and padded to the dressing room. Betsy had hung the white silk gown neatly on the back of the door to air before she put it away. Theo reached out to touch it softly, a little smile on her lips. She told herself she would never discard this gown, it was so full of wonderful memories.

Yawning a little, she wondered what Lucas was doing today. She had an appointment to drive in the park later with the dowager and Lucy Blake in that lady's landau. The sea green carriage dress and the chipped straw hat, she decided.

It was a glorious afternoon but when Theo was summoned, she discovered only Lady Blake waiting for her, wearing her usual quiet expression.

"Do not tell me the dowager is ill, Lucy," Theo said as

she took her place and the groom shut the door and put up the steps before he took his customary place behind.

"No, she was forced to cry off when an old friend came to call on her unexpectedly. I left them enjoying a tea tray and having the most comfortable gossip about everyone they have ever known.

"Tell me, did you enjoy the gala last evening?"

"It was wonderful." Theo sighed. "I had every waltz with Canford, and Maitland Grant was most attentive too. They both took me in to the most sumptuous supper."

Then catching sight of her friend's beautiful, composed face, she said, "I am sorry you were not there. I am sure you would have enjoyed it as well. Tell me, Lucy, why don't you ever go to parties? You have been out of mourning such a long time, I am sure no one would take it amiss."

For a moment, she thought the woman beside her was going to refuse to answer, but at last Lucy said, "I have no wish for parties, I suppose."

"But you are still young!" Theo exclaimed, wondering if she was about to be rebuffed, yet still unable to stop. "It is not right when you are so beautiful. You should marry again, have children . . ."

"Please, Theo, no more," Lucy interrupted sounding stifled. "I know you mean well, but I cannot tell you why. Not you, or anyone."

"I'm sorry. I did not mean to make you uncomfortable," Theo whispered, suddenly mindful of the groom clinging to the perch behind. Her wretched tongue!

Lucy patted her hand, then called her attention to a most unusual outfit worn by a lady in a party of strollers they were passing. Theo knew the subject would not be discussed again.

Still, she could not help but wonder what had happened to Lucy Blake to turn her into a recluse. True, she had opened her home to Theo and the dowager, but many times she had remained there while the two of them went shopping or made calls. And there had been all those days she did not come downstairs at all, not even for dinner. Faith

Abbott had bullied her into going to see a doctor but the medicine he gave her, and the regimen he recommended, did not appear to do her much good. Theo did not think Lucy was physically ill. There were no symptoms that she could discover, but something had to be wrong. And since Lucy dressed in the first stare, why did she then choose to live in a dark, cheerless house when she had inherited a fortune and could change it, or move somewhere else, any time she wished? It was a puzzle and Theo wished she could help.

Then all thoughts of Lucy Blake left her mind as the landau turned a corner and she saw her husband walking on the pavement with Lady Mary Williams on one arm, and her mother on the other. His phaeton was drawn up at the side of the road; she recognized the green-and-gold livery the grooms wore at once. What was he doing here, smiling down at the girl so intimately and saying something that made her smile in return, she wondered. He had not mentioned an appointment, but then, she had not seen him all day. Where had he been? What had he been doing?

Theo glanced at her companion, wondering if she had noticed, but Lucy was looking off into space, as if she were still considering the questions she had been asked by her inquisitive new friend.

Theo began to talk then about the gala, a party she was to attend next week, and a bonnet she had recently ordered. Lucy did not seem to notice how feverish this one-sided conversation was, or if she did, was too kind to mention it.

When their carriage came around the second time, Canford's phaeton was nowhere in sight, nor were he or his companions. Theo was relieved. She was sure if she had seen them there still, she would have ordered a halt, climbed down, and marched over to demand to know what was going on, she was so overcome with jealousy.

She did not find the earl at Canford House when she returned there; indeed, she did not see him until just before dinner was served. He asked her about her day pleasantly, but he volunteered nothing of his own, and Theo, having promised herself not to ask about his meeting with the Williamses, found she had nothing to say.

"Are you sure you are feeling well, Countess?" he asked as the servants prepared the next course at the sideboard. "Perhaps last night was too much for you? You were fast asleep when I came in."

Theo flashed a warning look as the butler approached bearing a dish of veal collops with capers in a wine sauce. She began to talk of her cousin Charlie Talbott then and his Bermuda adventure as she took some vegetables from a platter a footman offered, determined the servants would discover nothing amiss.

When they had retreated to the back of the house again, Canford said, "No, truly, Theo, you do look a little worn to me this evening. I suggest an early night. Mait asked me to join him and some friends for an evening of cards. I'll probably be late. I won't disturb you when I come in."

"Of course," she managed to say, raising her napkin to hide her quivering lips.

It seemed to take an age for them to finish dinner and for the earl to call for his hat and gloves. Theo rose when he did, saying she thought she'd look for a book to read.

"Perhaps one of those volumes of sermons some Whitney procured years ago that so intrigued your sister Violet?" Canford said. "Well, they'll be sure to put you to sleep."

Theo managed to laugh with him a little, marveling at her playacting, but when the door closed behind him, she was quick to retire to the library and shut the door.

She did not look at the shelves, instead she curled up in Lucas's big chair by the fire to stare into the flames, desperately trying to find some logical explanation for the meeting she had observed in the park, and the way Lucas had deserted her so carelessly tonight. He had not kissed her good night, but then he never did, so there was nothing to remark there. But he had said he wouldn't disturb her when he came in. How that had set her nerves to jangling!

Last night at the gala had been wonderful. He had been so warm and attentive to her, so seemingly content. Had Lady Mary Williams been there? Theo could not remember, it had been so crowded. But perhaps Lucas had met the girl during the set he had allowed Maitland Grant to dance with her. Perhaps it had been then the two had made an arrangement for this afternoon.

Theo called herself every kind of fool. How silly she was. Lady Mary had been with her *mother* this afternoon. Surely that lady would not be a party to any clandestine meetings between her daughter and a married man, no matter how rich and titled. Of course not, for what would be the use? Unless they're hoping I die, Theo told herself glumly. At that, she had to smile. Really, she thought, love did have a way of making perfectly normal people toss all common sense to the wind. Here I am acting like a ninny simply because Lucas greeted two old acquaintances kindly. But did he have to step down from his phaeton to do that, she asked herself, feeling despair again.

Besides, he *had* left her tonight. Thinking it over dispassionately, she told herself it could have been merely the act of a thoughtful man, concerned she seemed so tired and determined to make sure she had a good night's rest. On the other hand, it could have been the act of a man who only wanted to see his friends to play cards, drink, and exchange male gossip without any of the propriety necessary in a woman's company. Lucas had been with her most of the time since her arrival at Canford House. She told herself that of course she understood. She had always needed time to herself too.

He is *not* getting tired of me, he is *not* still yearning for Lady Mary, and I must stop acting like a pea goose, Theo told herself sternly. Still, she had trouble concentrating on the book she finally selected, and at last she gave up the attempt and took herself off to bed, determined not to lie there staring at the ceiling waiting for Canford to come home.

Instead, she lay there imagining him naked in the arms of some seductive temptress or attacked by a band of robbers on his way home and left for dead in the gutter, or knocked down and crushed by a runaway team in the dark, dangerous London streets.

She did not have a restful night.

19

Theo was surprised Lucas was still at home when she came down the following morning, for she had slept well past her usual time. He was seated at the table reading the early post when she came in.

As soon as she had selected her breakfast and the butler had poured her a cup of coffee, Canford dismissed him. Theo felt apprehensive for no reason she could discern. Still she said, "There is something you wish to say to me privately, m'lord?" determined to get to whatever trouble was coming as soon as possible.

"There is indeed," he answered soberly without the trace of a smile. "I have been thinking of this off and on a long time—for almost the entire length of our marriage, in fact. Then yesterday it suddenly occurred to me that when April comes, we will have been married for six months—half a year—and April is only a couple of days away.

"I did not go to Mait Grant's last night to play cards. I went to my club, found a quiet room, and barricaded myself behind a newspaper while I spent the evening thinking. Of us. Of our situation."

"Is it that you are concerned because I am not in the family way yet?" Theo asked, putting down the fork she had yet to use.

"No. I am concerned about how you must feel about me, considering how you treat me."

"I—I don't understand. How I *treat* you?"

"I don't mean your manners, ma'am. They are charming. I mean how you behave when we are making love."

If it seemed at all incongruous to Theo to be discussing such a subject in a bright cheerful breakfast room, she did not say so. Instead, speechless, she stared at him till at last he went on. "Because you act as if you didn't care whether I ever came to you or not. And afterwards, I can tell you can hardly wait for me to be gone, as if I had been some unpleasant *chore* you had been forced to endure.

"I've tried to ignore your coldness. I've told myself that of course you'll be different as soon as you become accustomed. But it's almost six months now—six months!—and you haven't changed. And no, I don't think I'm the greatest lover the world has ever known, but I do know I am not distasteful; repulsive. Still, you have certainly managed to humble me, Theo.

"It's ironic, isn't it? I picked you out to be my wife so carefully, and you turn out to be completely lacking in passion. What a joke on me that is."

He did not sound at all amused, but Theo had barely heard the end of his speech.

"You picked me *carefully*?" she asked. "What do you mean?"

"But of course I did," he told her. "A marriage, especially one of convenience, is a serious matter. I chose you first because you come from a good family with impeccable lineage—(I knew it, Theo thought glumly)—and then because your mother has been so prolific. I wanted children and certainly I had to have an heir. But I also chose you because I thought we would deal well together."

"How could you know anything of that, sir?" she dared to say. "We had never met before the final arrangements for our marriage had been formalized."

"That's true, but one evening at a party last spring, I chanced to be standing near a door that was slightly ajar and I heard you and your cousin, Charles Talbott, discussing some of the guests. Your comments were so apt, so lively and full of fun. And you had such a delightful laugh."

"You should not have listened," Theo reprimanded him, feeling flustered. "We did not know anyone was there and it was a private conversation."

Dismally, she wondered if he had overheard anything about himself, for several times she and Charlie had made mock of his air of calm superiority.

"Other gentlemen faced me. It was impossible for me to go away," he replied. "Besides, after I heard what you had to say about Mrs. Farnton, how could I? She does look exactly like a poodle, doesn't she? I think it is those long side curls she wears, and the fluffy topknot she sports. But do you really think Sir Harold Anders resembles a beagle? I would have said a bulldog myself. Those jowls! Of course I didn't like being compared to a thoroughbred horse, used to being coddled and made much of, but when I thought it over, I conceded that perhaps you had a point. But don't you think my behavior could be excused since I came into the title when I was only eight?

"That evening was the first time I noticed you, singled you out from all the scores of eager young things being puffed off that Season. You were unique. Since then I have come to admire your spirit, even what you call your wretched tongue. And how many women could laugh at being kidnapped by their husbands and embarrassed before their friends?

"But we stray from the subject. I have known ever since Christmas that you preferred Maitland Grant to me."

"Oh, Lucas, I don't prefer him, I don't," she cried, still trying to grasp everything he had said, and not at all sure she could have heard him correctly.

"Then why do you always have such a warm smile for him? Why did you spend so much time with him at Lansmere?"

"But you yourself told me several times I wasn't to hang on your sleeve," Theo said in her own defense. She felt as if she might burst from joy. Lucas had been jealous. *Lucas,* the top-of-the-trees, most singular Earl of Canford!

"Besides, you were so busy with your sweet Patsy, what

was I to do? I had so looked forward to being beside you when we brought in the Yule log, but you never made a move in my direction. And later too, it was all Patsy and her broken fingernail, the poor, poor dear.

"As for my coldness, well, I knew you didn't love me. That what we did together was only for breeding purposes. That left to yourself, you wouldn't have wanted to even touch me. I felt like a worthy mare, brought to be serviced by that thoroughbred Charlie and I compared you to. How could I welcome you? How could I relax and enjoy it as you once suggested? How could I possibly do that, knowing what I did?"

She took a deep breath when he showed no sign of wanting to interrupt her, only stared at her with an arrested expression. But then, what could he say? she asked herself. What she had told him was only the truth. Determined to be brave, she went on. "When we were at Lansmere, I heard two of the women discussing our marriage and how stunned they were you had chosen me. They said I was not at all beautiful, not even passing pretty—well, I know that. They also said I was not worthy of you, that I was a nobody—awkward, ill-dressed, and gauche. And I'm well aware those spectacles I have to wear to read make me look ugly."

"Sometime I would like to know who dared to speak of you that way," he said quietly. "But never mind that now. Go on, please."

"One of them said it was too bad you had to rush the wedding because it had to take place on October first, to honor your deathbed promise to your mother, for otherwise you might have had the woman you really loved."

"And who might that woman be? Did they mention her name?"

Theo bent her head and began pleating her napkin so she would not have to look at him and see the guilt on his face. "Oh yes, they mentioned it. It was Lady Mary Williams, of course. I gather you did try for her first, but she would not be pressured into a hasty marriage."

He stared at her for a moment, then, to her complete astonishment, he started to laugh. She wondered if he had lost his mind. And then she wondered if he had felt as she did now, the night he kidnapped her from Lucy's dining room and she had laughed at him.

"Lady Mary," he said at last. "I, marry Lady Mary?"

This made him laugh again and Theo was beginning to get annoyed.

"My sweet wife, I would not marry Lady Mary Williams if you gave me a fortune to do it," he said when he had control of himself.

"Whyever not? She is so beautiful," Theo demanded. "Are you making mock of me, sir?"

"Not at all. Tell me, have you ever heard her speak?"

Theo thought hard. Certainly she had not this year, for she had only been close to her the one time. She could not remember talking to her last Season either. Could it be that lovely girl had a speech defect, or a harsh, unmusical voice that had grated on Lucas's nerves? "No, I don't believe I ever have," she finally admitted.

"I am not surprised. The young lady never does speak. I think she probably feels her beauty and her smile are enough. But once, when I teased her to it, her remarks were so vapid, so commonplace, I wished I had allowed her to maintain her sphinxlike silence. Marry her and spend the rest of my life being bored? Not likely. Whoever said that was all about in their heads.

"Incidentally, you are not ill-dressed now, are you? And you have never been gauche. I have always considered you a handsome woman, with or without your spectacles. As for being a nobody, you should have remembered you were the Countess of Canford.

"But we digress. To return to our original discussion, I had thought we were getting closer, you and I. And when your family came, horrible as the visit was, they seemed to bring us together, to stand united against the fray, as it were. But now they're gone, and I can't ignore this problem of ours any longer.

"Tell me, Theo, do you want me to divorce you?"

When she only stared at him, he went on. "It will take a while, for I'm not sure I can arrange to have Parliament take up the issue this session. But I would not keep you tied to me if you cannot bear me and have formed a disgust for me. And I think you must have, the way you act in bed. You needn't worry. I'll see to it you're well provided for, and although it must be a crim. cons. case, privately I'll take all the blame. You see, I don't happen to think it fair to either of us to have to spend our lives in a joyless farce of a marriage."

Theo's throat was clogged with tears, but she managed to say, "Oh no, Lucas, I don't want a divorce, I don't. But perhaps you do?"

He considered her carefully before he said, "No. In spite of everything, I find I do not."

"But you don't love me, do you?" she asked, knowing full well the answer to that question.

"I wouldn't lie to you. Certainly I didn't love you when we first wed. How could I, any more than you, love a stranger? As for how I feel now, I am not sure. I've grown fond of you—we've been through a lot and there are times when I've thought it would be impossible to live without you. That's why it has taken me so long to bring this subject up, I suppose. Because what if I offered you your freedom and you accepted it? But is all that love? I don't know."

"But you see, I do," she said, throwing caution to the winds. "I mean, I do love you. I fell in love with you the night you first came to me at Canford Hall. But knowing you were only being kind to me, and loving me because you had to, to get your heir, I could not tell you. I was so afraid the ardor I felt would disgust you, feeling as indifferent towards me as you did. I can't tell you how hard it was not to touch you, kiss you back, remain silent and still when I longed to . . ."

He had started to get up and come to her, that familiar glint in his eye, when a discreet knock interrupted them. Looking annoyed, he took his seat again. Theo had not taken her eyes from his face, but the butler's words brought her sharply to attention.

"The Duchess of Lansmere, m'lord, m'lady."

Theo was dumbstruck as the duchess, huge now with child, entered the room. Fortunately the earl was made of stronger stuff. Rising quickly, he went to his sister with outstretched hands. "My dear Genie. What are you doing here in London, and so near your time too. Is there anything wrong?"

The duchess shrugged, her pretty mouth set in a grimace. "No, there's nothing wrong except for this endless, endless time I've been enduring," she said. "Oh, give you good day, Theodora."

"Do sit down, ma'am," Theo invited, rising to pull out a chair for their unexpected guest.

"But why did you come?" Canford persisted. "Is the duke with you?"

"Yes, he's here. He didn't want to bring me, but I insisted. I've been strangely restless this past week. I thought I would scream at the funereal pace he insisted we travel."

"But of course he did," the earl said smoothly. "There was your well-being and that of the child's to consider. You know the state of the roads."

She shrugged again and said, her face petulant, "I've come up to see the doctor. At least that's what I told His Grace. And yes, I know, we could have sent for the doctor, but I wanted to be in town. The baby is not due for another three weeks, and I don't know how I'm to bear it. But you wouldn't understand, either of you."

"Would you care for some coffee or a cup of tea, ma'am? Perhaps something to eat?" Theo said.

"No, nothing. If I eat I feel as if I'm going to choke."

She pressed both hands to her distended abdomen then and groaned. "Oh, do stop!" she commanded. "This child is as restless as I am. I am constantly being pummeled by him."

"You're so sure it is a boy?" Lucas teased.

"It had better be," Her Grace snapped. "I can assure you I've no intention of going through *this* ever again."

"Where is the duke now?" Lucas asked, anxious to change the subject.

"We arrived in town late yesterday. This morning he went off to his club, leaving me alone without another thought. I never realized how selfish and uncaring and downright unperceptive men could be.

"It was then I decided to call on you and find out how the Season is progressing. I could hardly go anywhere else except to family, the way I look. This will be the first Season I've missed, you know," she confided to Theo. "It is so hard."

Theo thought her as selfish as she had claimed her husband to be, but of course she did not say so. Still, she could not help wishing Eugenia had not come at just this particular moment, when she and Lucas had been so close—so very, very close—to resolving all their problems. As the duchess continued to bemoan her hard luck, Theo stole a glance at her husband, to find him also regarding her, a little smile on his lips.

"And I don't know what I've said that you could possibly find amusing," his fond sister snapped at him. The smile disappeared.

"I do beg your pardon, Genie. I was thinking of something else," he apologized. Theo looked down at the table lest the love she felt showed in her eyes.

Eugenia pressed her abdomen again, then struggled to her feet. "I must retire for a moment," she said with as much dignity as she could muster. "Theodora, would you assist me?"

Theo's heart sank. She had hoped that while the duchess attended to her needs, she and Lucas could share a few stolen kisses. Alas, she thought as she led the way from the room, it was not to be. But soon. Surely this tiresome, arrogant woman would go home soon.

"I see you have not changed this room any from my mother's time," Eugenia remarked on the way to the dressing room. "It is rather tired-looking, wouldn't you say?"

"I couldn't agree more. I just haven't had the time as yet."

"Perhaps my mother-in-law will advise you, as I am told she did with your ensembles. I have it on good authority the two of you are as thick as thieves."

"Your good authority being Lady Dalseny, no doubt," Theo replied in an even voice. She had no intention of ever letting Lucas know it was his sister who had said all those horrid things about her, but she had suddenly decided she would take no more of her snide remarks. "Yes, I am fond of the dowager duchess. She has been very good to me. I hope we will always be friends."

"Hmmph," the duchess muttered, entering the dressing room and shutting the door firmly in Theo's face.

Theo went to her dressing table and sat down to stare at her reflection in the mirror. It was strange. She had been sure she must look different, but she could discern no noticeable change even though her thoughts were chaotic with joy. Lucas had said he didn't know if what he felt for her was love, but that he had not wanted to live without her. Well, Theo told herself with a big smile, love or not, she would be more than happy to settle for that. And possibly, now she was free to show him how much she loved him, he might discover that, yes, indeed, he did love her after all.

She began to daydream about the future and it was some minutes later before she realized the duchess had been in the dressing room for quite some time. Going to the door and knocking, she said, "Are you all right, ma'am? Is there anything I can do for you?"

The answer when it came sounded a little flustered. "Ah, no, um, I'll be out shortly."

Theo was turning away again when she heard the armoire door close. She frowned. Was it possible Eugenia had been going through her clothes and inspecting them?

She realized it was entirely possible, for as well as gossiping about her friendship with the dowager, Lady Dalseny had probably relayed all the information she had about the new wardrobe Theo had been assembling. She had seen her several times at a distance in the park, and once on Bond Street, although she had managed to avoid having to speak to her.

But who would have thought Eugenia Abbott would stoop to prying through another woman's belongings? It appeared not even the most proper duchesses were immune to such a human emotion as curiosity, and how satisfying it was to know that.

20

To both Theo and the earl's disappointment, the Duchess of Lansmere showed no inclination to quit their premises and return to her own opulent town house in Berkeley Square. Instead, she settled down in the drawing room for a long visit. Theo knew Lucas must be longing to escape all his sister's confidences about childbearing and its demands, but he did not want to leave her. It made her feel heady with the power she had so recently acquired.

Half an hour later, the butler announced the arrival of the Meredith family. The two ladies who were increasing stared at each other frankly, each wondering if it was possible she looked as hideous as the other did. Theo was careful not to look at Lucas lest she dissolve in very inappropriate laughter, especially when he excused himself almost at once, claiming that a great deal of neglected correspondence awaited him in the library. He told Theo later he felt as if he had been rolled up, horse, foot, and guns, and he was not ashamed to admit it.

As soon as he left, the little boys both began to tell Theo about an afternoon at the Royal Exchange they had enjoyed, inspecting the menagerie there, while Gwyneth pulled on her skirt to get her attention, screaming about a calico kitten she had recently acquired. Marietta looked sulky, Violet saintly. Theo was not surprised to see that the Duchess of Lansmere appeared stunned, not only at the number of the company, but their noisy, undisciplined manners, and she was ashamed.

Still, she made the introductions calmly. Mrs. Meredith

attempted a curtsy before she said, "Marietta, you and Violet take the children to the garden."

Theo longed to beg them to be careful of the flower beds, but she did not wish to call any more attention to her family's lack of gentility.

When the room had emptied of children, Fanny Meredith said in a complaining voice, "Well, since it has become plain to me you were never going to call on me in Upper Brook Street, there was nothing for it but to come to you, Theo. It is too bad I had to do so when it is so near my time, and with all the children too. Well, I did leave baby Donald at home with the new nursemaid, and of course Teddy is nowhere about. Remind me to ask you later what Canford could possibly have said to him. He's been as sullen as a bear ever since he arrived in town."

"I see you are also in the family way, Your Grace. When do you expect to be confined?"

"Not for three weeks yet," Eugenia confessed, her eyes wide. "Er, tell me, ma'am, how many children do you have?"

Mrs. Meredith simpered and hid her face behind her handkerchief for a moment. "This new one will make ten. Of course I did lose three babies, so I suppose you could say I've had thirteen."

"Thirteen," the duchess echoed, looking stunned. "My word."

"This is your first, my dear? Well, there's nothing to worry about. The first is apt to take a bit longer than the others, but that's no never mind. Still, I daresay you'll be glad to get it over with, won't you?"

"Yes, indeed I will," Eugenia confided, putting her hand to the small of her back and rubbing it. "I've had the most painful backaches the last few days. And there is no position that is comfortable in bed."

"I know. I always feel like a beached whale," Mrs. Meredith said in sympathy.

"Excuse me, Mama, Your Grace," Theo said. "I want to ask Cook to send the children some refreshments. Would you care for a tea tray?"

The ladies agreed that would be delightful and Theo went away. She was tempted to interrupt Lucas in the library, but she knew she had better not. She had callers and it was obvious her mother was piqued at what she felt was her daughter's willful neglect. She dared not stay away for many minutes.

When she came back to the drawing room, she found her two guests still discussing babies and lying in, although, Theo saw as she took her seat, as the authority, her mother was doing most of the talking. The duchess sat back looking horrified at the things she was hearing. Only the arrival of the tea tray stopped these revelations, and Theo was quick to change the subject as soon as the footman left the room, by asking how the measle victims were faring at Pobryn Abbey.

"Very well, according to the doctor. I've suggested the boys come to town as soon as they are well," Fanny Meredith said. "There is so much to do here, and we have taken the house until the fifteenth of May.

"Of course," she added, tossing her head, "I would not have done so if I had known I was never to see you, daughter."

"Mama, I cannot be at your beck and call anymore," Theo was stung into saying. "You know that. I am married now."

"Well, I think it is a dreadful shame." Turning to Eugenia, she said, "You should know, Your Grace, I am used to depending on Theo in all things. When she left me, I was bereft, lost, even."

"Do have another muffin, Mama," Theo urged, holding out the plate. "Cook makes such delicious muffins."

"And don't try and change the subject, miss," her fond mama retorted. "You know why I cannot depend on Marietta, and Violet is still a little girl. It is too bad you had to leave me, and that I will always maintain, Canford or no Canford."

It seemed a long time to Theo before the children returned from the garden because William's knee was bleeding from a fall he had had. Theo took him to her room to clean him up, bandage the knee, and kiss his tears away. When they returned to the others, she discovered Lucas had come back and was offering to have the butler fetch a couple of hackneys for the Merediths.

"There's no need to put yourself out, m'lord," Fanny Meredith said grandly, although she had had no intention of leaving so soon. "I have my own carriage to convey us."

She struggled to her feet, pausing for a moment to catch her breath, her hand to her heart.

"Now you take care, Your Grace," she said to the duchess, who unlike herself showed no signs of leaving. "I wish you well, indeed I do."

"Thank you, ma'am," Eugenia said faintly.

"As for you miss, I shall be expecting you to be more attentive," she said, turning to her eldest daughter. "I was telling Theo it is too bad she feels she must neglect her dear mama to gad about with you, sir," she added, her tone belligerent. "Selfish, I call it."

"Really?" Lucas murmured. "I am sure you are wrong, ma'am. Theo is my wife. Her place is beside me, whether or not I am gadding about, as you put it, or not. Give you good day. And you, you young scamp, put down that cloisonné box you are holding and do it carefully, sir."

Lester gave him his angelic smile but he did as he was bade, and after the children had made their bows and curtsies, they left the room, all talking at once at the top of their lungs.

"How on earth does she stand it without going mad?" Eugenia asked in a weak voice. "I should never be able to cope. And the noise!"

"What do you say to a drive in the park, Genie," her brother suggested. "The fresh air will do you good, and when you are tired, you can drop us here before you go on to Berkeley Square."

Theo was amused at the way Lucas was so carefully arranging for them to be alone soon, and she gave him a little smile congratulating him on the feat.

"Oh very well," Eugenia said, frowning a little. Theo saw her hand go to her back again as she rose, and she wondered if Eugenia might not be better off going directly home. She did not suggest it however, something she was to regret later.

The duchess had come on her morning call in the duke's large traveling carriage, complete with his coachman and two grooms up behind. After the earl had lifted his sister to her seat, he offered his hand to his wife. "Soon, Theo," he whispered for her ears alone. "I promise you it will be soon."

"Your method of clearing a drawing room is matchless, my dear," she whispered back. "I was so impressed."

She took her seat beside the duchess while Canford sat facing back across from them. Theo felt his leg pressing hers under cover of her muslin skirt, and she smiled.

She turned her attention to her sister-in-law as the carriage started down Park Lane to the Stanhope Gates. Eugenia was turning this way and that as if trying to find a comfortable spot. Theo was surprised. The duke's carriage was luxurious, well sprung, and with thickly padded seats.

"You are not comfortable, ma'am?" she asked, holding out her hand.

"Of course I'm not," Eugenia snapped. "What a stupid thing to say!"

"I cannot allow you to speak to my wife that way, Genie," Canford said, his voice as cold as a wind off a glacier. "She is concerned for you, and you should be grateful. Perhaps it would be better if we got out here and you went home and sought your bed."

"No, it wouldn't," his sister said. "I—I apologize. I didn't mean to be so abrupt."

"I understand," Theo told her. "This is a difficult time for you."

She saw Eugenia bite her lip, as if to stifle another acerbic remark, and she wondered why she herself sounded so inane. But of course, she told herself as the team checked before turning into the Stanhope Gates, I am hardly thinking of her. How could I when Lucas is right there across from me, so handsome and dear and positively *smoldering*? I daresay there isn't a woman in London who would be able to think of anyone but him in the same situation. She turned to look out the window, to slow her breathing.

"There's no one but cits here at this time of day," the duchess complained, peering from her own window. "I have always maintained the King should reserve this largest of London's parks just for the elite. We should not be forced to associate with such as they."

She pointed with scorn to a little boy rolling a hoop and his watchful mother. They were both dressed poorly.

"They deserve the same fresh air and greenery as we do," Lucas said mildly.

"Then let them have their own park," Eugenia insisted. She leaned forward and moved her torso this way and that. "This wretched ache," she complained. "I swear it grows stronger every minute."

Theo suddenly had a most unpleasant thought, but before she could demand they take the duchess home immediately, Eugenia gasped and looked down at her lap in dismay.

"What's the matter?" Lucas asked. "Where did that water come from?"

Quickly, Theo checked to see where they were in the park. To her chagrin, she saw they had come quite a distance from the gates, and even as she pondered their chances, the duchess cried out and clasped her abdomen.

"We must get her home; have the doctor fetched," Lucas said, reaching for the check rein.

Eugenia moaned and Theo put her arm around her. "There's no time for that. The baby is coming now. Quickly, Lucas, tell the coachman to find a quiet place away from any traffic."

After he had done so, she said, "I'll need your shirt and your neckcloth. No, don't argue. I'm sure they are cleaner than anything the servants might be wearing. Hurry!"

As his sister began to moan louder, he stripped off his coat.

"Yes, my dear, it's all right," Theo said. "You'll be better soon, my word on it."

"This is the best I can do, m'lord," the coachman called down. He had pulled the carriage onto the grass near a small copse.

"Quickly, Lucas, get out and take the men some distance away, to give Eugenia some privacy," Theo ordered. For once the sight of his bare chest did not stir her. After he had handed her his shirt and cravat and obeyed, Theo released the duchess to remove her own petticoat. They would have to make do as best they could. Then she raised the duchess's skirts and took off her sodden petticoat as well.

"What are you doing?" Eugenia demanded, sounding close to hysteria. "Stop that at once. Oooh, the *pain*!"

"You can't have a baby and preserve your modesty, ma'am. But don't worry, I've sent the men away. It is just the two of us."

"Sent them away? No, no! I must get home and have the doctor come."

"There's no time for that now, I'm afraid," Theo said as she inspected her. "Your baby is coming now."

"But you can't help me. You're only a young bride!"

"Yes, I can," Theo said, holding her hands tightly. "I had to deliver my brother Will three years ago. He came too fast for us to get the midwife for my mother. Trust me. I know what to do."

Theo hoped she sounded more confident than she felt. Three years ago her mother had told her what to do—she prayed she would remember her instructions—and Mrs. Meredith had had an easy birth. Please God, Theo prayed, don't let there be any complications. Please.

She reached for her reticule. She did not have any scissors with her, but the cord that drew the bag closed was thin and it would have to serve until they could reach a doctor.

"Now then, Genie, we must make you as comfortable as possible," she said, trying to sound calm and in control. "Here, let me move to the opposite seat and you stretch out as best you can. Hang on to the sidestrap when you feel a pain coming."

"I can't," the duchess moaned. "Oh, this pain is killing me!"

"No, it's not," Theo said. "You're doing very well."

"But I can't have my baby in a carriage in the park," Eugenia panted. "I'm a duchess! It's not fitting. Oh, I am so ashamed. How will I ever face anyone ever again?"

"I vow you'll be the toast of London, ma'am," Theo told her just before another pain rippled through her body and she stifled a scream. "Imagine such heroism. Alone with only an ignorant girl to help you."

"But you said you knew what to do," the duchess cried.

"Of course I do," Theo retorted. "But the *ton* won't know that, will they? No, they'll think only of your bravery giving the duke his child, and they'll hold you up as a shining example, revere you even," she added quickly as Eugenia twisted and moaned. It was obvious she had no interest in heirs or cutting a dash in society just now.

"No, you mustn't fight the pain," Theo instructed, remembering what her mother had done. "When you feel it building, take a deep breath and let it out slowly. You make it worse trying to escape it, and there's no way you can anyway. It's almost time. It will soon be over."

As she spoke, she wiped the duchess's brow with Lucas's neckcloth, wishing his man had not starched it quite so heavily. Eugenia was going to need it later.

Another relentless pain shook the duchess then and Theo focused all her attention on her as Eugenia screamed her husband's name.

Some little distance away, Lucas Whitney stood with the two grooms and the coachman in uneasy camaraderie. When he heard his sister scream, he started to go to her.

"No, no, m'lord, you don't want to go back there, nor do the ladies want ye to," the coachman said kindly. He was an older man with a face that looked as if he had seen everything in his time. He took Lucas's arm and added,

"That's women's work, that is, and best ye leave 'em to get on with it."

"But she is in such pain," Lucas muttered, mopping his brow. "And Theo, the countess, you know, is only a new bride. What does she, a nineteen-year-old, know of birthing?"

"Well, it's my opinion most women know what ter do by instinctlike," the coachman replied. "At least they know a deal more than we do, m'lord, or so my wife is always tellin' me."

The duchess screamed again and Lucas's face went white. Then over that sound came the wail of a baby and all four men broke into wide grins.

"There now, what did I tell ye, sir?" the coachman said. "I'd say both those ladies deserved a medal.

"No, no, don't go to them jess yet, m'lord," he added when the earl would have gone and offered his aid. "Let them get things shipshape. They'll call when they're ready."

The baby continued to wail, and it was several minutes before the earl heard his wife's voice calling him. When he reached the carriage, she leaned out the window and said, "Genie has had a beautiful baby boy, Lucas. I think we can get her home now, but go slowly. And you must ride on the perch. It is a bit, er, disordered in here, and Genie is feeling a little shy."

Lucas nodded, his eyes never leaving her face. "You are awesome," he said. "Is Genie all right?"

"I'm fine," his sister said weakly. "Thanks to Theo, I'm fine. Oh, please, can we go home now?"

Fortunately none of the *haute ton* was on hand to remark the Earl of Canford seated high on the perch beside the coachman, wearing nothing over his breeches but a coat of navy superfine, nor was there anyone to question the stately passage of the carriage as the team was walked back to Berkeley Square. Once there, Theo sent one of the grooms running for the doctor, and the other for Eugenia's maid and a blanket. A few minutes later an exhausted Duchess of Lansmere, holding her son close, was carried tenderly inside.

She was followed by Theo, who was somewhat the worse for wear. Lucas frowned when he saw her blood-splattered muslin.

"You'll have to go home and get me another gown," Theo told him. "I can't walk the streets like this."

The duchess heard her and said, "Oh no, you must not leave me, Theo. I need you beside me, indeed I do. Promise me you'll stay, promise."

Theo looked up at her husband and shook her head ruefully. He smiled, a little grimly perhaps, but still he smiled even as he nodded in resignation. Taking his arm, Theo leaned close and said, "You should never have told me 'soon,' sir. It tempted fate."

21

The doctor, although not happy to have his particular field of expertise invaded by an amateur, and this one only a slip of a girl at that, deigned to be complimentary. After seeing to the baby and examining the duchess while Theo stood beside her, holding her hand to give her courage, he said, "Of course it was a very good thing there were no complications, Your Grace. And fortunate that the birth was so quick. It is rarely so with first children, except among the lower classes."

Theo felt Genie's hand tighten and heard her indrawn breath and she frowned a warning. The doctor did not notice. He went on with his dissertation before he left copious instructions with the nurses he had brought with him before he finally bowed himself away.

"Send them out," the duchess muttered between her teeth, her eyes glittering. Theo hastened to do so.

"Did you hear him, Theo?" the new mother demanded. "He as much as told me I was no better than a peasant! Oh, the shame of it. And what will Forrestal think when he hears? It will be all over town in a twinkling, I know it will. Oh, how dreadful it is, how truly dreadful."

"Genie, stop that," Theo interrupted, sitting down on the bed and forcing the girl to meet her eye. "Now you tell me, and honestly if you please, would you really have wanted the agony you were in to go on for hours, days even, because such a thing would be more fitting? You can't really believe that childbirth gets more painful according to *rank*, can you, with the Queen in the worst pain of all? Because that isn't so, besides being just plain silly."

The duchess frowned. "Well, no, of course I wouldn't have wanted more pain," she admitted. "Still, it would have been better if it hadn't been quite so hasty."

"No, it wouldn't," Theo said bluntly. "You were lucky. Most women would be thrilled to have a child born as easily as yours was."

She rose as Forrestal Abbott rushed in and knelt beside the bed to take his wife into his arms. Touched by the expression she saw on his face, Theo moved away to the window embrasure and stood with her back to the room, staring down into the square.

She only heard the two new parents murmuring together distantly, for her thoughts were elsewhere. She knew Lucas had returned to Park Lane earlier, as soon as a new shirt and cravat had been delivered to Berkeley Square. As well, an awed Betsy had come and brought her a fresh gown, helped her into it, and seen to it she had a glass of wine and a biscuit before the duchess began calling for her again. Theo felt weary, but she knew it was only a reaction to all the emotion she had been treated to this most memorable day.

When would she and Lucas be together and alone, she wondered. How long would she be expected to remain here beside the suddenly dependent Eugenia? It was really astonishing. The duchess had never liked her, why, look how she had maligned her at Lansmere. But now it appeared she wanted her to be her best friend and confidante. And that was all very well except Theo wanted to be with her husband. Alone. Just the two of them. Far away from all this drama and confusion. In his arms, now she was free to love him as she had longed to do.

Well, she told herself, Eugenia has no more hold on me than my mother does, less perhaps. And she is safe now, with the nurses and her maid to care for her. I will stay just a little longer and then I will insist on going home.

"My dear sister, how can I ever thank you?" the duke said close behind her. She turned and saw him smiling down at her, his eyes suspiciously bright. "You were so good. I don't know what my darling wife would have done if you hadn't been there. We can never, ever thank you."

"Have you seen the baby, Your Grace?" Theo asked, a little overwhelmed by all this praise. "He is beautiful."

"Yes, but he is so small," the duke whispered, leaning closer.

"I do assure you he did not seem so to your wife. Besides, he is a very good size, sir. Believe me."

"But why did he come so early?" the duke persisted, still whispering so as not to disturb his wife, who lay with her eyes closed now, half asleep.

"I think everyone probably miscalculated," Theo said. "That often happens."

"How does it come about that you are so knowledgeable about such things, and you so young?" he asked. Theo explained about her many brothers and sisters, although she did not mention she had delivered one of them. She told herself she must remind Eugenia not to mention it either. Somehow she knew that wouldn't be a problem, for she was sure the new mother would soon be basking in everyone's admiration, and enjoying her new notoriety.

When the Earl of Canford returned to his own home, he found several messages from Upper Brook Street awaiting his wife. After reading them, he stood for a moment in the hall, tapping them against his thigh. Suddenly he smiled, dropped the notes on the hall table, and left the house again.

His first destination was Portman Square. He was fortunate to find Lady Blake and her elderly guest at home. Not noticing the strained atmosphere, he lost no time acquainting them with the news of the Lansmere heir, and Theo's part in his arrival.

"My word, what a redoubtable girl she is," Faith Abbott said in a stunned voice, putting aside whatever had been troubling her. "She certainly has hidden talents, doesn't she, Lucy? I must go to Eugenia at once. You say Theo is still with her? Good. I shall be able to thank her for her help as well as see the baby."

"Please tell my sister how wonderful and brave she was, ma'am," the earl said. "She was crying when she told me that having the heir to Lansmere in a carriage was not at all the sort of thing a proper duchess would do."

"If only Eugenia would forget she *is* a duchess, things would go much better for her—and everyone else," the dowager said tartly. "But I shall certainly praise her to the skies. Are you off then, m'lord? Can't you wait and escort me to Lansmere House?"

"I'm afraid I must beg off, Your Grace, although I do intend to go there eventually. There is another call I must make first. Give you good day, m'ladies."

The earl strode briskly along the pavement, his long legs making short work of the little distance between Portman Square and Upper Brook Street.

He was fortunate enough to find Mrs. Meredith at home alone. She told him all the children, with the exception of Marietta, had gone to Hyde Park for the afternoon, attended by her footman.

Taking a seat across from her, Canford proceeded to read the lady a stern lecture on her past behavior. She stared at him, mouth agape, as he told her how much at fault she had been to demand her daughter's constant attention.

"Every day there are more messages from you," he concluded. "Should you care to hear them again? As I recall, one just said, 'Come at once!' Another that Lester had been naughty. A third mentioned mice in the kitchens, a fourth demanded Theo stop Violet from reading the Bible aloud every evening for it was driving you insane. And what did you think Theo could do about Marietta and Teddy's sullen attitudes? Today you mentioned you were out of a certain shade of embroidery thread and asked Theo to procure it for you immediately. And the last ordered her to come over and tell the cook the custard last evening had tasted burnt. Enough, madam. Enough, I say."

"Well, I never did," Mrs. Meredith exclaimed when he paused for breath. "To think you would come here and say such things, m'lord, and me so near my time too. I am shocked, *shocked,* I say."

"I hope you are, ma'am," he said relentlessly. "Shocked enough that you will remember that such never-ending attention as you seem to require will not be forthcoming in the future. It will do no good for you to keep sending your endless pleas to Canford House. Theo is not going to drop everything to rush to your side. Not anymore. It is more than time you take up your responsibilities and learn to cope by yourself and I suggest you do so."

Mrs. Meredith had to resort to her handkerchief to wipe away her tears. "So cruel, so hard," she complained. "And I'm *not* demanding. If I were, surely Theo would have told me of it, for we are the best of friends."

"Theo didn't tell you because she did not know herself before she married. It only became clear when you came to London and started ordering her about again. Remember Theo is your daughter, ma'am, not your best friend, and as my countess, she is certainly not your slave."

When Canford left the rented house several minutes later, his face was set even though he had accomplished all he had come for. Behind him, he left a chastened, weeping Fanny Meredith. He regretted that, but at least he had the satisfaction of knowing the woman would think twice before she demanded anything of his wife again.

Lansmere House was quiet when the butler admitted him, all the excited whispering among the servants stilled, and the bustle of people running up and down the stairs, absent. He found the duke in his library and was happy to join him in a glass of burgundy to toast his son and heir.

"Genie is feeling better?" he asked, after the child's good looks, sturdy frame, and certain intelligence had been duly acknowledged.

"Much better," Lansmere assured him. "I left her sleeping, the baby beside her. He was sleeping too. Do you know, Canford, I think he is going to have my nose."

"Good for him," the earl murmured. "And what of Theo? Is she still with the duchess?"

The duke nodded. "The strangest thing! Y'know, from some of the things Eugenia let fall during the Christmas visit, I didn't think she liked your bride very much. But now she can hardly bear to have her out of her sight. It was only with the greatest reluctance she let her go to have a short rest, and she made me promise that Theo would remain here tonight. I do hope you will agree that your sister deserves to be humored in this."

"Humored, eh?" Canford said, his voice noncommittal. Then he leaned forward. He spoke uninterrupted for several minutes. At last the duke nodded, and then he rose and shook the earl's hand.

"Certainly, old fellow, consider it done," he said. "Why don't you sit here at my desk and write your messages? I just heard my mother's voice. I don't want her rushing upstairs and waking Eugenia or the baby, and unless I intercept her, that is exactly what she'll do. Excuse me."

He almost ran from the room and Lucas Whitney smiled. He would be willing to wager a fortune that the duke wanted to be the first to acquaint his mother with the baby's sterling qualities, and that the two of them would spend at least one happy hour discussing the child and its miraculous delivery.

As he pulled a sheet of the duke's hot-pressed paper toward him and dipped a quill in the ink pot, the earl forgot them, so intent was he on his own plans. Several minutes later, he sent for Theo's maid, and when the girl left him, she was wearing a broad smile.

Theo woke from her nap much refreshed. A cheerful Betsy told her the duchess was still asleep, but that the dowager duchess had called and asked to see her. Theo washed her face and hands and had Betsy restyle her hair before she went down to greet the lady.

"My dear, dear child, what a heroine you are," Faith Abbott declared after she had given her a hearty kiss. "How on earth did you know what to do?"

Theo confided the source of her expertise, but begged the elderly lady not to say anything about it. "It would be embarrassing to my mother, you see," she concluded. "Better to let the *ton* assume Her Grace and I somehow muddled through despite our ignorance. And truly, it was an easy birth, although I beg you don't say so to Genie."

"Not a word," her friend agreed. "I am so anxious to see her and the baby. Forrestal has been telling me all about him—endlessly, in fact. By the time that infant wakes I expect him to be walking, talking, and fluent in both Latin and Greek, since I understand he is such an outstanding child, miles ahead of any others."

Theo laughed, but in reality she was deeply disappointed Lucas had not come back to Lansmere House. She had hoped he would demand that she return to their own home. But the afternoon lengthened and he did not come. Since she was busy with the duchess, reading her all the notes that suddenly began pouring in along with floral tributes and gifts for the new baby, she did not have time to brood. But when evening came and there was still no sign of him, she spoke of her desire to go home.

The duke and his mother were in the room at the time, the dowager cuddling her first grandchild and cooing to him.

"No, no, you must not leave me," Eugenia cried. "Forrestal, make her stay. I cannot bear it, if Theo is not with me."

"I hope you will see fit to remain, my dear," the duke hastened to say. "I spoke to Canford earlier, y'know. He was agreeable to you spending the night. In fact, he had everything you will need sent over earlier."

"He was? He did?" Theo asked, confused.

"Oh yes, he said he quite understood Eugenia had the prior claim. He told me to tell you he would see you tomorrow and to be sure you got a very good night's sleep."

Theo turned away and pretended to rearrange some yellow roses. She hoped the blush she could feel on her cheeks was not too noticeable.

"I think you should stay too," the dowager said as she handed the baby to a waiting nurse most reluctantly. "Eugenia should not be distraught just now, should she? Forrestal has arranged for you to have dinner up here with her. We will leave you to rest and enjoy it, for too much company is not good for a new mother, you know."

Resigned, Theo swallowed her disappointment and prepared to listen to the duchess relive for yet one more time the earthshaking event of the day. But much later, when Eugenia had been settled for the night, she felt restless, and she wandered down to the drawing room in search of company. The dowager was there, sitting alone before a little fire, a pensive look on her face.

"All is well?" she asked as she waved Theo to a chair.

"Yes. Genie has gone to sleep and so has the baby. At least for now. Why are you sitting here alone, ma'am, and looking so sad, I might add?"

"The duke has gone to his club. To tell the truth, I did nothing to stop him, for much as I love my grandson, after hearing all about him throughout dinner, I really didn't think I could bear Forrestal to begin again over the brandy." She sighed. "And yes, I suppose I do look sad. It is Lucy."

Theo leaned forward. "What of her?" she asked.

"She finally spoke to me today, just before Canford came. It seems she has been sorely depressed these past two years. She said nothing seems to help, not a change of scene or new friends, or lots of activity. She did say it had helped her a little when we were intent on solving your problems, but now she has returned to her usual apathy. That apathy is why she has not bothered to redecorate that ghastly house, nor done anything about selling it, or the estate in Cornwall. That is a great old mansion near the coast. Lucy says she has not returned to it since she buried her late husband there.

"I was just sitting here wondering how I could help the

poor girl. It is such a shame that one as beautiful and good
as she is should have her life devastated this way. But you
know, Theo, no matter how hard I try, I can't think what to
do."

"Was there another man involved somehow?" Theo ventured to ask. "I remember you saying once there must have
been."

"She did not say, and I—well, I did not care to press her
for I felt it important to get over the ground there as easily
as I could. She had never confided in me before and our
rapport was still so tentative."

"Perhaps she will talk to you again sometime, ma'am,"
Theo told her. "I think you are the most comfortable person
to talk to I have ever known. And you never tell people
what to do for their own good, or suggest their worries are
stupid, or insist they do everything your way."

"Thank you, dear," the dowager said, her eyes dancing
with amusement at this unusual compliment. "I have asked
Lucy to come and stay with me at the dower house at Lansmere. It is lovely there in the summer. I expect we will remove to it shortly, for Lucy is certainly not enjoying the
Season, and I have no heart for it this year. Besides, the
family will be there. I know the duke intends to move Eugenia and the baby as soon as they are able to travel safely.
London is no place for a newborn in the hot weather."

"I shall miss you both," Theo said, now looking a little
sad herself.

Her friend chuckled. "Perhaps you will, just a little. But I
imagine that handsome husband of yours will keep you so
busy, you won't have time to think of us, and that is how it
should be.

"And now, my dear, isn't it time you sought your bed? If
you are to get that good night's sleep Canford was so insis-
tent on, that is?"

22

Theo had been sure she would have trouble sleeping, for she was in a strange bed in a strange house without Lucas, and she had napped during the day. To her surprise, she dropped off almost at once after she had blown a kiss from the window in the direction of Park Lane.

She slept so soundly she never even heard the baby crying during the night. Still, just before dawn she woke with a start, her heart pounding as someone sat down on her bed. Her eyes flew open and although she could see nothing in the blackness that still cloaked the room, she knew without a doubt that the intruder was Lucas.

"Are you awake, Theo?" his deep voice teased. "Did you get that good night's sleep I ordered? I hope so. We have quite a day ahead of us."

Theo held up her arms and after a heartbeat of hesitation, the earl bent and gathered her into his arms. Just before he kissed her, he said, "I promised myself I wouldn't do this. It is too dangerous, you see, for you have no idea how it tempts me to join you there in bed. But if I did, it would upset all my careful plans."

His kiss was deep and searching, and as warm and intimate as she remembered. Theo reveled in it, her arms tight around him and her hands buried in his hair.

"I knew it would be dangerous," Lucas said unevenly when he let her go at last. "Come on, now, you seductive wench, no more dallying. Get up and dress. We must be gone."

"But where are we going?" Theo asked, propping herself up on one elbow.

"You'll find out all in good time, my girl."

"No, tell me."

"Absolutely not. Kidnappers don't apprise their victims of their destination."

"Horrors, kidnapped again! Aren't you beginning to make a habit of that particular crime? But at least there's no one to see what you're about this time."

"There will be, if you don't hurry," he told her, throwing back the covers. "You'll find Betsy in the dressing room with some breakfast. I'm so glad you didn't take Lady Blake's advice and engage a superior abigail. I find Betsy makes such a good, willing accomplice. I'll wait for you at the foot of the stairs. Hurry now!"

He was gone before Theo could ask another question, and she had a number of them in mind. Still, she padded obediently to the dressing room, still feeling his mouth on hers and sure her skin must be glowing where he had touched her, it was so sensitive even now.

As she washed and cleaned her teeth, and let Betsy put up her hair and help her into her habit, the matching hat and shining boots, she wondered where Lucas was taking her, and on horseback too. Not that it mattered, of course, as long as he was going there with her. And actually, even without that powerful incentive, she was not at all reluctant to leave London now. As she ate a muffin, a piece of fruit, and drank a cup of coffee, she thought of her mother and the coming birth and she knew she had had quite enough of babies for a while. Then there was Eugenia, who showed signs of growing as demanding as Fanny Meredith had ever been. Much better for her to play least in sight and hope to be forgotten.

As she took her crop and leather gloves from Betsy, Theo wondered if there was something about her that signaled other people that here was someone who could be put to good use, even overworked if need be, in their service. She hoped that was not the case as she kissed Betsy lightly and gathered up her train to run down the stairs where Lucas paced to and fro, impatiently waiting for her. She had to smile at how her heart lifted at the sight of him. Surely there had never been anyone who had been as anxious to be kidnapped as she.

It was cool and barely light with a dampness in the air left over from the night mists when she and Lucas let themselves out of the duke's mansion. Theo fought an urge to laugh from the sheer joy she felt, sneaking out of Lansmere House like a naughty little girl running away to escape punishment for some dire misdeed. But when Lucas lifted her to the saddle as a silent groom held the bridles of their two mounts, the way she felt was not something any little girl would ever know. Once mounted himself, Lucas waved the groom away and they set out, the horses' hooves clattering loudly on the cobblestones in the brief quiet between dark and light that was all London ever knew before it woke and stretched to commence yet another hectic, noisy day.

Theo looked to her husband, riding abreast, and saw from the flash of his white teeth that he was not only watching her too but smiling, as she knew she must be, now they had made good their escape. Still, she did not really take a deep breath or relax until Lansmere House was out of sight. And it wasn't until they were on a road leading out of London that she felt safe from someone calling them to a halt and ordering them to return.

There were only a few people abroad this early, but those who were looked curiously at the two thoroughbred horses with their handsome riders up, who trotted past in the chill gray light.

"What would you have done if it had rained today?" Theo thought to ask when they checked to let a milkman's horse and wagon plod across the street ahead of them.

"But I wouldn't let it rain," he said smugly. "Not today."

Theo laughed at him. It was growing ever lighter and now it was possible for her to make out his features.

"I wish you wouldn't look at me in quite that way, Theo," he said. "Not just yet anyway. It's unsettling."

As they left town the country roads and the villages they passed through became more crowded with traffic heading in the opposite direction. First they were edged to the side of the road by a herd of cattle, a little later by a flock of sheep. The sheep were attended not only by their shepherd but by a dog busy keeping them all together as they were driven to the slaughterhouses at Smithfield. As well, carriages and coaches were on the road in increasing numbers, and drays and carts filled with the wood and coal, or fresh produce, eggs, milk, and cheese necessary for the inhabitants of London. Theo saw a gaggle of geese, their webbed feet tarred to enable them to make the long march from their home ponds to end eventually on some rich man's dinner table, while their feathers stuffed his bed and pillows.

All Theo's senses seemed heightened. The smell of the animals was sharper than usual, and she heard the noises they made, the sounds of their owners' voices calling, the crack of a whip more clearly. And she could see the clear definition between lights and shadows as they fell across the road. Even colors were brighter—the grass, the sky, the glossy coat of Lucas's chestnut. As the sun rose higher to warm the air it reminded her that it was the first of April today. Six months since her wedding day. But she told herself today was her real wedding day, and she knew she would consider it so for as long as she lived.

Lucas did not call a halt until almost nine, when they stopped at a coaching inn near Uxbridge. To Theo's surprise, fresh horses awaited them there, not the usual job horses either, but stock from the earl's own stable. Theo wondered how he had managed it, but she did not ask as he escorted her to a private parlor and told her to rest. It was some time before he returned and when he did, he tossed his hat and gloves on a chair and smiled at her. "Do you suppose it's safe now to say 'alone at last'?" he asked as he held out his hand to her.

Theo took it shyly. "I believe it might be indeed," she said, studying his face as to memorize it anew. "I missed you yesterday. I couldn't understand why you didn't come and insist I return to Canford House. Rescue me."

"Ah, but I had something better in mind," he told her. "Besides, after your adventure with Genie, I dared not take a chance, remaining in London. You haven't forgotten your mother, have you? And she so near her time, as she keeps reminding us so often? Well, I could not risk a preemptory message from her, ordering you to her side to assist at yet another birth. I never thought when I married you, I was getting a midwife, which *I*, thank heavens, have no use for at all. All I wanted was a wife."

"And you shall have one," Theo told him. "I promise."

She held her face up to be kissed, but when someone knocked on the door, Lucas put her away from him. "I've ordered coffee and some rolls. We'll stop later for a more substantial meal," he said as he admitted a maid carrying a tray.

After the girl had gone and Lucas had served her, Theo said, "But of course. I just remembered."

"Remembered what?" he asked, stirring cream into his coffee.

"That you have an unreasonable dislike for making love in inns, of course," she explained, her eyes sparkling. "I see there'll be no kisses for me until we reach our destination. But where are we going? Can you tell me now?"

"Why, to Canford, where else?" he said. "Even stopping for frequent rests and to eat, we'll arrive there by late afternoon."

He studied her carefully before he added, "But if you feel yourself tiring, you must let me know, do you hear? We don't have to sleep at Canford tonight."

Yes we do, Theo thought but she only nodded.

"I wonder how Genie is doing," she said moments later. "I hope she doesn't feel I abandoned her."

"She won't. I explained everything to Lansmere and I left Genie a note explaining your absence. If she's angry with anyone it will be me, for I took all the blame. I also notified your father of our destination, wrote your mother, and the dowager duchess and Lady Blake, and—who else? Oh yes, your mantua maker, the man who makes your sandals, and the lady who fashions your very becoming hats, all of whom will have to send their wares to the country."

He reached across the table and captured her hands. "You see, my dear, I needed you with me. Alone with me."

Slowly, holding her eye, he raised her hands and kissed them one after the other.

"I think we should be on our way, don't you?" Theo asked, feeling breathless. "I assure you I am perfectly rested, sir."

All through the day they rode, and being April, the weather was changeable. Sometimes there was brilliant sunshine, sometimes a breeze came up and brought clouds that covered the sun. Once a brief shower drove them to seek shelter in an empty barn near the road. Theo was not used to riding such a long distance, but she did not call a halt. The earl's horses were chosen for their smooth gaits and good manners, and although she felt a little stiff whenever they stopped and she dismounted, that feeling left her when she moved about. At every halt fresh horses were there waiting for them, and the meal the earl had ordered at a charming little inn called The Duck and Dog, where he was obviously well-known, was delicious. He even insisted Theo lie down there for half an hour to rest, and he left her to make sure she did.

When they reached the stone columns that marked the entrance to Canford at last, the earl began to walk his horse and Theo slowed to keep pace.

"Not much further now, Countess," he said. "You have certainly been a game 'un."

"Nonsense," she said. "Oh, look at the daffodils! I didn't know the drive was lined with them. Aren't they lovely?"

She admired the drifts of yellow trumpets extending from the drive itself deep into the woods on either side. The earl admired her, for the daffodils were an old story to him.

"They've been here for as long as I can remember," he told her. "Once, when I was a little boy, I picked such a huge armful of them for my mother I could hardly carry

them and I left a trail of flowers behind me all the way back
to the house. Rather like Hansel and Gretel."

"There is so much I don't know about you," Theo said.
"So much I have to learn."

"Well, there's a lifetime to do so," he replied, stopping
as Canford came into view before them, tall and stately, its
walls and towers and windows golden from the westering
sun reflected in the quiet lake that fronted it. Theo sighed.
I've come home, she thought. At last.

Grooms came running from the stables to take charge of
the horses, and Lucas lifted her down and put his arm
around her to help her up the steps. Oates stood at the front
door waiting for them, his face wreathed in a broad smile.

"Welcome, m'lord, m'lady," he said, bowing. "Welcome
home."

Theo gave her gloves, hat, and riding crop to a footman
while Lucas had a few words with the butler. At the sound
of his voice, the spaniels began to bark from somewhere
deep in the house, and moments later, Molly came racing
through the hall to dance around him, tail wagging madly.
The young dogs of her first litter cavorted in imitation.
When the earl took Theo to the library they were escorted
there by the dogs.

She knelt to pet them as Lucas poured them both some
wine. He was shadowed by Molly, although she looked
back often at Theo, as if upset she must divide her loyalty.

"How the puppies have grown," Theo said.

"Yes. We'll see how well they've taken to training tomorrow," Lucas told her, handing her a glass brimming
with deep red wine and lifting his own to her in a silent
toast.

Theo took a sip before she looked around and chose a
seat. For some reason she was feeling shy now. Shy and
nervous and hesitant. The silences between them seemed
too long, their words when they finally spoke, banal. What
was the matter with her, she wondered. This was Lucas—
her beloved Lucas—and this was what she had been wait-

ing for all day. Why should she feel so uncertain, even frightened?

"What are you thinking, Theo?" Lucas asked as he sat down across from her. "You look different to me somehow."

"I won't lie to you," she said slowly. "It is the strangest thing. Now we are here, together, free of everything and everyone that ever came between us—now we're alone—I don't know what to do or even what to say to you. It's as if it were the early days of our marriage all over again. Even the dogs are with us just as they were the first night I came to Canford."

His face showed nothing of his feelings. "Does it seem like that to you? I wouldn't know," he said.

Sunshine streamed through the library windows. It would be some time before nightfall. Theo wondered why Lucas did not come and take her in his arms and kiss her—make all this easier. But then she realized that he was waiting for her to signal the beginning of their lovemaking; that this time she must take the lead.

Taking a deep breath, she set her glass down and went to the door. Holding it open, she said, "We would like the dogs removed now, Oates."

Two footmen materialized almost at once, to leash the spaniels and lead them away. Theo remained by the door until they were gone. Then, still not looking at Lucas, she said, "Please see to it the earl and I are not disturbed, Oates. Not for any reason."

His murmured assent came just before she closed the door firmly and turned to lean back and rest her shoulders against the wood.

Lucas was standing now, watching her gravely. "I find I can't wait for dark for you to come to my bed," she made herself say, never taking her eyes from his face. "And I've no appetite for dinner."

"There'll be no formal dinner this evening," he told her. "I've arranged for a light supper to be brought to our rooms at whatever hour we care to order it. If we ever do."

"I see," she said, and all the hesitation, all the nervousness she had been feeling, disappeared. Reaching up, she began to unbutton the jacket of her habit. Lucas stood very still, watching her. When the last button was undone, Theo removed the jacket and dropped it on a chair before she untied the stock she wore at her neck and began to unbutton her white lawn shirt.

She moved away from the door then, going to him slowly, her eyes intent on his. When she reached him, she took his face between her hands, trying to show him by her expression how much she loved him.

Then as he swept her into his arms at last, she remembered his words to her, their first time together.

"Now, m'lord," she said. *"Now."*